THE COVEN OF THE SPRING

Jeff Lovell

TotalRecall Publications, Inc.

TotalRecall Publications, Inc.
1103 Middlecreek
Friendswood, Texas 77546
281-992-3131   281-482-5390 Fax
www.totalrecallpress.com

Copyright © 2013 by: Jeff Lovell
Edited by
All rights reserved
ISBN: 978-1-59095-114-9
UPC: 6-43977-21140-8

Printed in the United States of America with simultaneous printings in Australia, Canada, and United Kingdom.

FIRST EDITION
1   2   3   4   5   6   7   8   9   10

To Laurie Rossi of Fairview, New Mexico, a colleague for many years and the editor of all my books. No one knows grammar and syntax better than she and she's been invaluable to me as a friend and expert.

Author Jeff Lovell

is a native Chicagoan, with 3 degrees from the University of Illinois and an earned doctorate from Vanderbilt University. Jeff taught high school writing and literature for thirty three years and sponsored the school paper, Student Council and several other activities. He ran the drama program at two high schools, teaching and directing and designing sets, lighting and costumes. His specialty in his career focused on Shakespeare. Since he retired from education, Jeff has served as a theatre and film critic for a television station and appears frequently to review theatre and literature.

Preface

An ancient secret emerges to terrify and destroy. Three people join together to destroy the cult that possesses the secret.

Chapter One

November, 1:00 P. M.
Winnetka, Illinois

The driveway gates opened at the same tedious speed as always, but Grace DeRosa sat waiting for them almost blind with impatience, drumming her fingers on her Jaguar's steering wheel. She pulled into the long driveway and sped up the hill toward the garage, far faster than she would have under most circumstances. Grace didn't open the garage. She couldn't spare the time.

She leapt from the car and slammed the door, noting somewhere in her distraction that it didn't quite crash shut. Something had gotten caught in the door, she realized in some part of her brain.

To hell with it. Car doors and slow gates didn't matter now.

Ironic, she thought, as she unlocked the front door and flew up the steps toward her bedroom. A great irony because she knew that people at work liked to call her—behind her back—The Ice Queen: cool, thorough, precise. Nothing rattled Grace DeRosa, no amount of work daunted her, and she kept herself above office politics.

Yeah, sure. The cold, soulless bitch. That's what they thought. People didn't know the depth of her passion. Nor did she ever—ever—lift her private veil to give them a peek.

She wondered what her co-workers would think if they could see The Ice Queen now. How different would she seem to them now that she had only—what? An hour? Perhaps only minutes?—to live?

The man from the Coven of the Spring, that disgusting cult of death would arrive in a few moments. At least one of them, at her invitation even, was coming to—she couldn't bring herself to say the word. No. She had to figure out how to separate her mind from her body.

Protect Crissy, she thought. *Don't let them get my daughter. No, no. Focus on her. Focus.*

What have I done? She thought for maybe the thousandth time. *Why did I do it?*

Grace DeRosa took some deep breaths, struggling to gain some control. She kicked off her Fiorentini and Baker high heels, stripped off her Donna Karan business suit and her Adrianna Papell blouse, and then went to the closet where she hung the suit up. Force of habit, she thought.

Then she pushed into the lavish wardrobe of clothes, not paying any attention to the cachet of beautiful scents she kept there mingling with the musty smell of the cedar lining of the closet. Deep in the back of the closet, from a secret drawer no one except she even knew about, she pulled out the ivory negligee, so silky to the touch that it threatened to run through her fingers like quicksilver. She'd found the lingerie in a tiny store in the ancient town of Salem, Massachusetts, and knew at once that the lovely garment would charm her husband. She'd been saving it for a special occasion and smiled even now to think of how it would have bewitched him.

Then the coarse reality struck again. Now she wouldn't wear it for him. Now it would help her seduce the man who would come to her home soon to rip-off from her what she had always intended and even insisted to be the exclusive and unique property of her husband.

She allowed herself a mordant smile at the irony. In junior high school, high school, and in college she'd personified The Ugly Duckling legend: poor complexion, overweight, unmerciful shyness. She'd never been invited to Homecoming, never been asked to Prom, never invited to parties. She was far too convinced of her own shortcomings to want to climb out of her shell.

But then something had happened. She fell in love, she thought with a rueful smile.

She met Jim in a graduate level organic chemistry class at the University of Illinois when they were thrown together as lab partners. After the first class Grace DeRosa went back to her dorm room and looked at herself in the mirror.

She saw a frizzy haired, out of condition, overweight slob. She wore clothes that were so unattractive that homeless people living under a bridge would have rejected them.

Then, for the first time, the determination that would make her a towering success in life emerged. Grace made up her mind and changed everything in that moment. She altered her high fat, starchy, high carbohydrate diet and lost 20 pounds in a matter of a few weeks. For the first time in her life, she began working out, using the exquisite IMPE building on the south end of the University of Illinois campus.

During that time she made her way to a beauty college in Urbana and told them she couldn't stand how she looked. Some of the delighted students at the college transformed her hair style, added some highlights, gave her a stunning manicure, and worked with her on make-up.

She had to laugh as she looked in the mirror two months after her decision. The change had been dramatic. Then her friend Janice came in.

"Yow!" Janice had said. She complimented Grace in lavish terms about the transformation. "But," she said, "we have to get you going with some clothes." Janice knew a good used clothing store in Champaign and, for a minor investment, helped Grace build a wardrobe that flattered a now beautiful figure, styled in colors that complimented her complexion and hair.

The next weekend she went on a double date with Janice's boyfriend and his roommate, the first date of her life. Grace saw him several times in the next few weeks, she remembered. She had balked at his suggestion of a sexual relationship although she liked the idea, for she had a deep interest in her lab partner.

The graduate college sponsored a dance one Thursday night. Grace had turned down a few early offers, saying she already had a date. She did it with a gentle grace that seemed to say that she regretted the fact that she couldn't go, and that she'd welcome a future offer.

Then, as she'd planned, Jim asked her. As they began to date, she decided that her evaluation of him as her potential life partner was right on the nose. A whirlwind romance—Grace could think of no other term to describe it—ensued, and a few weeks after the dance, he proposed and she accepted.

They both got their master's degrees a few months later.

They were married three weeks after that.

The memory of that tumultuous, if speedy, romance brought a smile to her lips—

Then Grace DeRosa jolted back to reality in her beautiful Winnetka, Illinois home. She loved her marriage, her home, her job, but all that meant so much to her stood threatened and in imminent danger of vanishing. She herself had a strong chance of dying in the next few moments.

The negligee adjusted, she rushed into her bathroom and looked at herself in the mirror. The hair adjustment. More makeup, especially the lips and eyes. Floss, then minty toothpaste and a violent brushing. Mouthwash, so bitter and acerbic as to burn her lips.

Her always logical mind spewed out conflicting messages. She'd never been unable to think her way out of a situation. Never. Grace DeRosa, the best student in her class, every class, all her life, couldn't think of a way out of this one. Nothing academic presented too great a challenge, her college professors thought. Her graduate school professors had all but begged her to pursue a doctorate and to take up a career in academia, doing chemical research at the University level.

Now, she didn't know how to think her way out of this. She'd be found in the bed, defiled, debauched, and humiliated. Her husband's primary memory of her would be that of her as a traitor, a whore, unfaithful and unworthy of his love and devotion.

Scared? Yes. This situation terrified her to the point of making her nauseous and sick to her stomach. This creep from the Coven planned to adulterate her and then rip away whatever was left of her soul.

A tear fell onto the granite countertop in her lavish washroom. The washroom and her bedroom were close to works of art which she'd planned and decorated with all the precision and care that she could muster. Tiffany shaded brass lamps stood on the bedside tables, a gorgeous chandelier she'd imported from Wales hung from the ceiling, and exquisite statuary and watercolors adorned the walls. The centerpiece was a king-sized canopy bed, made from hand-rubbed walnut, a special order from the craftsmen at the Amana colonies in Central Iowa. She'd waited almost a year for the expert woodworkers to build the bed. The cost had been high, but Grace felt that it added so much beauty and grace to her bedroom and the house that it was worth every penny. She and her husband Jim had built this huge sumptuous house with its magnificent furnishings together, planning to fill it with children —

—At least, *she'd* planned to fill it with children; she could never be sure if Jim shared her enthusiasm for children. To her intense disappointment, she had never been able to conceive a child.

Her stomach hurt again, thinking of how she and Jim had tried for months, then years, to have children of their own. They'd tried everything—fertility specialists, trips to clinics, pills, shots—but nothing had worked. At last they decided to adopt.

Grace, loving and with a patience and acumen born out of a lifetime of disappointment, had set up an adoption through an agency. After an agonizing wait, she and her husband became the parents of a beautiful baby.

They had adopted an infant daughter, who became the light

and joy of Grace's life. Grace named their child Clarisse, which had been shortened to the nickname Crissy. When the girl was learning to talk, her infant tongue could by no means pronounce 'Clarisse', but she did manage to say 'Crissy', and that's how she'd come to be known.

Grace smiled as she thought about how she'd watched Crissy develop into a fine young woman. Tall, slim and beautiful, with exotic blue eyes and long, honey colored hair, Crissy got superb grades in school. She also participated in student council, athletics and drama. The girl also read as much as she could, all manner of books, and Grace took delight in how her daughter loved to learn and how she received wonderful grades in school—

And again Grace jerked back to reality. Now she had to face it head on. Grace needed to die to save the girl. Then Jim would have to become a murderer, also to save the girl.

Somewhere in her brain the comprehension of her betrayal of her husband came alive and began to speak to her in a small but insistent voice in her mind. *Be quiet*, she whispered aloud through clenched teeth.

No, Grace, the little voice said. *You're the one who wounded your daughter. Your husband doesn't deserve to be involved in this.*

The voice spoke the truth and she knew it. Jim would become another victim of her arrogance, just like his wife and his daughter. But how else could she protect Crissy? What could she do? She couldn't let them have her!

The members of this unspeakable cult seemed incapable of pity, morality or mercy, a cell of despicable humans. If they *were* still human somewhere in those twisted souls, she sneered. Maybe not.

They called themselves The Coven of the Spring. The name implied witchcraft and, Grace thought, they deserved the sobriquet: an insulated and obscure group of witches. Their talent—if it could be called that—came from drinking the water of a clandestine well not far from Salem, Massachusetts.

The members of the Coven included the worst dregs of society, worse than any street hoodlums, motorcycle gangs, or terrorist cells.

She scoffed with her contempt for the worthless members of the cult. At least she wouldn't have to face them again. She'd be dead.

Her mind raged with her indignation about the cult. She saw them as arrogant, self-absorbed, and concerned for themselves and their own desires and comforts to the exclusion of all others.

She tried to think of something else. Calm down, she thought. Nonetheless, Grace's anger increased as she thought about her drive home that afternoon. Almost wild with urgency, she'd all but hit that stupid woman who cut her off in a rusty beater of a car. The woman darted out of a side street, blowing right through a stop sign. She'd almost wrecked Grace's lovely Jaguar—

Then Grace froze. In her blinding rage and fear she hadn't thought about it. Grace had acquired an extraordinary mental power from the well. She'd tried to smack the woman hard, with a vindictive rage and desire for vengeance, to send a bolt of terror exploding into the other driver's mind, but the Jolt she'd tried hadn't worked.

Her mind, which had been praised to the heavens in every school she had ever attended, flashed with the speed of light through the whole encounter.

Why didn't the Jolt work? It had *always* worked. It worked not five minutes later when she'd whacked that doltish gas station attendant. But. . .

She thought. What was different?

And then, like the sun appearing across a mountain range, the truth materialized. She knew what to do. Of course. She saw the solution to her dilemma. The plan formed in moments. Maybe she *could* save herself. Why hadn't she thought of it before?

No time to worry about that now. She had to tell her daughter. But how could she do that? If she tried to give Crissy a remote jolt, the girl would know it and would block Grace's thoughts.

Her thoughts racing, she ran to the stairs, the exotic high heels clicking on the oak floor. Down the steps to the lower level. Down the hall to her private office. Boot the computer. Extract the external hard drive from its secret hiding place, a little safe that not even her husband knew about. Bring up the Word program.

Come on, come on!

She connected the external hard drive and opened her personal diary file. As quick as though she typed in a new message, her nimble fingers flying across the keyboard with an urgency born of fear and exigency. So alert was she that she typed without any mistakes.

Save the message to the hard drive. Delete the message from the computer. Hurry, hurry!

Disconnect the hard drive. Back into the hiding place.

Now she began deleting the files from her computer. Come on!

As the computer worked, Grace ran upstairs, shuffling a little in the striking high heels she thought would entice the lascivious brute from the coven. She hurried to the garage and threw on the light switch above her husband's work bench. Her senses reached such a heightened pitch that the stale garage odors of gasoline, motor oil and other lubricants almost overwhelmed her.

She scanned the rack of tools, the pliers, the wrenches, the screwdrivers. Where were the damn things? At last she found what she needed and dug out a couple of them. She ran back into the house. Out in the backyard and quick practice. Up to the spare bedroom, where she hid her cache of weapons where she could get her hands on it in an instant. Then back downstairs to check on the computer.

The computer hadn't quite finished cleaning her diary files when the doorbell rang.

She never prayed much. Now, at what could be the end of her life, she turned to prayer: *Oh God, I'm sorry*, she whispered as she walked up the stairs to the first floor. *Please help me, give me courage.*

She crossed the foyer, her feet weighing fifty pounds each, continuing to murmur, *Please help me protect Crissy. My dear girl, the joy of my life…*

She reached the front door. She turned the knob and pulled the door open.

Chapter 2

Clarisse DeRosa—whom everyone called "Crissy" except Mrs. Stinson, her 159-year-old English Lit teacher who, for some reason, insisted on calling her "Miss DeRosa" or "Clarisse"—got off the school bus, as angry and disgusted as she'd been for weeks.

She tapped in the entrance code on the numeric pad located on the left pillar, its identical stone companion opposite on the other side of the drive. The gate swung open and she walked up the long drive to the house where she'd lived her entire life, certainly as long as she could remember. She'd gotten used to the magnificent building, the immaculate grounds, the lovely trees and landscaping. In the spring and summer the smell of the flowering crab trees, as well as her mother's beautiful flower gardens combined with the sounds of bees and birds, would be all but overwhelming.

The anticipation of the beautiful sights and smells might have cheered someone else up, but, boy, they sure didn't work on her today.

Crissy's school bus ride home enhanced her anger, leaving her grumpy, hungry, tired and annoyed. She muttered to herself as she thought about the stupid school bus which had broken down on the way home, and how she'd had to sit on that stupid bus for almost an hour and a half while they got another stupid bus to come and pick them up and haul them home. She'd managed to redeem the time by doing her AP Calculus homework and helping a couple of freshman girls with their algebra.

Despite the bad mood, Crissy smiled to herself. She loved to help other kids like that. Those little girls, a couple of years younger than Crissy, seemed to hero worship her. Crissy noticed with amusement that they tried to dress and talk like she did. That attention flattered her.

She'd been thinking, like the last few weeks, that maybe she'd like to be a teacher. Her counselor had been talking to her about college, encouraging her to look at some catalogs, read up on some schools, and get an idea of where she might want to point her interest.

Of course Mom and Dad would want her to go to the University of Illinois, where they had both been honor students as undergraduates and as graduate students, but she felt pretty sure they'd credit her decision if she wanted to go somewhere else. Crissy had even been thinking about going to a community college for a couple of years, to work and build up a bank account.

She wouldn't major in math, though. Oh, she did okay in math and sciences, A's and B's, as she did in all her subjects. However she preferred American and British Literature and Shakespeare and the social sciences like psychology and sociology the most.

Her academic preferences left her a little puzzled, she had to admit. Her mother and father were outstanding scientists and researchers. The University, both undergraduate and graduate school, and the company for which they worked regarded both of them as brilliant at their jobs. Crissy's work in math and the sciences didn't reflect the luster of her parents.

Then her mood took a downturn again as she thought about the rest of the day. The worst part—she'd been angry about it all afternoon—came at lunch when that creep Alex had tried to talk her into going out with him again.

She'd become much more objective about her ex-boyfriend since she'd broken off with him, telling him she didn't want to see him anymore. Today, he looked like he should be living behind a dumpster in an alley: the ubiquitous baseball hat pulled low over his eyes, ripped jeans—which was a laugh since his parents had enough money to fill up several dump trucks—and a sweatshirt with some sort of dorky message on the front, and he was redolent with a combined odor of yesterday's sweat socks, despicable aftershave and a giant sized, if stale, order of cafeteria tater tots.

She would never set out to be rude to anyone, of course. Impoliteness went against her nature, and, besides, her mom had taught her manners all her life and impressed on her many times that in all situations she needed to be kind.

But Alex's intentions weren't nice. She began to suspect after a few months that he wasn't in love with her. She'd used her ability to jolt him and find out what he wanted out of their relationship. He just wanted to—

She shuddered to think of herself in a sexual situation with that stinky Doofus. Yuck.

Crissy's mind now registered that her mom's car sat in the drive. Mom hadn't put it in the garage. Not only that, she'd left open the driver's side door. Just a crack, to be sure, but Crissy could see that the dome light of the beautiful Hunter's Green

Jaguar sedan hadn't gone out.

Now that puzzled her. Mom always put her car in the garage. Crissy's mother was almost maniacal about her precision, her care, her concern and attention to detail in everything she did. Mom cleaned the house like a woman possessed, maintaining a spotless, unimpeachable beauty: gleaming hardwood floors, kitchen cabinets polished to shine, spotless rugs and flawless upholstery on the furniture. Mom kept the Jaguar immaculate inside and out, and for her to leave the car out of the garage with a dome light on seemed bizarre, seemed out of character for her.

Crissy, on the other hand, all but drove her meticulous mother to exasperation with her messy bedroom and casual dress. Mother and daughter didn't much resemble each other in that regard, either. Except when she was going to exercise, Mom always left the house dressed like a high fashion model in exquisite suits and shoes, with flawless nails and beautiful dark blond hair.

Crissy had quit chewing her nails in fourth grade, she remembered, but didn't think her hands would ever be as beautiful and expressive as her mother's.

Crissy grinned. She decided she would have some fun at dinner giving her mom "The Business" about leaving the car open, dome light on, and not in the garage.

The girl opened the car door and caught the faint luxurious smell of the leather seats and her mom's expensive French perfume. Crissy saw that the seat belt buckle had fallen into the space between the door and the car's frame. She tucked the belt away and shut the door. The light faded out at once.

Then Crissy forgot about the car and walked to the front

door. She started to slide her house key into the lock—

—the door swung open as she pushed on the key. Crissy's mouth dropped open in surprise.

Mom left the front door open? She wouldn't do that. Never. Besides, it was cold outside.

With some apprehension, Crissy walked into the large, two story stone-floored foyer. No lights were on and the afternoon light in November was dim. Again she cursed the waste of time on the stupid school bus, sitting by the side of the road until the stupid bus company could bring another stupid bus to rescue them.

Crissy DeRosa hated riding the school bus, always had. She had a couple of dramatic memories of all but being dragged away from her mother when she had to go to kindergarten and first grade. She'd given up the dramatics for many years, of course, but now that she'd gotten her driver's license, she wanted her own car.

Crissy brightened a little at the thought. Maybe after dinner she'd again ask—well, okay, nag—Dad about letting her get a car of her own. She had money saved from birthdays, a little waitress job, and a small allowance. Yeah, sure, she intended to use the money for college, but if she had her own car she wouldn't have to fool with that stupid school bus anymore. She smiled, seeing herself behind the wheel of a Corvette, or an early model Trans-Am, but she'd take a small Toyota at this point.

"Mom?"

No answer. Down the flight of stairs to the basement, where Mom had her home office. "Mom?"

Still no answer.

Well, maybe Mom had drawn herself a whirlpool. Yeah, that could be. Dad had put in a Jacuzzi for a present on one of Mom's birthdays and sometimes Mom liked to indulge herself when she came home from a tough day at work. She'd fill the tub with blazing hot water, dump in some fragrant oils and bath salts—yeah, that could be it. Mom wouldn't hear an atomic attack over the sound of the whirlpool.

But she would have locked the doors. Again Crissy felt that nagging concern, which now began to turn into anxiety. What could have been wrong that Mom wouldn't have checked her car and the front door?

Crissy looked for the mail on the antique marble and mahogany table that stood in the hallway where Mom always dumped it when she came in. But she didn't find any mail on the table. That's weird, thought Crissy. Mom always stopped at the foot of the driveway at the mailbox embedded in one of the driveway's brick pillars and picked up the mail.

Puzzled, Crissy zipped her parka again and walked to the end of the driveway. She looked in the mailbox and found a stack of bills and other correspondence, a few fliers from department stores and some other junk. She riffled through the pile as she walked back up to the house but found nothing addressed to her. Strange. Mom always got the mail.

Crissy walked in the front door and again listened for any sound that would have given a hint of where to look for her mother. "Mom?" she tried again.

Still no answer.

Okay, now this had become real goofy. Mom had to be here in the house somewhere. Yeah, okay, she had been a fitness fanatic since college—running, cycling, weights, stretching. But her routine never varied. Mom always jogged in the neighborhood in the morning, usually three to five miles. Then Mom would stop at the health club on the way home from work.

Crissy again smiled with a little pride as she returned her thoughts to her beautiful mother. It was no accident Mom had a trim, lovely figure and soft, radiant skin that glowed. She really took a serious approach to exercise and proper diet, not like her friends' parents, some of whom dripped with money. They'd probably hire someone to exercise for them if they could.

But Crissy felt pretty sure that Mom wasn't out somewhere exercising. The car sat in the drive and it would have been a long walk to the health club.

Crissy hung up her parka on the hallway clothes hook and shivered. The house felt cold and silent, almost sullen, the result of the front door standing ajar. She heard the furnace running and knew that the house would be comfortable in a few minutes. She walked upstairs to the bedroom level. "Mom?" No answer.

Now Crissy became scared. Mom *ought* to be in the house, but she always responded to Crissy's greeting. She wouldn't go and visit a neighbor, she'd have to drive to the store or the health club, and this silence *felt* uncharacteristic. Mom always greeted her at the door, and she liked to snap on some music on the Bose system in the house.

Crissy went into her bedroom and changed out of her school clothes. She even hung up the dress she'd worn that day. She turned away and grinned, thinking that Mom would be shocked, but proud of her daughter for that. She slipped into jeans and a sweatshirt and heavy wool socks, what her mom called Crissy's uniform.

She reached into her book bag—a knapsack that she carried instead of a purse—and rummaged around for her cell phone. It took a little while, but she pulled it out, flipped it open and checked it. As usual she felt a bit annoyed at her high school. The dumb school wouldn't let students turn them on during school.

Yeah, right, she thought. We're all drug dealers, using our cell phones to call connections in Cartagena or Tehran or something.

But yes, she *had* turned the cell phone on when she left school. No, no one had left a message.

Okay, now it became official. Crissy DeRosa admitted that this situation scared her. Mom verged on being overprotective with her daughter, and she would never be the type who'd just vanish. Crissy hurried down the long hallway to her parents' bedroom. Maybe, she thought, maybe I should call the police?

She looked in. No Mom. Then she peeked into the open door of their bathroom—

The Jacuzzi stood there empty, as dry as an autumn leaf.

Crissy stood, staring for several moments at the Jacuzzi, not sure how to proceed. She'd been all but certain that she'd find her mom in the tub. What in—

At last she rallied. Okay. She would call Dad at work. Yeah, why didn't she think of that to begin with? Of course he didn't like to be interrupted on the job, but this behavior went completely out of character for her mother. Sure, Crissy thought, he'd know where Mom had gone.

Crissy left the beautiful bathroom and walked back down the hall to the stairway, intending to grab her cell phone. As she passed the guest room, a flash of white on the floor caught the corner of her eye. But it didn't register for a few moments, until she reached the stairs. Then she realized that she'd seen something lying on the floor of the bedroom. The smell of that exotic French perfume Mom wore on special occasions struck her senses. Crissy realized what she'd seen on the floor.

She turned and dashed back to the doorway of the guest room. Crissy looked in the room and saw her mother lying sprawled on her back. Mom's eyes were open, but she wasn't moving. She didn't even seem to be breathing.

"Mom?" Crissy ran over and knelt by her mother. She took her wrist and couldn't find a pulse. She started to shake her mother.

"Mom!!!"

Chapter Three

The lakefront of Chicago, Illinois
Three Months Later

At the time in his life when he thought things couldn't get worse, Clay Foster saw a girl try to kill herself. She jumped into Lake Michigan about 50 yards from him.

He'd parked in a lot near the Lake and climbed out of his 1963 Corvette, his prized possession. The lake wind blasted the warmth of the car off him as he let his dog out. He pulled an old towel from the 'Vette's trunk and wrapped it around his neck as a makeshift scarf. He tucked it into the jacket of his sweat suit. Then he re-tied the draw string of his hooded sweatshirt.

He started running down to the path that led by the lake. He'd run through a nice park, a fair distance from Lake Shore Drive.

The mist of the waves striking the beaches froze in his nostrils, but he didn't mind. At least that was better than the stench of the dead alewives in the summer. Clay thought for an unpleasant moment about the invasion of the tiny herring-like fish that occurred when he was young. When the St. Laurence seaway opened the Great Lakes to the Atlantic Ocean, the Alewives had migrated down to the Chicago area and for years died in ghastly numbers. Their tiny bodies rotted away on the beaches, the stench of death everywhere, almost overwhelming the beautiful lakeshore all summer.

He grinned a little to think about his grandfather who had lived on the Lake in Michigan City, Indiana, about thirty miles southeast across the lake from where he was now. Papa and his neighbor went down to the beach with rakes and raked up the dead fish on an evening when the wind was blowing offshore out into the lake, away from the houses that lined the shore about three miles down the beach road from the center of town.

They made three huge piles of dead fish, poured barbeque starter fluid over the piles, tossed matches and backed up, secure in the knowledge that they'd rid the beach of disease, death, insect infestation and, in particular, the ghastly stench that the rotten bodies produced.

Everything went as it was supposed to until the wind shifted direction and began to blow off the lake right at the houses.

Clay grinned as he thought about the people leaving in their cars, shaking their fists, threatening Papa with lynching. At least it got rid of the fish for a few days. A fresh batch of dead alewives covered the beach within a week.

Clay chuckled at the memory, but he still wondered what he could have been thinking of when he'd come over here. He'd been working on rehabbing a townhouse in the Hyde Park area, not far from the lake. He'd been wallpapering and painting the house all day. He'd begun to notice that the old place, as he transformed it from a wreck into a showplace, was starting to feel like home to him.

Nonetheless, he decided that he needed a break from the rehabilitation effort. He went up to the master bedroom where he'd camped out, put on his jogging clothes and tied up his shoes. Then he hooked up his dog and headed out the door, intending to run a neighborhood route that would allow him to stay out of the icy East Wind most of the time.

Then, for some reason, he decided to drive from his Hyde Park house over to the lake. He went back into the house and retrieved his billfold and keys. Then he opened the garage and started up the Corvette. He sat for a moment, letting the synthetic oil flow around the engine. He took care of his car as if it was a prized possession, which, he grinned, it was. Then, he dropped the stick shift into reverse, backed down the short drive and drove over to the promontory.

Clay stretched a little, figuring this would be a great day to strain a muscle if he wasn't careful. As he did, and began a slow warm-up jog, he couldn't shake off the strange thoughts as he ran along the Chicago Lakefront not far from the Museum of Science and Industry. "How stupid am I?" he said aloud. "Why did I come over here today?" His cheeks burned and his legs felt the chill through the cotton sweat pants.

Huh. Thirty-five degrees, Chicago style gale off the lake, gray cloudy sky—all in all, absolute misery for running, even if you're a guy who doesn't feel his life means anything anymore, and who doesn't have much to live for, and whose children hate him, and whose ex-wife wished he was dead—

Damn it, Gail, he said to himself. Why couldn't we have worked it out? He missed his ex-wife, while he hated her for what she'd done, hated himself for screwing up his marriage, and for never seeing his kids.

As usual, he winced as he thought about his failed marriage. The pain never seemed to get any better. He'd met Gail when they were seniors in high school, they'd dated throughout college, and she'd been waiting when he came home from the Navy, where he'd served as a S.E.A.L. She'd been a rock of support in his business ventures, and they'd worked together for several years at rebuilding businesses.

They'd been a great team. Yeah, he knew things like organization structures, delegation of authority, hiring and firing. Gail, on the other hand, managed money with a brilliance that would have done credit to a CPA and handled employees with compassion and instinctive skill that would defuse awkward situations. He'd marvel to see her handle hostile customers, who, after talking to her for a few moments, would relax and let her make things right. He smiled even now to think of the pride he took in his talented wife.

Then, she'd met the rich guy named Steve in their condo association.

Their affair began when he asked her to get a drink with him after a condominium board meeting. She thought the whole group was going out, but it wound up being just her and Steve. One drink had become several drinks.

With the booze working to lower her inhibitions, she yielded when he invited her back to his house. She gave in without much of a struggle when he took her to bed for exotic sex that lasted all night.

As she drove home in the morning, she realized that she didn't feel any guilt or regret, but only anger at Clay. Indeed, she hadn't enjoyed lovemaking that much since the early days of her marriage to Clay. In those days, they had made love with a frenetic, athletic joy. The sex with the new man had thrilled her, and she wanted to replicate that for the next several years.

Clay, frantic with worry when his wife didn't come home,

had called the police of their small town. She found Clay and the police waiting at the door when she pulled the car into the driveway. His relief turned in a few moments to monumental hurt and emotional pain that wouldn't be relieved for a long while.

Gail dismissed the police, and then turned back to her husband. He listened in bewilderment as she told him that she'd had enough of his crazy hours, his neglect, his thoughtlessness and his lack of cooperation in raising their two daughters. She went on for some time and asked him for a divorce, which began the process that would end her marriage to Clay. Within a few months of beginning the affair, Gail had emerged free and clear of Clay for good.

When she at last dumped Clay, she married Mr. Right almost at once and took the children to live with her and Steve. She and the family moved to Lake Geneva, Wisconsin, and now he never saw his children anymore.

Clay, at 6-2 and 200 pounds, was well built and good-looking in his late 30's. When his marriage fell apart, he'd been devastated, unable to work, read, or do anything other than sit and contemplate his life. He sort of rallied when the divorce reached an end, and he assumed he'd be able to meet a ton of attractive women.

But it hadn't happened. He had met several women, gone on several dates, but no flame had been struck with any of them. He knew he'd never gotten over Gail.

***

Clay's dog, Hephzibah, nudged his leg. Okay, to be fair, someone did care about him. He had to grin. She was his best friend, he thought.

He grinned as he thought about the dog comforting him through the divorce. She would come to him in the midst of his depressed moods, sleep next to him on his bed, and curl up on the couch with him as he watched a news show in the evening.

Hephzibah — whom he called 'Hep' most of the time — was about three years old, and she'd developed into a fine dog, a terrific companion and well, to be frank, the only affection he ever received came from her.

He hadn't exactly adopted her, in the sense of going to a shelter or a breeder or pet store. On the contrary, he'd found her in the forest preserve, cringing, crying and terrified. Some idiot had taken her out into the woods, tied her to a tree off the path, and left her to die.

Clay heard the puppy crying that cold, raw day in early spring as he ran along the forest preserve path. He made a concerted effort to ignore the pathetic whelping but found he just couldn't let it go. After running twenty yards past the sound, he sighed and turned back.

Off the path, which the forest preserve district packed with limestone screenings, he found the ground spongy and close to impossible to struggle through. His Nikes sank ankle deep into the muck and he had to pull hard to keep going.

He found the puppy about ten or twelve yards off the path, straining at the clothesline tied around her neck, her eyes wide with fear and confusion.

"All right, little guy," he said. "All right." He approached and the puppy almost wagged herself in two. Clay called out, but no one answered.

He looked around and decided he had to make an executive

decision. He began tugging at the knots, which the puppy, straining in terror, had yanked into sullen wet lumps. He remembered the small folding knife on his key chain. Even though he kept the little blade as sharp as a scalpel, it took some effort to cut away the sodden clothesline. The puppy cried as he picked her up.

The day, chilly and overcast with a cold north wind, and chilly, left the dog freezing cold and shivering. He had no way of telling how long she'd been there either. The filth and the mud that had caked into her short fur would be difficult to clean off. He made a good effort with the towel he wore around his neck, wiping the little dog down with it and then wrapping her up in it.

The puppy was still shivering, so he unzipped his jacket and pulled it off. Now *he* began trembling as the wind penetrated the hooded sweatshirt he wore under the jacket. "Who would do such a terrible thing to you, Pup?" he asked the little dog as he wrapped her in his coat.

He tucked the puppy under his arm and struggled through the swampy mud back to the path. Off balance, he fell to his knees once or twice and got soaked with wet mud. At last he reached the path, scraped away as much mud off his shoes as he could with a stick, and took off toward his car which he'd parked about a mile away from where he'd found the dog. Someone had really wanted the little creature dead, he decided.

Then he considered the situation. No, not just dead. Someone wanted the little creature to suffer, to starve to death or die of pneumonia. What kind of person would do that? He struggled to rid himself of the thought that someone might have gotten a sadistic pleasure out of thinking of a helpless creature dying hopeless and terrified.

Arriving at the car within ten minutes, he found a blanket in the trunk and wrapped the dog up. He took his cell phone from its cradle on the dash and speed-dialed his college buddy Terry Osborne. Terry had gone on after college to become a veterinarian and now ran a clinic not far away.

It took a few moments for the vet to reach the phone and Terry gave his friend a good natured cursing for a few moments. "What is this?" he asked. "I got work to do, unlike *some* people I could mention."

"Look, Ter—" began Clay.

"Yeah, look," said Terry. "I hope you're calling to make arrangements to pay me back the twenty bucks you owe me."

"No, I'm not," said Clay. "And what's more I don't owe you a penny."

His friend gave a snort of contempt, ready to continue the teasing, but Clay interrupted. "Wait a second, Ter," he said. "I've got an emergency with an animal here." Terry grew serious at once.

Clay headed the car out of the parking lot and drove hard as he talked to Terry, explaining the puppy's condition. "My God," he said. "Someone tied the little guy to a tree and left her?" Clay confirmed it and Terry told him to bring the dog right over to the office.

Krystal, Terry's assistant and receptionist, had a warm bath for the puppy waiting when Clay arrived. She gave Clay a few rags and a spray cleaner to clean the mud off of his shoes and sweatpants while she bathed the dog with gentle earnestness, cooing and stroking the creature.

"This poor little thing's scared to death," said Krystal.

"Not just cold."

"Yeah," said Clay. He told the story of finding the animal. Krystal shook her head with mute anger and disgust.

"I bet they figured a coyote would get her," she said.

"What?" choked Clay. "Coyotes in this area?"

"Yeah," shrugged Krystal. "A lot of people are telling us they've seen them in the preserves. They might even have thought a pack of wild dogs would kill her." She dried the little animal with a blow dryer and fed her a few handfuls of high protein dog food. The puppy gobbled the food and Krystal gave her some more.

As Clay stroked the little dog's fur, she interrupted her meal long enough to turn and lick his hand. "Oh brother," said Clay, realizing he'd fallen in love with the puppy.

Terry came in to see the puppy a few moments later. He and Clay shook hands while Clay told the story. "Is that why you look like a bum?" asked Terry.

Clay chuckled. "I suppose so," he said.

Terry grinned. He told Crystal to get his college buddy a set of green surgical scrubs to change into while he started a workup on the dog.

Clay took a quick shower in Terry's office and changed into the scrubs. He returned as Terry finished his examination. Spotting Clay, he pulled his stethoscope out of his ears and sighed.

"I'm afraid she's got a fair case of pneumonia," he said. "It doesn't look real good." The puppy coughed and Clay groaned. "I'm sorry, Buddy."

"How bad?" asked Clay.

"Bad enough," said Terry. "I should probably put her down.

I'd hate to do it, but — " his voice trailed away.

"Damn," Clay muttered, and winced as the puppy looked up into his eyes. "Do you have to?"

Terry hesitated and thought about it. "Well, no," he admitted. "If she belonged to a family, I'd probably work with her a bit. Some antibiotic and tender loving care would take care of it. Everything besides the lungs—heart, kidneys, like that— seem pretty good. She's a sweet little thing, too, Bro."

"You know anyone who'd take her in?"

Terry shrugged. "We get calls every once in a while," he said. "We have people come in, looking to adopt a dog to replace an animal, yeah. But Clay, she likes you, I can see that. Why not take her yourself?"

Clay made a feeble protest at first, but he knew that he really wanted to keep the dog. He certainly didn't want her to die. He'd grown up with dogs in the house, but Gail didn't like animals. It had been a bone of contention between them before, when he'd asked about getting a dog some years ago. She'd dug in her heels and resisted with a hostility he hadn't anticipated at the time.

Okay," he said. "Gail won't want her, but—"

"I thought I could see that light in your eyes," Terry chuckled. "Good for you. What's her name?"

Clay thought. "Let's go biblical," he decided. "Hephzibah."

Terry laughed. "Why not Jezebel?"

"Hephzibah," affirmed Clay. "Hep for short."

So the little dog had a name. Terry put her age at about three months.

In retrospect Clay couldn't imagine why he'd bothered to dispute with his friend. He'd fallen in love with the puppy and could see that she'd make a wonderful family pet. He knew the puppy's intelligence, gentleness, and sweet disposition.

Gail didn't see the dog in the same way he did. Clay called Gail's reaction on the nose. She protested with an astounding vigor.

"What do you mean, you adopted a dog?" she snarled.

"Well, see, I was jogging in the woods, and…" he began to relate the story finding the puppy tied up off the trail, but realized that she wasn't overly interested in the narrative.

"You know I don't want a dog," she said. "And you brought this thing home anyway?"

"Well, see, I didn't think I could just leave her in the woods," he whined. "She was tied to a tree, scared to death, and trembling with cold and terror."

"So why didn't you let Terry put her down?" she asked. "Or let someone else adopt her?"

"You'll find she's really a sweet little thing, Gail," he said. "At least give her a chance. She's got short fur, so she won't shed much—"

"No," she interrupted. "Not a chance. Take that thing right back to Terry."

"But. . ." he began.

"I hate dogs, cats, guinea pigs, anything with four legs and fur. . ." she retorted, and the fight, which had become a characteristic of their deteriorating marriage, lurched into a higher gear.

At last, Gail seemed to relent. The puppy, oblivious to the tension she'd caused, went about the business of being a puppy. Gail's scowl of fury abated a little when she saw Hephzibah playing with some little toy Clay had bought for her on the way home. After chewing on it, the puppy took the toy in her mouth, tossed it in the air, and then bounced around as if stalking it. When she'd seize it, she'd toss it and stalk it again.

Gail, making it clear that she didn't approve, agreed Hephzibah could stay. "But only," she asserted, "as long as I don't have to take care of the damned thing." Clay agreed to the conditions and the puppy had a home.

Clay's daughters came home from school and giggled with pleasure at the puppy. Clay devoted a good deal of time to teaching them how to play with Hephzibah, how to feed her, take care of her and make sure she was walked and let out into the yard and how to clean up after her. The puppy, remarkable in her intelligence, required little time to housebreak and train, and she learned commands with apparent ease and enthusiasm. It seemed to Clay that Gail had even begun to enjoy having her in the house.

***

Clay, jogging along the lakeshore in a violent windstorm, grimaced as he remembered the fury on Gail's face that day. He watched Hephzibah running up ahead of him. During the three and a half years since he'd adopted the scrawny little puppy, she had grown into a beautiful dog. Terry thought that she had yellow labrador and white shepherd in her ancestry, but at forty pounds, she was small for both breeds. "I'm pretty sure she also has other breeds mingled in, too," Terry shrugged.

"So she's a little mutt, huh?" Clay said.

Terry chuckled. "She's going to be a terrific mutt for you, partner."

Clay looked around and saw no one else had come out on the

promontory. Of course not, he thought, on a crummy day like this. He decided to let the dog run off the leash for a little while. He clicked his tongue and Hep stopped, turned to him and sat. Clay grinned to himself. He'd become convinced early on that Hep's intelligence ranked her above him on the food chain.

He knelt and pulled back the clip, and Hep took off, happy and bouncing and looking back at him from time to time. They came near the promontory and the rocks piled on the shore out into the lake.

Lots of family history here, he thought with a grin. When his uncle Bob and his cronies were on summer break while they were in high school, they would dive off the rocks and swim out to the Crib, the water treatment plant that stood at least a mile out in the lake.

Clay recalled the family fable about his dad's first encounter with Lake Michigan and chuckled to himself. His dad had grown up in Southern California and when Dad first came to Chicago to live, he went swimming with Clay's Uncle Bob. Dad, a fine swimmer, dove off the promontory into Lake Michigan and, according to the family legend, jumped back out with such haste that his swim suit didn't get wet. Uncle Bob would laugh as he related Dad's shrieks of disbelief at the polar frigidity of the lake even in July.

Jeez, Clay thought. *How cold would it be today?*

And what the hell was I thinking of to come over here? Again he found himself mystified at why he would have driven over to the lake in a wind that almost amounted to a gale.

Checking on Hep, he saw her about 50 yards off, having a wonderful time sniffing, chasing leaves, pawing at sticks. Huh, he thought. At least one of us is having a good time. He started to whistle...

But Hep stopped and turned to the rocks. She barked several times and ran toward the lake. Clay groaned. What if Hep had seen some other dog owner with his dog—

And then Clay saw what she was barking at. A girl in her mid to late teens, tall with a slim lovely figure, staggered out onto the Promontory. *Could she be drunk?* He wondered. He stared as she shrugged off her camel hair topcoat and stood for a few moments, wearing only a sheer white slip in the freezing wind. As Clay watched in bewilderment, she walked to the edge of the rocks. She slipped off a pair of jogging shoes.

What the hell? thought Clay. The girl looked like she planned to. . .

Her knees buckled and she fell into Lake Michigan.

Clay shrieked "No!" and sprinted to the rocks, tearing off the sweat suit as he went. He sat on a rock and stripped down to his jogging shorts and yanked off his shoes and socks. When he'd served as a Navy SEAL he had a lot of cold water experience and he was no stranger to it. It had been part of his qualifying for the SEALs, lying in freezing cold surf. Later, he'd worn a wet suit in cold water from Northern California up to Alaska.

Now it was him against a near ice-cold lake. Cold water training and experience were quite a few years ago.

He saw the steel gray waves smashing on the rocks, but no sign of the girl. He stood and scanned, watching for anything that would indicate—

There. He saw the flash of blond hair about fifteen yards out.

"Don't think, Clay," he murmured to himself as he ran to edge of the rocks. "Go get her."

He launched himself into the shallow surface dive of a

trained lifeguard that kept his head above water. He had to bite back a scream as the 35 degree water surged around him. The dive carried him five or six yards out and he fell into a swift crawl, never taking his eyes off the spot he'd seen the blond hair.

A surface dive into the gray, freezing water took him down a few feet. Visibility couldn't have been much worse as he pinwheeled, trying to catch a glimpse...

Then he saw a flash of white a few yards away: it was the girl's body sinking away from him into the black abyss. He grabbed a lungful of air and struck out.

He covered the distance to the young woman in moments. He gave a silent prayer of thanks that she faced away from him.

His lungs near bursting, he wrapped his right arm around her from the right side of her neck to her left armpit and grasped. He felt a slight movement, he thought, but it could have been only a spasm caused by the god-awful current.

Then he kicked for the surface. The swim upward, at the most ten or twelve feet, seemed to last forever, but his head broke the surface and he gasped air.

He turned and saw that they were about twenty yards out and maybe twenty-five from the rocks. Adrenaline surged through his body as he side-stroked to the rocks. Clay, a powerful swimmer and experienced lifeguard, pulled hard, but he felt that an eternity seemed to pass before he managed to reach the rocks and pulled her out.

Oh my God, please don't be dead, he breathed to the girl.

Somehow he climbed onto the slippery, freezing rocks, dragging the unconscious young woman up with him. He found some footing, picked her up and slung her over his shoulder. He managed to lift her out of the lake and bounced her on his shoulder in a desperate attempt to force water out of her lungs.

She remained unconscious and couldn't struggle. Clay saw at once he needed a paramedic crew, an ambulance and oxygen.

Stop and rest, his body told him. *Catch your breath.*

No, he told his body. Death from hypothermia waited for him just outside that red light that shone in his eyes. The girl hadn't resumed breathing and he knew he had to act fast.

He managed to keep going until he reached his clothes. He rubbed his skin hard with the rough towel, trying to dry off and get the circulation going again. He struggled into the hooded sweatshirt, his socks, and his shoes. Then he pulled on the sweat suit. His hands didn't function as they ought in the cold, but he yanked on the jersey work gloves and the black watch cap.

Breathing with labored pain, he ran to the edge of the rocks and grabbed the girl's coat that she'd discarded. To his relief, it hadn't gotten wet. He turned and hurried back to her. Pulling her up, he used the towel to give her what his granddad called a dutch rub, drying her as best he could. He managed to wrap her in her camel hair topcoat. Then he picked her up and headed back toward the path.

Where the hell did Hep go? He wondered in some obscure corner of his mind as he tried to gain control of the situation. He found a windbreak and stood gasping for air, knowing that he had to start CPR in moments.

He almost screamed with relief when he saw a man walking toward him. "Here!" he shrieked. "Help me!" He bent over the girl and saw that her lips had turned a dark blue. He realized that he might be too late to revive her, but he knew he couldn't fail to make the attempt to save her. He started chest compressions and controlled breathing in the girl's mouth, hoping the man would show up.

"Okay," said a voice.

"My phone," said Clay. He paused and reached into his pocket. He withdrew the cell phone and held it up. "Here! Call 9-1-1!" The man didn't take it. Clay fell back into the rhythm of the CPR and again yelled at the man to call 9-1-1. The man didn't respond.

To Clay's relief, the girl coughed and turned her head to the side. Clay turned her on her right side as she vomited out water and detritus. She hadn't regained consciousness, he saw, but she gasped and started to breathe on her own. Relieved, he looked up at the man who still stood there. "Take the phone, will you?" he yelled. "My hands are so cold I can't poke in the numbers!"

The man still had made no move to pick up the phone. "Damn it!" Clay screamed. "Call 9-1-1! This girl needs a hospital!" The man still didn't move. Clay, disgusted, grabbed the phone and flipped it open, not sure he could talk between his chattering teeth. He struggled to make his trembling fingers type in the emergency number. The man interrupted.

"Put down the phone!" yelled the man. Clay stopped and looked up in surprise. "Nice work, Idiot."

"What?" Clay stammered.

"Now you can put her back in the lake," said the man. "Pick her up. Let's go."

"Put her back? What. . .?" Clay stopped when he realized what the man held in his hand.

"What's the gun for?" Clay asked.

"You and this girl have to die," said the man, speaking with such dead calm that Clay had a hard time hearing him. "I can shoot you here or you can drown. Decide now."

Clay climbed to his feet. "Why do you want us to die?" He was playing for time, trying to figure this situation out. He saw, now, that the pistol was a small bore, likely a .22. Nonetheless it could be plenty lethal, he knew.

"Never mind," the man interrupted, waving the pistol. "What's it going to be—" But he didn't finish the question. Hephzibah slammed into the man's back, snarling and snapping at his throat.

"Oof," gasped the man as he staggered forward. Clay, shivering, stood riveted in place for just a moment, stunned with surprise that Hep had come to save him. In an instant, though, he recovered, took a deep breath, let out half of it and stepped in.

His first punch to the jaw snapped the thug's head back. A punch to the stomach drove out the man's breath and doubled him over. Clay's upper cut staggered him as Clay kicked the man's wrist. The gun fell to the ground and discharged.

In the next instant Clay had the pistol in his hand and pointed at the man, who lay stunned and struggling with an angry dog. "Hep," Clay yelled, "Down!" The dog stopped and backed away, showing her teeth, growling and barking. It occurred to Clay that he'd never seen her so transformed. He'd never been around a more gentle dog.

The man looked up and swallowed as he saw Clay holding the gun on him. "Know how to use that, Punk?" he asked.

"That's Mr. Punk to you, Buddy Boy," sneered Clay. "You bet I know how to use it. I've served in combat and I've shot guys who were a lot tougher than you. Get your butt out of here before I give you a new nostril."

Despite the beating he'd just endured, the man decided to take a tough stance. His face twisted into a bitter sneer of contempt. "Yeah, sure, I really believe you," he scoffed. "Why don't you take that gun and shove—"

Clay shot him in the right arm. Clay, a good shot, aimed to crease the man's shoulder. It would hurt, Clay knew.

The man stood stock still, shocked that Clay had pulled the trigger. He tried to stay belligerent, but then the pain of the wound in his upper arm hit. He clutched at the wound and began to cry.

"Hit the bricks, Creep," said Clay. "The next bullet will hurt a lot more. I'd recommend a hospital ASAP." The man turned and ran toward a parking lot. Clay watched him go, his finger still pressed on the trigger. *I could still put a bullet in the back of the bastard's skull*, he said to himself.

Despite his adventures in the Armed Forces, Clay knew that he was no killer. He had to make a deliberate effort to slide his trembling finger off the trigger as he watched the man start the car and take off. The man headed north on the Outer Drive. He'd probably make it to a hospital, Clay decided.

Clay flipped open the cell phone. He managed to suppress the shivering enough to tap in 9-1-1. It rang once and the operator picked up. Clay, now beginning to shiver beyond control, managed to blurt out: "Ambulance. Cops. Promontory." The operator said something as Clay sat down next to the unconscious girl. "Uh, huh," he said. "Hurry." Then he closed his eyes and lay down next to the young woman, hugging her as tight as he could. Hep lay down next to him, scared and concerned.

Chapter 4

Clay had vague impressions of police, an ambulance, the noise of the siren, then little else. He recovered consciousness in the Michael Reese Hospital Emergency Room an indeterminate time later. A tall Chicago cop stood over his bed.

"Hi," he said, his head feeling like someone had packed it with cotton. "You dirty copper, you'll never take me alive, see?"

"Works for me," said the cop. "I prefer it that way. Saves a lot of expense."

Clay chuckled and shook the cop's extended hand. "You did the celebrity impersonation pretty well," said the cop. "Bill Clinton, right?"

"Philistine," sneered Clay. "Jimmy Cagney. *Angels with Dirty Faces.*"

"Needs work," said the cop.

"I know," shrugged Clay.

"My name's Nolan," said the cop, handing him a business card.

Clay nodded. "Clay Foster," he returned. "I don't have a card. Or any identification for that matter. I left my billfold in my car, parked at the Promontory."

"Okay if I take a flyer here?" asked the cop and Clay nodded. "I'm guessing you were a SEAL?"

"Yeah," said Clay. "How'd you know?"

The cop shrugged. "Like I say, a guess, but an educated one. I served in the Marines myself."

"Semper Fi," smiled Clay. The cop looked a little surprised. "The Navy attached me to a Marine Unit for quite a bit of my hitch," Clay told him.

"You okay?" said the cop, his hand on his weapon. "You look terrible."

"Headache," said Clay. "Big time. But thanks for the compliment. Why don't you sit down?"

"Thanks, yeah, I will," the cop nodded with a grin and sat in a chair next to the bed. "I got your dog," he said. "Nice pooch."

"Yeah, she's a terrific pet," said Clay. "She saved my life and the girl's life as well." He explained how Hepzibah had jumped the thug in the park.

The cop smiled. "She's in my cruiser outside. I think she's asleep."

Clay nodded. "She's good at sleeping," he said. "Any time and any place will do." A nurse came over and handed him a couple of pills. "What's this?" he asked her.

"Tylenol," she smiled. "I heard you say you had a headache."

"Am I okay?" he asked her as he swallowed the pills with a big drink of water. He was surprised at how thirsty he felt.

"Yeah, but I'll have the doctor talk to you," the nurse nodded. "We want to keep you overnight."

"I left my wallet in my car, parked near the Promontory," he said. "I'll have to. . ."

"I can have my guys get it for you," said the cop, who Clay now realized was a Lieutenant.

Clay shivered, his body still struggling to throw off the lake chill. "Feeling okay?" asked the Cop.

"Yeah," said Clay. "I'm still frozen to the bone, I guess. Damn lake was cold."

"I'll bet it was, yeah," said Nolan.

Clay turned and saw his sweat suit hanging on a hook on a wall. "Keys in the jacket pocket," he noted. "A '62 Corvette," he added. "Deep blue with a black top." He gave directions to where he'd parked it. The lieutenant nodded and a patrolman came forward.

"Do I get to drive the 'Vette, Loot?" asked the patrolman.

"Only if you behave," said the Lieutenant. The patrolman grinned at Clay, found Clay's keys and departed.

Clay's mind cleared a little. "Do you know what's going on with the girl?" he asked.

The lieutenant shrugged. "She's pretty sick," he said. "They moved her to a room and they're pretty sure she'll make it. Still she's suffering from hypothermia, maybe a touch of pneumonia and she's shocky now."

"Yeah," said Clay.

"Want to tell me what happened?"

Clay shrugged. He began to relate what had taken place.

"I still can't believe you went into the Lake in March," said the Lieutenant, shaking his head.

"Not much choice," grunted Clay. "It was either go in or let the kid drown."

"You risked your life," said the Lieutenant. "Lot of guys wouldn't make that choice."

Clay shrugged. "I knew I could do it," he said. "I swam on the school teams in grade school, high school and college. I also got certified and worked as a lifeguard in high school. I've pulled a lot of people out over the years."

"Yeah?"

"Well, not so many the last several years, you know how it is."

"What about the blood?" asked the cop.

Clay tried to tell the story, aware of how bizarre the story had to sound to the policeman. "So why were two shots fired?" asked the lieutenant.

Clay tried to explain. The cop shook his head, looking puzzled by the story. He hauled out a notepad. "Can you describe the guy?"

Clay did his best to give a useful description, but his major memory was that of looking down the barrel of a handgun. "You'll want to check emergency rooms and 24 hour care places and that. I winged him and I think he needed stitches at least."

"Yeah, I'll get some guys on it," the cop nodded. "Do you own a gun?"

"Yeah," said Clay. "I own a Glock 19, a .9 mm. I keep it locked and unloaded in my safe at home. I got it because I work late at my projects sometimes. Yes, it's licensed."

"Okay," the cop said. "Anyone we can notify?"

"I suppose my ex-wife ought to know," said Clay. "She lives in Lake Geneva with her —ah — new husband."

"I got it," nodded the Lieutenant. "So you're divorced?"

"Yeah," Clay nodded. "I didn't want it and it got very bitter, but yes, I'm divorced."

The cop got the picture. He took the information, and stood. "Well," he said, clearing his throat. "You seem to be a hero, sir."

Clay raised his eyebrows. "I sure don't feel like a hero," he said. "As a matter of fact, I'm just feeling hungry now."

The cop smiled a little. "They're planning to keep you here overnight," he noted. "I imagine they'll bring you some chow pretty soon. What do you want us to do with your dog?"

"Call my neighbor, Scott Janess," Clay said, and gave the lieutenant his neighbor's address and phone number. "He'll come and get her, and then he'll keep her till I get out of here," he said. "Look, if you talk to him, tell him to bring me some clothes, will you? He's got a key to my townhouse." The cop nodded. He shook Clay's hand and started to go. Then he turned and walked back to the bedside.

"Listen," he said. "You did a helluva brave thing. A young woman who ought to be dead will live because of you. I want you to know that I appreciate it."

"Thanks," Clay said.

"If you get a chance to come by the station house," continued Nolan, pointing at his business card, "I know we've got a fair number of guys who'd like to shake your hand."

"Thanks for saying that," Clay nodded. "I appreciate it." The lieutenant left. An orderly came in a moment later.

"We've got a room for you, Sir," he said. "I'll take you up there now."

A few moments later the orderly wheeled him into a room where he transferred into the room's bed.

Clay lay back against the pillow, aware that he felt cold, tired and hungry. He tried to watch some idiotic sitcom, then the news, but his mind wouldn't focus.

He kept seeing a girl standing on the rocks on a cold gray day. The girl shed a coat and fell into the steel gray waves of Lake Michigan. Then the dive. The rescue. The swim to the rocks. The fight with the thug. Over and over...

Dinner arrived and he ate like a maniac, his headache fading. He felt pretty good once he finished and thought he'd get up. He made it to the bathroom and back before he realized that he didn't really feel like walking around. He felt a little weak and more than a little dizzy.

***

At nine that night, Clay switched off the light and tried to sleep. He'd just about dozed off when someone knocked and the door opened.

A tall woman, perhaps a few years younger than he, stood framed in the light from the hall. She stared into his room for a few moments. She had a lovely shape, he noticed, but he couldn't quite see her face.

"Mr. Foster," she said.

Clay reached up and flipped the light back on. "Yes," he nodded, "but my name is Clay. Mr. Foster is my dad." He held out his hand. She walked forward and took it. He motioned her to a chair next to the bed and caught a tiny whiff of a pleasant perfume that added to the woman's already powerful attractiveness.

"I'm Dr. Sharon Gray," she said. "I'm a consulting psychologist here at the hospital. I had to come in and thank you."

"For what?" he asked, as she released his hand and sat down.

"For saving my daughter," she said. "Clarisse."

"That's her name?"

Sharon nodded. "You risked your life," she noted. In the

dim light from the hallway, he saw a tear sparkle on her cheek. "To save someone you didn't know at all."

"I'm no hero," Clay said. "Anybody would have done it. I just happened to be there…"

"No," she said. "Almost nobody would have jumped into a near freezing Lake Michigan in that weather to save a girl he didn't even know or had never even laid eyes on before. I don't know how to thank you…" The woman choked and then began to cry in earnest.

Clay paused for a moment before replying. The woman wore the clothes of a professional: a gray suit with a modest skirt and a pale gray blouse with matching high heels. She had the same honey colored hair as Clarisse and Clay thought he might see a resemblance between the two. She also had very beautiful knees, he couldn't help but notice.

"Have you gone in to see her?" asked Clay, trying to shrug off the intense attraction he felt for her.

"Yes," the woman stammered, "but she's been fading in and out of consciousness."

"So what?" smiled Clay. "I don't think that's important at all. Go and spend the night with her in the room. They'll bring in a cot for you."

"She wouldn't even know I was there."

"I think you're wrong there," said Clay. "I think she'd sense that someone who loves her was sitting next to her, stroking her hair, loving her and being kind."

Sharon stared at him for a few moments and gave him a smile. The teeth were white and even and beautiful. "You're tired, aren't you," said the woman.

"Yeah, I feel a little bushed," said Clay. "It's been a pretty emotional day. But if you need to talk—"

"I do need to talk and I'd like to talk to you," she said. "But not tonight. Get some sleep—make that a lot of sleep—and I'll see you tomorrow."

"Okay," he said. "What time?"

"I don't know," she said. "I'll come as soon as I can."

"Swell," he said. "I'll look forward. . ."

But Sharon leaned forward and embraced him for a few moments. She leaned back and looked into his eyes, giving him a warm smile.

Then she leaned forward and kissed him. The kiss, at first gentle and warm, grew in passion and fervor until it far transcended normal gratitude. He returned the kiss and embrace for several of the best moments of his life.

"Wow," he managed to mumble when she drew back. "What was that all about?"

"I'll see you in the morning," she smiled. She turned and walked through the doorway into the hall.

Chapter 5

Clay didn't sleep too well, despite his exhaustion. He couldn't quite get his mind to shut down. He kept seeing teenaged girls falling into Lake Michigan and an attractive woman kissing him. He could almost smell that perfume on his pillow. What a day of contrasts, he thought.

He woke up a few times when nurses came in to check his temperature and blood pressure, then had to fight his way back to sleep. He gave up the struggle to stay asleep about 7:00 A. M. when a pretty young Hispanic woman brought a tray of breakfast into his room. He tried to say "hi", but started to cough.

"Uh, oh," said the young woman. "That doesn't sound good."

"I wouldn't presume to disagree," he said. "I went swimming in Lake Michigan yesterday."

"I know," she said. "The story got splashed all over the news. In fact, I'm feeling honored to meet you."

Clay almost choked on a swallow of orange juice. "What?" he gasped between coughs.

"Yeah, it was the lead story on a couple of broadcasts last night," she smiled. "You went into the Lake to save a girl, they said. My name is Marisol," she added, extending her hand. He took it for a few moments.

"I'm pleased to meet you, Marisol," said Clay, who coughed again and managed a smile. Oh, no, just what I need, he groaned to himself. Reporters and cameras and interviews.

"Please, you need to make an effort to eat," said the girl. "You're going to need it."

He looked up. "Did you just say 'I'm going to need it?'" he asked.

"Yeah, I'm afraid so," she grinned. "You've got a whole bunch of reporters waiting downstairs. They want to interview you and take your picture and like that." With a wave she gave him another smile and left.

Clay sighed and tucked into the breakfast, which included juice, pancakes, bacon and a fruit cup. His hunger pangs subsided a bit, but he could have eaten another tray full without difficulty.

His coughing seemed to relax as he sipped at the coffee. He almost never drank coffee, but the warmth felt good.

A young doctor came in and identified herself as Dr. Hazlitt. Clay introduced himself and groaned again as the doctor told him about the news stories on local TV. "Please," he said. "Tell me I don't have to face a phalanx of reporters this morning."

"Your modesty does you credit," she assured him. "But I'm afraid a whole lot of people want to meet you. It's a great human interest story." She set about examining him.

A few moments later, she straightened up. "How do you feel?" she asked.

"Okay," he shrugged. "A little cough. But how about the girl?"

"She's going to be okay, but she's got a touch of pneumonia," said Dr. Hazlitt. "Do you know who she is?"

"I don't think I've ever laid eyes on her before yesterday," he shrugged. "She was just a girl who jumped into the lake, as far as I knew."

"Tough," sympathized the doctor.

"Didn't her mother give you her name?"

"We don't know how to contact her mother," said Hazlitt.

"But—" Clay began, but paused. Again he felt the bewildering haze that seemed to surround the girl and her mother. Why wouldn't Sharon tell them about her daughter?

"I'm suspecting suicide, of course," said Dr. Hazlitt. "It seems that's the case."

"I don't think so," Clay said. He told her about the man with the gun. The story appeared to horrify the doctor, who shrugged a little. "Can I see her?

Hazlitt nodded. "Sure," she said. "In fact, when you want, you can get dressed and go home. I'll have them get your release ready. Did the nurse bring in your stuff?"

"I don't know," he said. He glanced at the closet.

"Okay, we've got them here at the nurses' station," she said. "The police brought in your wallet and keys, and your neighbor brought in a bag of clothes." She bid him goodbye and departed, telling him he could go home as soon as the release could be processed.

The nurse brought Clay a bag which contained his fresh clothes. As he laid them on the bed, he breathed a silent prayer of thanks. Even though his jogging clothes had dried out overnight, he didn't relish putting them back on. Yech.

Clay took a long shower. He stood in the hot, hot water, shampooed and shaved, letting his body throw off the lingering chill of the lake. He dried off and dressed, feeling better than he had since he'd gone out to jog yesterday morning.

But all the time the thought kept nagging him. Why hadn't the girl's mother identified her daughter?

A nurse came in with an envelope containing his wallet and keys. He had to sign some forms, and the hospital staff assured him he could go home as soon as they finished processing his insurance stuff.

Clay felt okay except for the recurring cough. He decided to try to find the young woman. His first stop at the nurse's station helped out. "What's her name?" asked the woman at the computer.

"I don't know," he admitted. "She's the girl who went into the lake, and I think her first name is Clarisse. That's all I—"

"That's all we know, too," she said. She wrote a number on a slip of paper. "She's in this room." Clay thanked her, but again felt a little puzzled. The girl's mother had been here. Why hadn't she given her name to the hospital staff?

Clay decided to get it over with and took the elevator to the lobby. The director of public relations met him and led him to a room where he took a half hour or so to talk with the press. Pictures and questions began to become repetitive and he thanked the group, but pleaded that he wanted to go and see the young woman he'd saved.

Clay went up to the girl's floor and found the room in a few moments. He peeked in the open door.

The girl lay on the bed, staring out the window at the grey, sullen March day. Clay knocked. She turned her head and saw him and then turned away.

"What do you want?" she asked, her tone sullen.

"I wanted to meet the young woman I pulled out of the Lake

yesterday," Clay said.

She turned back, lightning flashing from her eyes. Clay straightened with surprise as she snapped at him. "You!" she snarled. "Big hero, right? Why didn't you just let me die? It's what I wanted!"

"I know," said Clay. "I saw you go in. I know how serious you were."

"But...why? Why did you interfere?" she lashed out.

Clay paused for a moment. "I don't know," he said. "Maybe because I'm so lonely and scared myself."

The girl had been ready to retort. She choked on the words, though. He saw tears form in her eyes and walked over to her bed. He sat on the edge and took her hand. "It's okay, Clarisse," he said. She looked up and he noticed that she had lovely blue eyes, so deep as to verge on violet.

"You know my name?" she sobbed. "How. . ."

"I met someone who knows you," he began. "I just. . ." Then he stopped, seeing that the terrified girl needed comforting. He leaned over and hugged her, but her tears wouldn't quit. "Okay, Clarisse," he said. "Okay." He embraced the girl and just let her cry.

In a few minutes she calmed a bit and struggled to get herself under control. "Want to hear my duck joke, Clarisse?" he asked.

She smiled a little. "Sure," she said. "But call me Crissy. Everyone does."

"Hang on a minute," he said, going through an elaborate pantomime of lighting a huge cigar. "So this duck goes into an expensive restaurant, see?" he asked, taking a few puffs at the imaginary cigar.

"Got the picture," said the girl. "And watch where you're waving that cigar."

"So the duck hops up on a table," he went on. "A waitress goes over to shoo it away, but it turns out the duck can talk. 'Bring me a glass of swamp water and a raw fish,' it says."

Crissy nodded and Clay went on. "'Uh, huh,' says the waitress, stunned that the duck can talk of course. 'And how do you plan to pay for this? Cash?'"

"'Nah,' says the duck. 'Just put it on my bill.'"

Crissy gasped, then groaned. "Oh brother," she said, and giggled. "That's terrible."

"Want to hear another?"

"No thank you," said the girl. "In my weakened condition I can't take too much hilarity."

Clay chuckled and enjoyed hearing the girl laugh at the terrible joke. "Can we talk now?" he asked.

"Sure," said Crissy. "I'm Crissy DeRosa." She stretched out her hand. Clay's eyebrows went up a little. That wasn't the mother's surname.

"Clay Foster," he told her. He took her hand. "I saw you go in during my run along the lakefront."

"Why on earth did you go to the lakefront to run?" she asked. "I've never seen a worse day there."

He laughed. "That was tame compared to some weather even in the summer," he smiled. But again that question nagged him. Why *had* he gone over to the lakefront to run?

"But you saw me jump in?"

"Yeah," said Clay. "Well, my dog saw you, and I sort of followed her. You didn't jump in, either."

"What do you mean?" she asked, puzzled.

He explained how she'd slipped off her coat, walked to the edge of the rocks, and fallen in, as if she'd fainted. Crissy didn't say anything.

"I thought dogs had to be leashed over there," she said, after considering for a few moment.

"Yeah, they do," said Clay, wondering why she'd changed the subject. "But I let her go when I saw no one else was out there. She saw a squirrel and took off. The squirrel looked up and saw her coming. The squirrel's face turned white—And that isn't easy to do, you know, when you have a face covered with gray fur—"

"I suppose not," giggled Crissy.

"—But then Hep saw you, and took off toward you," he said, and related what he could of the rescue.

When he finished, she sat in silence for a minute or two. "You went into Lake Michigan in March to save me," said Crissy, her voice quavering, almost in a whisper. "You dove into that freezing, wild water."

"Well, yeah, I did," he said. "I didn't want you to die all alone in a cold lake."

"I am grateful, Clay," she said. "Thank you."

He smiled. "It's okay." He saw that she once again had tears forming in her eyes and changed the subject. He chatted Crissy up about some storms that he'd seen on the Lake. She listened, her interest apparent.

As they talked, he didn't pick up much depression, or hatred of her life or anger or bitterness. She seemed to be a very intelligent and warm person with a fine sense of humor, by no means suicidal.

"Got a place to go when you get out of here?" he asked.

She shook her head. "I don't think so," she said. "I've been living in my Grandma's apartment. But I guess I can't go back there if they've found me."

They? thought Clay. But he said, "No friends?" She shook her head. "What about your Mom and Dad?"

"No," she said. "That could never work."

"Clarisse," he said, "I know that's not altogether true."

"How would you know that?" said the girl.

"Your Mom came and saw me last night," he said.

Clarisse did a double take and stared. "What do you mean?"

"I mean, I lay in the hospital room. The door opened, a woman came in. She told me her name, Sharon something." He decided not to tell her that her mother had given him one of the most erotic kisses of his entire life. She didn't need to hear that, he decided. "So we visited, she said she'd see me today, said we'd talk some more—"

She interrupted. "You didn't see my Mom," said Crissy.

"What?" asked Clay, his mouth open. "But. . ."

She waved a hand. "My Mom's been dead for five months. Also her name wasn't Sharon."

Clay noticed that this whole conversation had taken on a surreal quality that would have brought a smile of pride to the lips of Eugene Ionesco and Salvador Dali. He sat back in the lounge chair and stared at the girl in the bed.

"Crissy," he said at last. "Do you have any idea who came to see me last night, then?"

"What did she look like?" she asked.

"Tallish, reddish blond hair, sharp business suit, I couldn't see the color of her eyes, nice figure, a bit younger than me..."

"That's what my mom looked like, all right," said Crissy.

"But like I say, she's been dead..."

The girl choked on a sob as her beautiful eyes teared up.

"Still miss her, huh?" noted Clay.

"Yeah," she said. "But a few weeks before the end, Mom and Dad began to fight all the time. I always felt frightened to come home during that period."

"Hm," Clay said. Then he had a hunch. "Could you describe your Dad?"

She shuddered. "Do I have to?"

Clay shrugged. "Might help," he said.

"He's tall, a bit overweight, crew cut grey hair, stinks of liquor most of the time any more. . ."

"I met him," said Clay.

"*Met* him?"

"Yeah, he showed up at the Promontory," he said. "After I pulled you out of the lake he came over. I asked him to help, he drew a gun—"

"He what?" she gasped.

"He pulled a gun," said Clay. "It was a small caliber, like a .22. Hep attacked him from behind—"

"Who?"

"My dog, Hephzibah. Hep for short. She jumped him from behind, I got in a couple of punches and took away the gun."

"Oh my good God," groaned Crissy.

Clay nodded. "Anyway this guy wanted me to throw you back in the lake. Then jump in after you. He left after I shot him in the arm."

She'd been sitting with her mouth agape since he'd told her that he'd met her father. A few moments elapsed. Then she shrugged. "Cripes," she said. "I don't know why I'm surprised."

"You mean that I met your Dad?"

"Not exactly," she said. "I wonder why he didn't shoot you on the spot. He's pretty nuts. He might have figured that you were my boyfriend or something. He hates all of them. I think he drove my mother to kill herself. I've been trying to stay away from him."

"You mean this man's been trying to kill you right along?"

"Yeah," she said. "He's been after me since Mom died. I've been hiding with my grandmother in her apartment, but then Grandma died, and…well…" Her voice trailed off.

"Tough," he said, squeezing her hand.

"Thanks," she said, and managed a little smile. "Where did you get the name Hephzibah?"

"It's Biblical Hebrew," Clay smiled. "It comes from the Book of Second Kings in the Old Testament. Hephzibah was the mother of a King named Manasseh. The name means 'My delight is in you.'"

"Very nice," she smiled. "I wish I knew more about the Bible."

"How old are you?"

"I'll be eighteen," she shrugged.

"When?" he asked, trying to be serious.

"July," she shrugged again.

He managed not to smile. "When can you go home?" he asked.

"I think this afternoon," she said. "Not that it makes any difference. I don't have any place to go."

Clay couldn't help his surprise now. "What does that mean?"

"I mean, I'm like homeless, you know?" she said. "If I go

back to Grandma's apartment, my father will find me and kill me."

"You've got a place to go," he said. "You can come home with me."

She looked up, amazed. "What?"

"I've got a big condo," he smiled. "Three bedrooms, including one I don't ever use. It's got a bed, a closet, shades and drapes on the window, hardwood floors, and—now listen to this—a bathroom with running water and a flush john, even."

"Oh, wow!" she giggled.

"Now I know what you're thinking," he said. "It's too much, right? You're overwhelmed, right?"

Crissy giggled again and Clay again noticed how much he was enjoying her. Crissy, he decided, was an altogether charming and lovely young woman.

Wait a minute, he thought. This young woman tried to commit suicide? That seemed preposterous.

"Do you have a family?" she asked.

"No," he shook his head. "No, I got divorced some time ago. I bought the condo after my wife tossed me out. I got three bedrooms because I thought my children would come to see me. They never do, though."

"They don't like you?" she asked.

"Doesn't sound like it, I guess," he smiled. "Since the divorce has been finalized—a couple of years ago—I haven't laid eyes on them."

"Were you an abuser?" said the young woman.

"No," he smiled at the blunt question. "Just stupid. I'll tell you about it sometime. Think of it as a tale for a long winter night in front of the fireplace." She managed a little smile.

"You'll be safe with me there, anyhow," he went on. "Do you go to school?"

"Not now," she said. "I had to quit after Mom died, just before the start of the second semester of my senior year."

"Uh," he said.

"Yes?"

"Weren't you a little young to be a senior?"

She shrugged. "I skipped second grade," she said. "I've always been a good reader since I was about four, I think."

"Gotcha," he nodded. This information confirmed his impression that he was chatting with a pretty smart young woman.

A knock at the door made them turn. Dr. Hazlitt stood there. "Ah, Mr. Foster. Can you give us a moment?"

"Does he have to go?" said Crissy.

"Well, I think for purposes of modesty—" smiled the doctor.

"I've got some stuff to do, Crissy," said Clay. "I'll be back."

"Okay," she said. Then she added, her voice low and shy: "You promise?"

The question surprised Clay. "Yeah, I do," he said. "Tell you what. You get scared, call me in my room." He gave her the number and saw the big blue eyes tear up. He realized that the girl remained frightened and had come to trust him to protect her, just in the short time they'd been talking. "Okay," he said. "Let's try plan B. I'll wait here in the hall, okay?"

The girl swallowed, nodded and shook back the honey-colored hair. "Thank you, Clay," she said. Her violet eyes brimmed with tears but somehow sparkled at him. Even as disheveled as she looked, he couldn't help notice that she was one of the most beautiful young women he'd ever seen. *What could be going on inside that head?* He wondered.

He stepped into the hall and saw a lounge a few feet down from Crissy's room. He took a chair which allowed him to keep an eye on the room. A promise is a promise, he told himself.

"Is she okay?" said a voice from the other side of the room. He looked up. Sharon Gray stood in the corner, leaning against the wall. He saw at once that she resembled the girl in the hospital room a few feet away: height, figure, and hair color were all but identical in the two. In particular he noticed that Sharon had the same exotic eyes as Crissy, so blue they verged on violet. Again she wore the suit of a professional, though today she'd put her hair up in an attractive style.

"Yes, she seems to be all right, no ill effects," he agreed. "The doctor's with her now." Sharon nodded. He paused for a moment. "Excuse me for asking a very rude question," he said.

She looked him in the eye. Then, she wavered and looked at the floor. "Why am I not dead?"

"Yes," he said. "That's the question. I imagine you get that a lot."

"I think you're the only one who knows," said Sharon.

"Why's that?" he asked.

"You met her father yesterday," she said.

"The thug in the park," he said.

"The same," she said. "He's violent, as you saw, and killing her seems to have become his life's work. I wanted to take her out of state to live—" she paused and choked a little.

"Uh-huh," said Clay, trying to encourage her a little.

She gained a little control and wiped at her eyes with a handkerchief. "He couldn't find her for several months. But when her grandmother died, he saw the obituary and figured out how to find her."

"Oh," he said. He started to ask a question, but that moment the door to Crissy's room opened and the doctor emerged. She turned and spotted Clay and came over to him. She nodded at Sharon but didn't address her.

"I thought yesterday she might have a slight pneumonia," said Dr. Hazlitt. "But that doesn't seem to be the case. I think a touch of malnourishment together with the lingering effects of hypothermia. . ." her voice trailed off and she paused for a few seconds, gathering some thoughts.

"You were saying?" asked Clay.

"In a suicide situation I almost always suspect some drug use," said Dr. Hazlitt, shuffling through some papers on her clipboard. "I'm sorry to be blunt, because I can see the affection you have for her. Still I'd like to do a tox screen on her, but we need parental permission." Clay cut a swift glance at Sharon, who shook her head just a little to say "Don't say anything."

Dr. Hazlitt looked up. "I think a few good meals, some rest and a few good nights' sleep would be my prescription right now."

"That could be a problem," said Clay, turning back to Dr. Hazlitt. "She's afraid to go back to her apartment. So I asked her to move in with me for a few days anyhow, until we can—you know—find a proper place for her."

"A beautiful teenaged girl living in your house?" said Dr. Hazlitt, her eyebrows raised.

"I know what you're saying," nodded Clay. "But I have a friend I can invite in."

"A chaperone, sort of?" smiled Dr. Hazlitt.

"Yes," nodded Clay. Hazlitt looked at her clipboard and

made a note on it. Clay took the opportunity to glance at Sharon, who nodded with a little smile.

"You can go home now," Hazlitt said. "Could you pick Crissy up this evening? I'd like to keep her just a bit longer."

"I think I might wait with her until she's ready to go also," said Clay. "She's pretty scared."

Hazlitt thought for a second, and then agreed. "Yes, she did seem more confident when you were around. Okay."

After a few more pleasantries, Clay shook hands with Hazlitt. He glanced back to Sharon who sat looking unconcerned, as if the conversation meant nothing to her. Hazlitt departed and Clay stood and walked over to Sharon.

"Is that okay with you?" asked Clay, sitting next to her. "I mean, with Crissy coming to live with me?"

She hesitated, looking for the right words. "Can I come as well?" asked Sharon.

"Huh?" said Clay. "You mean—er—live at my house too?"

Sharon nodded. "Please, just for a time, until she's better."

"Well, I don't know—"

"Please, Mr. Foster," pleaded Sharon. "I'll be happy to pay room and board—"

"No, that's not what I meant," he said. "You're welcome and I'd be glad for your help. I intended to say that I've never been the parent of a teenager before, and I don't know what to do."

"I'm no expert either," said Sharon, "but I really want to stay as close to her as I can."

"I get it," Clay nodded. "Are you going to tell her now?"

Sharon considered, but then shook her head. Clay pulled a business card from his wallet and handed it to her. "You can go there now if you wish..." he offered.

"Okay," she said. She started down the hallway, but then turned and came back. "Why are you doing this?" she asked. "I mean, you're extending yourself for two people you don't even know?"

He thought. "I'm a little tired of living all alone, I guess," he said.

Sharon smiled and reached up her hand to his cheek. "You're a very kind person, Clay Foster," she said. "I'm so grateful to you." She drew his lips to hers and gave him another kiss, this one brief and gentle, but full of gratitude. When she drew back, he again stared into her eyes, realizing that this woman had the most striking eyes he'd ever seen.

She gave him a beautiful smile, and then she turned and started down the hallway.

Clay returned to Crissy's room. He knocked, though the door had been left ajar. "Can I come in?"

"Yeah," said her voice. He walked in and found her lying on the bed. He pulled a chair up next to her and took her hand.

"You stayed around, like you said you would," she noted.

"Does that surprise you?" he asked. "That someone would make a promise and keep it?"

She shrugged. "A little, I guess," she said.

"You can count on it," he affirmed.

She nodded thanks again. "If it weren't for you I'd be at the bottom of Lake Michigan."

"So do you want to hear the plans?" he asked, stroking the back of her hand with his thumb. She looked up.

"We have some plans?" she asked.

"I mean what I said. I want you to come and live with me," he said. "For a while, I think, like we discussed."

She shrugged. "Are you sure?"

"Yeah," he said. "Just until we can figure out what to do with you and how to keep you safe. Me and Hephzibah."

She wrinkled up her face. "Your dog?"

"Hephzibah. Hep for short," he nodded. Crissy smiled. "She's a yellow Lab and white shepherd mix. Can you walk?"

"Yeah. . ." A little look of fear crossed her face.

"Listen to me," he said. "I'm not leaving the hospital, not until you're ready. I'll stay with you until the doctors let you come home too. Promise."

"Okay," the girl smiled. Then she sat up, leaned to him and hugged him. "Thank you," she whispered. "I've been so scared so long. . ."

He nodded. "Is that why you jumped into Lake Michigan in 35 degree water?"

She hesitated. "Sort of," she said. "Yeah, I guess that's part of it." She looked reluctant to talk about the situation. He nodded. He didn't need to press her now and upset her. It could wait.

"Are you feeling okay?"

"Yeah, sure, I'm fine."

"Okay, come with me. I have to check out."

A little look of fear crossed her face. He changed the tone. "Listen to me," he said. "I'm not leaving the hospital, not while you're still here. I'll stay with you until the doctors let you go home, I promise."

"But..." she began.

"Yes?"

"Well, I feel terrible," she said. "I mean, I so appreciate you staying with me, but don't you have to go to work?"

"I work out of my house, and at this point I don't have anything to do that would be more important than you."

Crissy smiled. "Thank you," she said. "I've been scared so long…"

"Okay," he said. "We'll talk at home. You know how to play Gin Rummy?"

"Yeah, I guess," she said. "I'm not very good, though."

"Got any money?"

"Some," she said. "I have a bank account but I just have a few dollars with me. In my coat."

"That's just the way I like it," he cackled, rubbing his hands together. "A lousy Gin player with some money. I'll see if I can round up a deck of cards." He stepped out to the nurses' station a few feet down the hall and found that they could loan him a deck.

Two hours later, a package arrived for Crissy. "What's this?" she asked the nurse, puzzled.

"Dunno," said the nurse.

Crissy ripped it open and found a pair of jeans, a tee shirt with long sleeves and heavy socks, along with a pair of lime-green Crocs. The last thing she lifted out was a bag containing some lingerie. "'This ought to get you home,'" she read off the card.

"Any signature?" he asked.

She shook her head. "I guess I should change," she noted.

"Thank goodness," he said. She lifted an eyebrow. "I'm down a gazillion points in the game. You little fink. Next you're going to want the keys to my house."

Crissy laughed and went into the washroom. Typical of my luck with women, Clay sighed. The girl had hustled him at gin rummy. Sure. That had to be it.

He listened as Crissy turned on the shower in the washroom, then took the deck of cards and began to play a little solitaire.

She took a long shower. He imagined that the warmth felt good. He heard a hair dryer go on, also, and he chuckled to himself.

When Crissy came out, he did a double take. As he'd assumed, the girl was beautiful, like a magazine model, skin bright and glowing, her hair flowing in gentle waves down her back. "Holy Mackerel," he said.

"'Holy Mackerel?'" she asked, looking bemused.

"Do you listen to the Cubs games on radio?" he asked.

"No," she grinned. "White Sox fan."

"Yeah, me too," he agreed. "But the Cubs used to have a radio announcer who always said 'Holy Mackerel' when something dramatic happened. Guy named Vince Lloyd."

"Oh," she said. "What dramatic thing happened now?"

"You look beautiful," he said. Crissy looked at him for a long moment.

"Do you mean it?" she said, and her voice quavered just a little.

"Of course I do," he said. "Don't you ever get compliments?"

To his surprise, Crissy sat on the bed and began to cry. *Oh my God*, he thought. *What has this girl's life been like?*

He went to her and sat with her, just embracing her shoulders a little until the storm passed. He murmured comfort to her.

A knock at the door. Lieutenant Nolan came in. "Hello,

Foster," he said. "I didn't know if you'd hang around."

Clay introduced Crissy to the lieutenant. She shook his hand.

"Want to talk?" asked Nolan. Crissy shrugged okay. "I need to nail some stuff down, Miss DeRosa."

"Okay," she said. "Could you call me Crissy?"

"Sure," said Nolan. "I'd be honored. Anyhow we're still looking for this guy who tried to kill you and Foster at the Lake. I hear you think he's your father, huh?" Crissy nodded, and Clay excused himself to the hallway.

"I'll be right here, Crissy," he told her. She gave him a grateful smile. Nolan came out several minutes later, shaking his head. He came over and sat down next to Clay.

"This girl is no suicide," said Nolan.

"I agree," said Clay. "She strikes me as articulate, intelligent, and considering what happened to her, I think she's handling stuff very well."

"I guess she could be the greatest actress of all time," said Nolan.

"I'm not a psychiatrist," said Clay. "But I think the father had a lot to do with the jump into the Lake."

"Yeah, I agree," said Nolan. "No luck yet in finding the father. He wasn't at his house today when the Winnetka coppers went over there. You want me to call you when we find him?"

"Thanks, yeah," said Clay, and handed Nolan a business card. "I think the girl will want to know. She's pretty scared."

"I don't blame her," said Nolan. "This doesn't make sense, the father wanting to kill his daughter."

"He blames Crissy for his wife's death," Clay noted.

"Yeah," said Nolan. "I called the Winnetka police about that. They don't consider the girl a suspect in her mother's death. She never has been, not even close. No one there understands why the father thinks she did it."

They shook hands and Nolan took off. Clay went back into the room.

"Thank you for staying," Crissy said and Clay could see she meant it. "I appreciate how kind you've been to me and I don't feel scared when you're around. I'm a perfect stranger to you and . . ." her voice trailed off.

"Okay," he said. "I have a buddy I'd like you to meet, okay?"

"Who's that?" she said.

"My friend Scott, who's watching my dog for me."

"Why?"

"He's a counselor and social worker at a church we both attend. He helped me a lot when…"

When he didn't continue, she said, "When what?"

"When my marriage—uh—blew up a couple of years ago."

"Oh," said Crissy. "Why do you want me to meet him?"

"I'd like you to talk to him, you know, kind of unpack some stuff up there." He pointed to the girl's head. "He's very good, real kind, you know? And I'm sure he'd agree that anyone whose father has been trying to kill her needs all the support she can get."

"Thank you for being so considerate," she stammered. "But…"

"But what?"

"I couldn't pay him. I don't have any insurance, either…"

"Don't worry about that."

***

About an hour later, the nurse came in and told Crissy she could go home. Crissy looked up at Clay and raised an eyebrow. "Are you ready?" she asked.

"Sure," he said. "I mean, the company has been great, and all that, but—"

She giggled and Clay again enjoyed the relieved happiness he could hear in the laugh. He noticed that her confidence had gone up quite a bit in the last few hours. "I know what you're talking about," she said. "I can't wait to get out of here."

"Okay," he said. "Let me go down to my room, get my coat, and I'll come back and get you. You be okay for a few moments?"

She nodded and gave him a smile and a casual hand wave. "Yeah, don't worry," she said.

"Okay," he said. "You get your stuff together and I'll be right back."

He walked out, closing the door behind him. He returned to the lounge and found Sharon looking at a magazine. "I have to go down to my room," he said. "Will you keep an eye on her?"

"How about if I just go to your apartment? Maybe it'd be better if I met her there."

Clay considered. Oh, what am I worried about? What could happen in a few moments? "Sure, I guess," he shrugged. He gave her a business card with his address and told her where he'd hidden a spare key. She turned left and headed for the staircase at the end of the hall.

Clay rode the elevator to his floor and trooped down to his room where he collected his wallet, keys, and other stuff. He thanked the nurses at the station and went back up to Crissy's room. He knocked and opened the door a crack. "Okay to come in?" he said.

She didn't answer. He pushed the door open. The bathroom door stood open a little, and he rapped on it. No answer.

Now he became alarmed. He hurried down to the nurses' station. "Where's Crissy?" he asked.

The nurse smiled. "Oh, her father picked her up a minute or two ago. They should be in the lobby by now—"

Clay yelled, "Call the police. Now!" Then he broke into a dead sprint for the stairway.

Chapter 6

Clay shot down the stairs and emerged into the lobby. *Why the hell did Security let that guy in the hospital?* he wondered.

The elevator doors opened and Crissy stumbled out, impelled by a shove from the man who'd intimidated Clay at the Promontory. Clay took off across the lobby toward them. Crissy saw him and her eyes widened. "Clay!" she screamed.

Now the thug saw him and jerked her arm behind her. He tried to pull a pistol out of the pocket of his trench coat. "Don't try it, Jerk," he snarled. "Or I shoot the girl and she dies right here—"

But Clay didn't slow down. He dove at the pair from three feet away and crashed into Crissy, driving her father back. The gun came free as the father lost his balance. His arm struck the ground as he fell. The gun discharged into the ceiling and the lobby erupted into screaming confusion as the sound reverberated and the smell of exploded gunpowder permeated the air.

Clay took a shoulder roll and regained his feet at once. The father lay sprawled, struggling for breath and unable to get to his feet.

Clay launched a kick that would have broken the father's neck, but the father squirmed just enough to take the kick on his shoulder. He screamed as Clay's Nike tore open the gunshot wound he'd received yesterday. Clay dove for the gun and slapped it across the lobby floor.

By now the father gained his feet and screamed a profanity. Security guards streamed toward him and he ran to the door. An elderly gentleman had just about entered the revolving door but the father seized him and threw him aside.

The man staggered backward. Clay saw that he could either catch the gentleman or pursue the father. He took the former course. He grabbed the old man just before he landed hard on his back, and Clay went down with the old man on top of him.

It took a second or two for Clay to extricate himself, and then he was up again, speeding through the door in pursuit. He reached the sidewalk in time to see the father turn the corner of the hospital.

Clay ran to the corner, but by the time he arrived he saw no sign of the father. He stood there, stunned with surprise.

What the hell? Where did he go? The street lay wide open, the sidewalks were empty…

With a last look around, he turned back to the lobby of the hospital, puzzled.

How could he have vanished like that? There was no place to hide. The street was wide open. He'd only been a couple of seconds behind the man.

Crissy stood waiting for him next to a female security guard. The girl sobbed with relief when he walked in. "Crissy," he asked. "Are you all right?"

"Yes," she sobbed. "Just scared. Tell me he didn't hurt you?" she managed.

"No," Clay said, putting an arm around her shoulder and

embracing her. "No, I'm a little bruised but I'm okay. He went around a corner and just vanished." She looked at him in surprise. "Yeah," he went on. "He seemed to disappear."

Crissy bit her lip, looking puzzled. "And you were right behind him?" she asked.

"Well, yeah," he said. "I can't imagine..." His voice trailed off.

Crissy shook her head. "No, that can't be, can it?" she muttered, almost to herself.

"What do you mean?" he asked.

Crissy looked up. "Oh, sorry," she said. "I didn't mean to say that out loud."

Clay waited a second or two and asked, "What happened upstairs after I left the room?"

Crissy nodded and looked up. "Dad stormed into the room a few moments after you left," she said. "He pulled out the gun and pointed it at me. He told me to get going, that we had unfinished business at the lake."

Clay shuddered. "The nasty jerk," he snarled. "He must have been watching the room, waiting for me to leave."

Crissy nodded. "Yes, I think that's right," she said. "I don't think he wants to give up now on killing me."

Clay frowned. "I don't get this," he said. "I'm in way over my head. Why would your father be so intent on killing you?"

"I don't know," she pleaded. "He's been, like, out of his mind."

The police arrived and Clay again met Lieutenant Nolan. The interview went on for some time.

"How did my father know how to find us?" asked Crissy.

Nolan snorted. "Foster's picture has been all over the news

in the area here. I think Fox and CNN picked up the story for national distribution today. If your father didn't see it, he's blind."

"Oh," said Crissy.

"Are you ready to go, Foster?" asked Nolan.

"Yeah," said Clay.

A little later, Clay walked to his old Corvette, his arm around his ward. He kept his eyes roaming around the scene. "Where are we going?" she asked.

"Not far," he said. "I live in Hyde Park. Like I say, the house isn't what you'd call luxurious but I'm sure you'll be comfortable."

Crissy nodded. She gave him a broad grin as he unlocked his Sting Ray. The girl looked excited to sit in the leather.

"What a gorgeous car," she said. "I've never ridden in a Corvette."

"It's my prized possession," he agreed. "I got it from the estate of the original owner, who'd cared for it like it was one of his kids. At least my ex-wife didn't take this in the divorce settlement."

They lapsed into silence as they drove the short distance to his building. Clay let them in and stopped at his neighbor's apartment to pick up Hephzibah. At seeing him, the dog went unto spasms of joy accompanied by high pitched whining. She seized a shoe next to the door and brought it to her master. Then she rolled onto her back in a frenzy of greeting.

"What's this?" laughed Crissy.

"She's done it since I've had her. I think it's a characteristic of yellow labs. Whenever people come in, she brings them a little gift: a shoe, a hat, whatever comes to mouth. One time she brought me a can of corned beef hash." Crissy laughed and knelt to pet the dog which writhed on the floor in ecstatic greeting.

Clay led Crissy to his apartment and opened the door. "I'm home, June," he yelled.

"Who is June?" said Crissy.

"Oh, that's from the *Leave it to Beaver* sitcom. Jerry Mathers played Beaver Cleaver—no, he wasn't really a beaver, it was a nickname—Tony Dow portrayed his brother Wally, Barbara Billingsley sustained the role of the mom, whose name was 'June', and Hugh Beaumont performed the father, whose name was 'Ward'." Crissy grinned and complimented his grasp of 1950s TV trivia. "Anyhow," Clay went on, "Ward Cleaver always yelled 'I'm home, June,' when he came in."

Sharon walked in from the kitchen. Crissy smiled. "Hi," she said. "I'm Crissy."

"I know," said Sharon. She took the girl's outstretched hand. Then she sobbed and threw her arms around the young woman. She continued to cry as she embraced Crissy.

The emotional hug took Crissy by surprise, Clay saw. She hugged Sharon back, but with something of a reserve.

"I ordered pizza," said Sharon. "They'll deliver it in a half hour or so. I also picked up some pop, a six pack of beer, and a bottle of Chianti. Anything else you need?" she asked Clay.

"Well, no," he said. "I guess not." Sharon nodded, smiling and still holding Crissy in a light embrace. Clay still felt puzzled that Crissy had seemed so baffled by the greeting. "Crissy," he said. "Do you know this woman?"

"Other than we just met, no," shrugged Crissy.

Clay fixed Sharon with a pointed stare. "Er," she said,

dropping her hands. "Crissy, why don't you go up to the bedroom and get settled? I fixed up the guest room for you. First door on the left at the top of the steps. Come on, I'll show you."

"Thank you," smiled Crissy. "I'm grateful to both of you. I don't think Dad will be able to find us now, do you?"

"I think you can probably relax a little, yes, Crissy," Clay nodded. "Try not to be afraid."

She nodded and followed Sharon into the hall and up the steps. Sharon returned smiling in a few moments. "I bought her some outfits, you know, tee shirts, jeans, a couple of dresses, and pajamas as well as some toiletries like deodorant, toothpaste and floss, you know. . ." Her voice trailed off as she saw Clay staring at her. "Er," she said. "Is something wrong, Mr. Foster?"

"Her mother died six months ago, Sharon," he said. "If that's your name."

Sharon didn't look at him for some moments. "I am Sharon Gray, yes," Sharon nodded. "I can show you my identification if you need to see it. I didn't lie to you about that, I promise…"

"You promise," he nodded. "What else did you lie about?"

Sharon bit her lip, but didn't respond. She clasped her hands in front of her, and turned away, not speaking.

"Let me see if I understand this," he said. "I gave you access to my home, my keys, and all that, and you really aren't Crissy's Mom, is that right?"

Sharon walked over and looked up the steps. She turned back. "Okay. Look, please let me explain. You're right, I did lie in a way."

"You aren't Crissy's mother, are you?" he asked again.

"I don't know for sure," she shrugged.

"What does that mean?" he asked, by now baffled.

She took a deep breath. "I got pregnant at the age of fourteen," she said. "The father was an eighteen year old college boy who lived a couple of houses away in my neighborhood. He and his parents were moving out of state. I went to his going away party with some girls who were a lot older than me. I waited until my parents went to sleep and sneaked out of my house. My parents didn't know. The people who owned the house where the party was held weren't home."

"Oh, brother," he said. "Let me guess: lots of dope, lots of booze, I imagine?"

"Yes," said Sharon. "A typical teenage home alone party."

"I've got the picture," he said. "Go on."

"The guest of honor—talk about an irony, linking him in any way with honor—took an interest in me. We started to make out, and I didn't know how to handle it."

"Yeah, you were a little young," he said.

"He pulled me into this little room where they'd set up a couple of air mattresses. I tried to resist, I guess, a little. I remember that I tried to say 'no' a few times. Still he was an athlete at the high school, football and wrestling, so he was a lot stronger than me. It didn't take long for him to take all my clothes off."

Clay nodded. "I suppose he raped you then, huh?"

Sharon began to cry. A tear appeared on his cheek as she re-lived her worst memory. "It terrified me," she said. "It hurt so much. He claimed to know what he was doing, and not to worry. He told me it would get better as we went along, and it would only hurt for a few seconds. But it never hurt less and it didn't get better."

She paused and wiped her eyes. She looked back up the steps to make sure Crissy hadn't shown up. "I don't want her to hear this," she said. Clay understood and nodded. "It only lasted a couple of moments. He got up about a minute later and put his clothes back on and went back to the party. I could hear him laughing and joking about it with some of his disgusting buddies. In fact I can still close my eyes and hear it and see that room. They even applauded. I was so humiliated and ashamed that I was crying. I got dressed, and left the room and the party. I never saw him again."

"Never saw him again?" said Clay. "I thought you said he lived in your neighborhood."

"Oh, he timed this to perfection," she said. "He and his parents moved away the next day to some place in New England. I didn't think too much of him being gone. In fact I remember that I never wanted to see him again. I never have."

"Not surprising, I suppose," said Clay.

Sharon couldn't talk for a few moments. She blew her nose into a napkin and wiped at her eyes again. At last she managed to rally. "So that's how I got pregnant," she said. "Not a real romantic story."

"Well," Clay shrugged. "I guess if your story's true for a change..."

"I got pregnant, didn't I?" Sharon snapped. "Fourteen years old. I had no more idea of what to do than if I'd been assigned to command a nuclear submarine."

"Right," said Clay. "So..."

"My mom could see how distressed I was, of course," she said, still keeping an eye on the steps. "She noticed that I didn't have a period a few weeks later. At the time I didn't know what it meant, but I also began to get morning sickness. My Mother figured it out. Mom and Dad took me to the doctor a month or so after the party."

"Your pediatrician?" he asked.

"No," she said. "She found an obstetrician who did abortions."

"I see," he nodded. "And he ran a lot of tests, I suppose?"

"Yes," she said. "He told me the boy had gotten me pregnant."

"Uh, huh," Clay nodded. "So how did your Mom deal with that?"

"Mom insisted the doctor abort the baby right there," said Sharon. "Dad agreed wholeheartedly. They both told me that would be the best thing I could do. I agreed after some discussion, though I didn't like the idea. Then, when the nurses and doctors put my feet into the stirrups, and I heard them turn on that awful machine..." she shuddered, the horror of the memory overwhelming her for a moment.

Clay knew what she'd done. "I get it," he said. She looked at him for the first time in several minutes. "You bailed, huh?"

Sharon nodded. "I screamed and cried and thrashed. The doctor didn't want to proceed with me that upset, so they took my feet out of the stirrups and helped me up. I got dressed, and we went home."

She didn't go on for several moments, again choked by tears. *What a terrible memory*, thought Clay. He now felt sorry for this exquisite woman, and felt sorry that he'd pushed her into remembering this ghastly event. He waited. A few moments later, she went on.

"Mom and Dad nagged at me for a couple of weeks to reconsider, to go ahead and kill the baby. That continual demanding—nagging at me to get an abortion—caused a real and permanent rift between me and my parents. Mom and Dad were ashamed of me and didn't want their friends to know, so they sent me away for the pregnancy to a residential facility in Idaho."

"All by yourself?" asked Clay.

Sharon nodded. "It was a place for pregnant girls, a pretty discrete home off the beaten path," she said. "I lived there and went to school, such as it was, for several months. I didn't come home, and they didn't visit me until Crissy came along."

"So they were there for the birth?" Clay asked.

"Well, sort of," she said. "They waited out in the hall until I gave birth. They didn't support me or comfort me in the godawful pain, and terror, and all that. So I delivered all by myself, though of course with the help of a doctor and a couple of nurses. But I've never felt any more alone in my life."

"Uh, huh," he said.

"A few minutes after Crissy was born, my parents came into the delivery room and sat with me," she said. "It was a long and horrible labor. It left me so tired and beat up that I didn't know what to do. For a long time they tried to persuade me—well, browbeat me would be a better expression for what happened—to put her up for adoption."

She turned back and looked at him. "It might have been okay if I hadn't seen her," she said, and he saw the tears on her cheeks. "But the nurse didn't know that I'd made an agreement and she put Crissy in my arms. Then I wouldn't let go."

"Yeah," Clay nodded, and he felt real sympathy for this

lovely woman with the intense eyes. He recalled how his girls had been yanked away from him a year and a half before.

"They sent in a guy who claimed to be the hospital chaplain to see me. My parents came in with him. For an hour—well, it seemed longer than that—-they persuaded me—more like beat me up in the mental and emotional ways—to let her go. They told me I couldn't support her, I had my life ahead of me, I'd have children when I could handle it—I imagine you can hear the drill."

"I guess."

"At last they gave up trying to reason with me and they literally pulled her out of my arms. My father held me down and my mother peeled my arms and hands away. That wound has never healed. I'm still alienated from my parents."

"They're still ashamed of you?" asked Clay.

Sharon nodded. "No one would have ever called my relationship with my parents especially loving. It was never the kind of love a parent and child ought to share. I've always—and I mean from the earliest memories I have—well, I've had the feeling they were sorry they ever had me, that maybe they'd made a mistake. They never said it in any direct words, but I thought maybe Mom forgot to take her pill one day and conceived me by accident. On the other hand, maybe I put myself in the position to get pregnant just to pay them back. I can't deny it's possible."

"Geez, Sharon," said Clay.

"Now that I think of it, that could be why I'm so passionate to take care of Crissy," said Sharon. "I feel like she really needs to know that you and I love her and care for her."

"I guess I feel the same way," said Clay. "I wouldn't have a problem with that. God knows I miss my own kids so much since the divorce—"

Both paused for a few moments. "About my parents again," said Sharon. "To this day I don't see them very often, maybe once a year and sometimes not even that. I haven't had—and still don't want—much of a relationship with them. That seems to suit them fine, too. They never call out of the blue and ask me to come for dinner, or send me a birthday gift. In fact, one of the principal memories I have include them resenting having to give me any gifts, much less helping me with college."

"Uh, huh," said Clay.

"I don't blame you for being cynical," she said. "You think I lied to you, and I don't blame you for being mad."

"No, not angry," he said. "Mystified, or maybe bewildered, I think. One of those would be the better word."

It took a few moments for her to speak. "After they stole her away, I cried for two weeks. I went home and became a complete recluse," she said. "I went home, went to my classes at the high school, played on some teams, then went to college, then grad school."

"All by yourself, huh?"

"Yes," She nodded. "I'm sure I went into a deep depression. I lost myself in academics: I got sensational grades, which led to Scholarships and jobs. I just kept going until I earned a Ph. D. in Adolescent Psychology. I played on the softball and volleyball teams in high school, did well enough to get an athletic scholarship as well as my academic scholarships, so I just kept the achievement stuff going in college." She looked up at Clay and gave a little smile. "When I was a senior, I received honorable mention All American in softball, in fact. Also three years I got Academic All-American. But I always felt like an outsider and always kept to myself."

"And?"

"After I finished my bachelor's degree and graduate school I had a few jobs as a consulting psychologist," she said. "When I had time I started looking for Crissy."

"Uh, huh," he nodded. "Found her, too."

"Yes, but it took a long time," Sharon nodded. "Then, not too long ago, I managed to locate her. I couldn't bring myself to speak to her, so I hung around in the background, trying to keep her in sight, not having the nerve to come forward. Like yesterday."

"You mean you saw what happened at the Promontory?"

"No," she said. "I'm a consultant here at the hospital. They called me and asked me to come in. I rushed to the hospital and went right up to her room. You can imagine how I felt when I saw it was Crissy. I've had to maintain as low a profile as I can, since I have no legal right to her, you know. Still from time to time I've managed to send her little anonymous gifts."

"Like what?"

"Little birthday presents, a charm bracelet, subscriptions to magazines—anything that wouldn't be too obvious," she said. "I've stayed as close as I can, since my consulting business allows me enough flexibility to move around. I lost track of her for a couple of months when her mother died."

"Okay," said Clay. "Let's get serious here."

"What do you mean?" she asked.

"I mean, are you planning to tell her?" he asked. "That you're her real mother?"

Sharon turned back and looked up the stairs. "She doesn't

know she's adopted," she said. "She looked enough like her adopted mother that I'm sure she's never questioned it. I'm afraid that any more trauma…"

Clay nodded. "Okay," he said. "So what do you want from me?"

Sharon turned back and came over to the couch where he sat. She sat at his side and took his hand. When she spoke, her voice was pleading. "Please let me stay here with you," she said. "I'll pay room and board, help around the house, whatever. She can't go back to any place where that brute can get hold of her. I have to protect her."

Clay thought. "And that's all?"

"Not quite," Sharon shrugged. "I get the impression that she thinks we're lovers. If you want…" she swallowed. "…I think I can go along with that."

"Sharon…" he began, but stopped when they heard Crissy coming down the steps.

"What a nice room," she said. "Thanks, Sharon, for all the stuff you bought me. I don't know what to say. You guys have been so good to me…"

Clay stood and went over to the girl. "Come here," he said, and put an arm around her shoulder. Then he turned back to Sharon. "In my house we have honesty," he said. "It seems to me she needs to know the truth."

Crissy turned to Sharon and saw her face pale, tears on her cheeks, in clear distress. The young woman turned to Clay, bewildered. "What's going on?" she asked, puzzled. "What do you mean, the truth?"

"Clay, I can't—" began Sharon.

"Yes you can," he said. "This talk has been years in the

making."

"What talk?" said Crissy, raising her voice a little.

Sharon looked at her, then back at him. "I can't," she pleaded.

"Can't what?" said Crissy. "What is this, Clay?"

"You say it," Sharon said, wiping at her eyes, not able to look at her daughter.

"Sure?" said Clay. Sharon nodded. Crissy now began to look scared.

Clay took a deep breath. "Clarisse," he said. "I'd like to introduce you to your mother."

A profound silence settled in. After a few moments, Crissy stammered, "What?"

"See," said Clay, "I have to tell you a story about a fourteen year old girl. . ."

Chapter 7

Sometime later, things seemed to be reaching equilibrium. "Anyhow," said Sharon to Crissy, "I have no legal claim to you. You can say the word and I'll leave. You'll never see me again."

"Come on, Sharon," said Clay. "No one even suggested Crissy wants that."

Crissy stood and walked to the other side of the room. "Did you mean it when you said you regretted giving me up?"

"Oh yes," said Sharon. "Not one day has ever gone by that I haven't thought about you. All during high school, college, and graduate school I wondered about you and worried about you..." her voice trailed away and she seemed out of things to say.

"I need some time," said the young woman. "I'm feeling overwhelmed."

"Honey," said Sharon. "I'm so sorry. I never *wanted* to do that. I mean it when I say that my parents pulled you out of my arms—"

"People tell me I tried to kill myself," Crissy interrupted. "I have no idea why I would even consider doing that. I've never had a suicidal thought in my life. Then I met a man, a perfect stranger, who saved me from the lake and who has risked his life several times to save me."

"Wait a minute," said Clay. "You tried to drown yourself. Do you mean to say that you don't remember that?"

"I remember waking up in a hospital," she said. "Before that, I remember drinking a cup of green tea and reading a magazine at a bookstore. I have no memory of anything in between, not even jumping in the lake. Not at all. I think my father drugged me somehow."

Clay sat staring at the girl. "Did you come to the store with anyone?"

"No," she said. "I lived with my grandmother in her apartment until she died a few weeks ago. I stayed on in her apartment and I have a little job waiting tables at a coffee shop, but I don't have many friends."

"So when did you see your father last?" asked Clay, taking a stab.

"Before this latest thing, not since Mom died," shrugged Crissy. "I've been hiding from him as best I can."

"Did they do a tox screen on you in the hospital?" asked Sharon.

Crissy shrugged that she didn't know and turned to Clay. "Do you know?"

"No," said Clay. He spoke to Sharon. "The doctor suggested that Crissy might be using drugs—"

"Not a chance," snorted Crissy. "I hate the things and I don't even drink. I can't stand the feeling of being out of control of my mind and body. Not only that, I couldn't afford them anyhow."

"—But she said that she needed parental approval for the screen," Clay concluded.

"Huh," said Sharon. "Well, everything seems okay now—"

"Like hell," said Clay. "I haven't told you what happened

after you left the hospital." He related how Crissy's father had attempted to abduct her at the hospital.

Sharon stared. "Oh boy," she said.

"That nails it," Clay agreed.

"We have to get out of here," Sharon said, turning to Crissy. "Let's get you packed and we'll go off somewhere—"

"Wait a minute," Clay said. "You say you're her real mother. I'm prepared to believe that because you two look so much alike, and you seem like a nice person—"

"Thank you," snapped Sharon. "Where are you going with this?"

"I mean that until I know you better I'm not going to turn Crissy over to you," Clay asserted. "We only have your word for who you are."

"Oh for—" Sharon sighed.

"You have to see this makes sense, Sharon," said Clay. "I'm not ready to put anything past Crissy's father. What if he hired you?" Sharon sulked a bit, but at last had to admit that she couldn't see any sense in Crissy going with her on the basis of her assertion.

"Look, let's see what happens for a day or two," said Crissy.

"But someone just tried to kill you, from the sound of things," Sharon pleaded. "I gave you up once. I don't think I can do it again."

At that moment the doorbell rang. Hep leaped to her feet and ran to the front door. Clay looked through the peephole. "Pizza guy," he said. He opened the door, paid the delivery man and brought the pizza back into the living room.

They ate the pizza in strained silence. Sharon sipped a glass of wine and Clay and Crissy stayed with ginger ale.

Dinner concluded at about nine P.M. Sharon suggested that Crissy go to bed. "I don't want to seem naggy," she said. "And I know you're not a baby. But I think you've had a rough couple of days and you ought to get some rest. Try to sleep in a bit for a few days."

Crissy grinned and trooped off upstairs after a round of good nights and thank yous. Clay and Sharon sat staring at the fireplace, where the gas logs burned with a cozy light. "Where do you want to sleep?" Clay asked.

"Give me a blanket and a pillow," Sharon said. "I'll be fine here on the couch. Or if you'd feel more comfortable, I could go home and come back in the morning, or I could go to a hotel."

"And leave me alone with a lovely teenage girl? Just what I need," he snorted. "Most people in the neighborhood think I'm a nut anyhow. They'd probably conclude that I'm a pedophile."

Sharon chuckled. "Okay," she smiled. "I need some things out of my car."

"I'd better come with you," he said. "Why don't you pull the car into the garage, okay?"

She smiled. Clay kept watch as she pulled the car in next to his Corvette. He took a small suitcase out of the trunk and carried it inside for her. They went back into the living room and took their places next to the fireplace.

Clay didn't say much. He let himself relax and enjoy that lovely scent from her perfume. She seemed oblivious to the attraction he felt for her, which was good, he thought. He felt like he needed to maintain a professional distance while they were trying to keep Crissy safe.

"What do you do?" asked Sharon. "I mean, for a living?"

He shrugged. "I'm a re-builder," he said. "I take over failing businesses and make them prosperous."

"Like what?" she said.

"I'll give you an example. Ten years ago or so Gail—I mean, my ex-wife—" he added, sounding a little lame. Sharon smiled. "—Well, we bought a broken down marina on a lake in central Indiana. The owners hadn't done much with it and sold gas, a motor or two, some bait, stuff like that."

"Uh, huh," she nodded. "It sounds like a nice place."

"Yeah, it was," he said. "The lake was beautiful, nice homes all around, a good community and all that."

"Sounds like you should have stayed there the rest of your life, huh?" she smiled.

He nodded. "Maybe I should have," he said.

"So what happened?" she asked.

"Well, anyhow, Gail and I built the business up for four years," he said. "We sold it for ten dollars on the dollar we paid. It looked terrific, and I talked to the new owners not too long ago. It's still running well."

"Anything going on now?" she asked.

"Not exactly," he said. "Four or five years ago we bought a car wash, fixed it up, got it going also, not far from here. I sold that business after my divorce a couple of years ago. I cleared a very good profit with the sale, I mean, enough money so I didn't have to work for a little while, anyhow. The last couple of years I've found a new business, and even with the lousy home sale market, I've done pretty well. I've been re-habbing houses. Low interest mortgage rates, you know. I buy foreclosures, move in to them, and then go to work on them. I re-plumb, re-wire, put on siding, new carpet, paint, like that. I sell them for a good profit."

"You mean you bought this beautiful place as a project?" said Sharon.

"Yeah, I've thought I might sell this thing in a few months. I replaced the furnace and the air conditioner, I put a new roof on it, re-plumbed the place, re-wired and updated the electricity, and some other stuff," he said. "The last couple of weeks I've been redecorating, new paint, wall paper, and I've been re-doing the trim."

"You do nice work," she smiled.

He thanked her and went on. "I thought about selling it, but I have to admit I like this place. It feels like home to me. In fact it's the first time a place has felt like home in a long while."

Sharon sat staring into the fireplace. "Can I ask something else?" she said.

"Would I be correct in assuming you want to ask what happened to my marriage, since we appeared to be so successful in business?"

She hesitated for a second. "Okay, yes," she said.

He considered, and then shrugged. This woman had a unique gift of facilitating personal disclosure. He found himself telling her things he never dreamed that he would talk about on a first date. He trusted her and her implicit promise of confidentiality. "Okay," he said. "When I was married, I became a workaholic, you know what I mean. Like when I owned the car wash, I'd stay there, oh, ten to fourteen hours a day. That would be typical for me in any job. But Gail decided she'd had it."

"She wanted a divorce," nodded Sharon.

"Not at first," he said. He paused before he went on, again noting his surprise at the things he was telling this woman whom he'd known for about 24 hours. Opening up to her seemed quite reasonable, however. "She got herself elected to the board in our condo association. Several of the board members would go out for a drink after their meetings. She started to see one of the guys..." he paused. "Then began to sleep with the guy—" He broke off. The pain of the rejection from his wife hadn't faded yet.

"And decided to trade you in on a new model, huh?" she asked in a soft, gentle voice.

Clay thought for a few moments before he responded. "Yeah, I guess that pretty well summarizes it," said Clay. "She hired a terrific lawyer, and while mine was okay, he couldn't hold a kitchen match to hers. The judge gave her the house, the girls, monthly support, all that. I don't even see the kids now. Jerry Reed had a song that summarized it: *She Got the Gold Mine, I Got the Shaft*."

"I don't think I've heard it," Sharon grinned.

"One lyric is 'Well, they split it all down the middle, and then she got the better half, *She Got the Gold Mine...*"

Sharon joined in, "'*I Got the Shaft*."

"Right," said Clay. "Jerry Reed died in 2008. I miss him."

"Sounds like you got the shaft, all right," agreed Sharon. "Did she marry the guy she'd been chasing around with?"

"Yeah," he said. "The ink hadn't dried on the divorce decree before they announced their engagement. They got married a few weeks after that, though they'd been living together all through the divorce. That hurt worse, I think, than anything else. They seem pretty happy, I guess."

"And the court agreed that even with her adultery she should get the girls, huh?"

"Yeah," Clay shrugged. "What's more, the children are on her side. They don't even want to see me. I guess I can't blame them. I was a lousy father."

Sharon nodded. After a lengthy pause, during which she gazed into his eyes with warmth and sympathy, she said, "I'm worn out, Clay, you know? With your permission I think I'll brush my teeth and get right into the couch."

He chuckled a little. "Yeah, I'm bushed too. I'll take a look in on Crissy."

They said good night, though they didn't kiss, rather to his disappointment. He climbed the stairs to Crissy's room and saw her lying on her left side, sleeping in obvious peace and calm, a light snore emitting. He grinned at the peaceful look on her face and envied her ability to sleep. He himself hadn't slept through the night in three or more years.

Reaching his bedroom, he became aware of intense muscle ache, suppressed chill, and profound fatigue. He climbed into the shower in the bathroom off the master bedroom, trying to wash away the lingering chill of the icy lake still in his bones. The shower felt wonderful, but he found himself feeling a little guilty about leaving Sharon in the living room. The most profound of sleepers wouldn't describe the lumpy old couch as comfortable . He toweled off and examined his body in a full length mirror before going back into the bedroom.

The hot water had driven out the remaining cold, but he noticed the bruising that the waves had caused when they banged him against the rocks at the Promontory. He guessed that a couple of the contusions could be attributed to the scuffle with Crissy's father at the hospital.

Not the first bruises I've ever gotten, he muttered. I look like a rookie quarterback after a scrimmage with the first string defense.

The bruises, though, weren't as painful as the bruises on his psyche that Gail's departure had caused, or the misery of not seeing his children and how little his life meant to anyone at that point.

However having Crissy and Sharon around made him feel needed and worthwhile again, for the first time since Gail left. He liked Crissy a great deal. He found her bright, fun to be with, articulate—just a terrific young woman.

And now Sharon Gray had come into his life.

He hadn't thought much about women for the last couple of years. He'd find a date once in a while if he had to go to a wedding, or a banquet, but no one had emerged as a steady partner.

He laughed at the on-line dating sites on the internet when other people suggested them to him, but in his heart, he knew he didn't like them because they just reminded him of how lonely he felt all the time.

Yeah, he exercised so much for that reason. The pain diminished when he ran or lifted weights. He knew that he was just substituting physical pain for the emotional pain of loss.

For a couple of months after the divorce he'd done too much drinking, sure.

He'd never been much good with alcohol anyhow. One drink or a glass of wine was plenty. Anything more than that and he would wake up sick, hung over, and depressed.

Not only that, drinking didn't make the pain subside. So he gave up on the drinking, except for an occasional scotch or glass of wine.

Work didn't help much either. He shrugged, thinking that was probably because he didn't feel that he had a great deal to work for. He could go into a house and lose himself in project after project. But even as he worked, he'd think of Gail, his high school sweetheart and college love. She was the girl who'd been waiting for him when he came back from the service.

The girl whom he'd figured for the love of his life now slept with another man.

He brushed his teeth and headed back into the bedroom.

"Hi," said Sharon, looking up at him in the dim light from the bathroom. She lay in his king size bed and with the covers pulled up to her neck.

"Uh," he managed.

"I decided I couldn't sleep on that couch," she said.

"Uh," he burbled again.

"We don't have to make love," she said. "You have a preference for sides?"

He shook his head. "Do I need pajamas?" he managed.

"Oh, come on," she said, and turned back the covers on the other side of the bed. "Relax a little, will you?"

"In the circumstances, I think that would require no less than an intravenous drip of phenobarbital and a double shot of Hillbilly White Lightning," he said. He turned out the bathroom light and slipped into bed.

"You don't have any pajamas either, I notice," he said.

"They're on the floor next to the bed," she said. "Would you prefer that I…"

"No, I am certain that I wouldn't prefer," he asserted.

"Has it been a long time for you?" she said, as he stroked her breast.

"Three years at least," he said.

"Then it's way over—" Talking, however, ceased as a far more intense form of communication took over.

Chapter 8

Clay and Sharon lay side by side in the king size bed, both exhausted but invigorated at the same time. "Clay," she murmured.

"Um, hmm?"

"Are you awake?" she asked.

"Well, I think so," he said, smiling. "If I'm not, I'm living the best dream I've ever had."

"Three years?" she said. "You didn't seem to be far out of practice."

"Because of you," he said, stroking her hair.

Sharon smiled and rolled on her side. She stroked his face with her left hand and gave him one of those kisses that she'd given him in the hospital. She drew back after a few moments and he embraced her to him.

"You are," he said, pausing for emphasis, "the best kisser I've ever met."

"Thank you," she said. "You're better, I think."

"You're way too kind," he grinned.

"I hate to ask this," she said.

"I can imagine," he said. "But go ahead."

"Do you think we're safe here?" she asked.

He shrugged. "That nut father still wants Crissy, I'm sure," he said. "Though I haven't the least idea why. I'd guess he plans to bide his time."

"I think you're right," she said. "That's what I was thinking, too. Drat."

"I guess he wants me, too," he said.

"That doesn't seem farfetched, you're right," she agreed.

"I'm not afraid of him, Sharon," he asserted.

They went back into the delicious kissing for a little while. In a few moments they began making love again, with less urgency than the first time but with equal passion.

When they lay back again, they were winded, but contented.

"Thanks so much," he said.

She smiled. "Thanks?"

"I don't know what else to say to someone who's just given me something more valuable than anything I've received in years."

"Dear Clay," she smiled. "It seemed that you really needed this."

"That's for sure," he acknowledged.

She rolled on her back and stretched. "Could you get away?" she asked.

"For how long, do you think?" he asked.

"I don't know," she said. "Remember, we don't know why her father wants to kill her, or to what lengths he might go."

He reflected. "I might have to board Hep," he said. "Or, we could drive somewhere."

She thought about it. "I don't think so," she said. "Your Corvette wouldn't hold all three of us, and that wreck of mine wouldn't go very far without a lot of work—"

The phone rang. "What in—" muttered Clay. He pressed the illumination button on his digital watch. Almost midnight. He and Sharon had used the time well, he grinned. But who—

He picked up the phone. "Clay Foster," he said into the receiver.

"Bring the girl and the woman out. Now. If the three of you assume the position, I'll make it quick."

"Who is this?" snarled Clay.

"Never mind that. We've got the house surrounded. If we come in, we kill everyone anyhow."

Clay stared at the receiver. The voice went on. "You're not speaking, Hero," said the voice. "You're messing with stuff you can't imagine. Now: all three of you. You've got two minutes and then we come in." The phone went silent.

Clay jumped to his feet. "They found us," he said. "Get dressed. I'll get Crissy."

"What on earth…" stammered Sharon.

"Do what I say," he yelled. "It'll be okay but we have to hurry." He'd already jerked on underwear and socks. Within seconds he'd thrown on a sweat suit and pelted into Crissy's room.

"Crissy," he said, shaking her shoulder. "Wake up, Honey. You have to."

"Wha—" stammered the girl.

"Don't talk," he said. "Get dressed now. We have a big problem."

Then back to the bedroom. Sharon had put on her sweat suit and coat. "That'll do for now," he said. "Come on!"

He hurtled into the hallway where he found Crissy dressed and waiting. He grabbed a cord hanging from the ceiling and pulled down a stairway. "Up," he ordered, and Sharon and Crissy climbed into the attic. He slung Hep over his shoulder and followed them up. Then he pulled the staircase up.

"Follow me," he said, turning on a light bulb. He led them across a beam to another door and twisted the knob. The door opened and he led them through, yanking the door shut behind them. He turned on a light, revealing a finished attic with a bed on one side.

"It's okay," he assured the group. "Scott's going to be a bit shocked, though."

This attic had a door, which he flung open. Hep led the way through and down a set of steps. Scott staggered out of a bedroom down the hall. "Clay, what the hell—"

"No time, Scotty. Call the cops."

"Okay..." Then the group pelted past and down the steps to the main floor.

"This way," hissed Clay, opening a door and leading them into a basement.

Clay flipped on a light at the bottom of the basement steps and crossed to a door. A workbench stood there and he seized a battery powered work light and then opened the door and Hephzibah again led the way through.

"Clay," wheezed Sharon, almost out of breath. "Where are we going?"

"This old passageway leads from the carriage house to the main house," he said. "I parked my pick-up truck in the carriage house. Now shhh."

In moments they'd reached another door and Clay yanked it open. They went up a short flight of concrete steps and into a dark garage. Clay pulled the truck's door open and Hep hopped up into the seat, then into the back seat of the cab.

In moments they were inside and Clay used the remote to

open the door. He started the truck and drove into the alleyway turning left.

"I had the muffler replaced last week," he said. "We should be okay now. . ."

"Clay!" yelled Crissy.

Clay braked to a stop. He turned and looked back at the house. He saw flames spurting from the upper floors.

"Omigod!" he yelled and hauled out his cell phone. He dialed 9-1-1 and reported the fire. Then he called Scott and bellowed at him to clear the townhouse. Scott replied in a vague way that he'd smelled smoke, but yes he was okay.

"Damn it!" cried Clay, pounding his fist on the steering wheel. He pulled to the side as a fire engine clanged by, followed by a police cruiser and another truck.

Crissy sobbed. "My God," she said. "They wrecked your house, Clay. Just to get at me."

Clay took a deep breath and calmed down with an effort. "I have insurance," he said. "Things can be restored. I can't replace you, Honey." Crissy leaned forward and gave him an awkward hug and murmured her thanks.

"Where can we go?" asked Sharon.

"Outer Drive, then north, I think. Crissy's the only one who's gotten any sleep. I know a place we can hide for what's left of tonight."

Clay pushed the old truck hard onto the expressway, and then took I-90 north and west to Arlington Heights. He reached into the glovebox, extracted his Bluetooth and had Sharon rig it for him. Then she poked in a number he told her on his cell. A man answered in a few moments. "Craig, it's Clay," he said to his older brother. "I've got two women and Hep with me. We need to crash."

"You got your key?" asked Craig. Clay assented. "Okay, put the gals in the bedroom off the family room and you take the pullout. I'm going back to sleep. See you in the morning." He hung up.

Clay drove down a side street and into a driveway, concealing the truck behind a large house. He led them in.

"Where are we?" asked Sharon.

"My brother's house," Clay said. "He's used to me coming and going like this. Don't worry."

He let them in the back door with his key and showed Crissy and Sharon to a small bedroom with twin beds. He made sure they were comfortable, pulled out the sofa bed and climbed in. A few moments went by as he tried to decompress.

"Hi," said Sharon, standing next to the pullout.

"Hi," he grinned.

"Do you mind?" she said, indicating the bed.

"Not even in the slightest," he said. She slid in next to him and embraced him.

"Thank you," she said. "For everything."

"Hell, they wanted to kill me, too," he noted.

"I know," she said. "But you keep saving Crissy's life. I keep thinking…"

"Thinking what?" he asked, when she didn't go on.

"Come here," she said. "We'll talk in the morning. I hope the late morning."

They embraced for a few moments. Clay entertained an idea of making love again, but decided the fatigue he felt wouldn't enhance the effort. Clay, by now exhausted, fell into a deep, troubled sleep. His dreams were fiery, and filled with beautiful girls jumping into lakes, which turned to fire as they hit the water.

***

At 7:00 A. M., Clay's brother gave his shoulders a gentle shake and whispered to him. "Clay," he said. "Come on in the kitchen."

Clay dragged on his tee shirt and sweatpants and ran his fingers through his hair. He walked into the kitchen and Craig handed him a cup of coffee as he let Hep out into the backyard.

"You okay?" asked his older brother, his senior by two years.

"For the moment," he said. "I'm into something I never expected, Bro."

"The woman in the bed," said Craig. "It looks like you're pretty serious with her."

"Not sure where this could go," Clay shrugged. He gave Craig an outline of his life for the last two days.

"People at work said they saw you on the news, interviews, like that."

"Great," said Clay. "Just what I need."

Craig chuckled. "Most of the people in the country think you're a big hero."

"The Media haven't been here, have they?"

Craig shook his head. "No. At this point I haven't even been contacted."

"I want to let the two women sleep as long as they can," Clay said. "They've been under a lot of stress."

Craig nodded to the living room. "I take it the girl's the one you pulled out of the lake?"

"Yeah," Clay nodded. "Her father seems intent on killing her for some reason."

Craig's mouth dropped open in amazement. "He wants to kill that beautiful girl?"

Clay nodded and gave that little cough that had been plaguing him for a few days.

"What's with the cough?" queried Craig.

"Dunno," he said. Hep barked at the door to come in and Craig opened it.

"So what plans have you made, Clay?" Craig sipped at his coffee.

"I need to ditch the truck," said Clay. "Then rent a car and get the two gals away from here. That's as far as we've gotten."

Craig handed him the portable phone and reached into a kitchen drawer, from which he produced a copy of the yellow pages. Clay called a rental agency which would pick him and the girls up. He reserved a sport utility van and said he'd call just before the group would be ready to leave.

"You want to leave Hep?" asked Craig.

"I hate to trouble you, Craig…"

"Ah, Hep has never been a bother, don't worry," said his brother. "I've got a neighbor boy whose parents teach him at home. He'd be thrilled to come and walk her especially if I sweeten the offer with a couple of dollars…"

"Good morning," said Sharon, entering the kitchen. "Sorry to impose like this…" she began by way of apology to Craig. Craig waved the thanks off and Clay handled introductions. Sharon accepted a cup of coffee with gratitude and beamed good morning at Clay.

"Do we have any plans yet?" she asked.

Clay explained that he'd arranged for a rental car that he'd pick up when Crissy woke up. Sharon nodded. "Then where?" she asked.

"Not a clue at this moment," Clay said.

"Want to go to the cabin?" Craig suggested.

"Now there's an idea," said Clay, eyebrows raised. "Why didn't I think of that?"

"Where's this cabin?" asked Sharon.

"In Iowa," Clay responded. "You think we'd be okay?"

"Yeah, at least for a few days," said Craig. "Not many people outside the immediate group know where it is, after all. It's nothing fancy, Sharon," he said, turning to her. "But I think you'll be comfortable for a couple of days until the cops catch these creeps."

"They might think they killed us," Clay said. "That could be a break, I think."

"You think they might have figured we were killed in the fire?" asked Sharon.

"Maybe. I'm hoping that'll give us some lead time to get out of the state," he shrugged. "Let's head to the cabin and regroup, huh?"

"How far..." began Sharon.

"About four hours, maybe a bit longer," Clay said. "We'll take back roads across Illinois and into Iowa." Craig nodded and described a route he liked to take.

A few moments later, Craig had to leave for work. Clay stashed the truck in the garage and thanked his brother. "Sharon wanted to fix you guys some breakfast," Craig said. "I showed her where to find the eggs and such, so help yourself." With a handshake and a hug Craig departed for work.

Clay called the rental agency and an agent picked him up fifteen minutes later. Clay in turn dropped the agent off at the agency and returned to the house with the SUV.

Breakfast sat waiting and Crissy, looking haggard and tired, rubbed her eyes as she entered the kitchen.

"I'm sorry I had to wake you, Honey," said Sharon. "We need to eat and get going, though. You can go back to sleep in the car."

Crissy yawned and nodded, then drank a glass of orange juice.

After breakfast, Sharon and Clay cleaned the kitchen, then started to say goodbye to Hephzibah. "Do we have to leave her?" asked Crissy.

Clay looked at her. "You want her to come?"

"Well, yeah," said Crissy. "She saved my life, didn't she?" Clay nodded and grinned at the girl. "I owe her at the very least a big steak."

Sharon shrugged and agreed. Hephzibah, very excited, led the way to the rental car and the group set off.

Crissy fell asleep in a few moments, and after about an hour and a half Clay felt himself nodding over the steering wheel.

"Did you sleep last night?" Sharon asked.

"Not well," he admitted.

"Couldn't get comfortable?" she grinned.

"Hardly that," he snorted. "You feel terrific next to me. No, I kept having these wild dreams." He described the feeling.

"Hmm," she said. "Do you have a fever?"

"I don't know," he admitted. She placed a hand against his forehead.

"You seem okay," she said. "Any symptoms beside a cough?"

He shook his head. "Tired, of course, but. . ."

"Yeah," she said. "Want me to drive for a while?"

"Maybe that'd be a good idea," he admitted. "Let me take us into Iowa. We'll get some gas in Clinton and you can take over. It's only another forty-five minutes or so from the border."

Sharon pulled out a notepad from her purse and Clay described the route to the cabin. "It's pretty complicated," he said. "The cabin is pretty remote, but I think you'll love it."

They stopped over the border in Clinton, Iowa, and filled the car with gas, bought some snacks and walked Hephzibah. Once they got back on the road, Clay managed to nap, but couldn't quite fall into a deep sleep, dozing in and out.

When he woke, Sharon smiled and told him they were in the little town of Mount Vernon. Clay directed her into the deep country north of the town. Cornfields surrounded them for some time until Clay directed them down a dirt road. They saw a small cabin nestled in among some pines overlooking a small lake.

As the car came to a halt, Crissy woke from another nap, stretched and opened the car door. She breathed deep and kicked at some lingering snow in the driveway.

"Pretty," she said.

"Yeah," said Clay. "I used to spend all my summer vacations here. My grandparents left it to me and my brother. I don't get out here as much as I'd like, you know, a week here, a weekend there. . ."

"Very nice, yes," said Sharon. "How far to a grocery store?"

"Ten miles, maybe a little more," he grinned.

"Is there anything to do around here?" asked Crissy.

"Sleep, read, talk, play some games," grinned Clay. "But

we'll go out for dinner in a little while after we clean up."

He looked at the sky. "No," he said. "Maybe we should go now."

"Why?" asked Sharon. Then she looked at the sky. "Oh," she said. "A late season snowstorm, you think?"

"Wouldn't surprise me."

A half hour later the snow started. They were in a shopping center on the outskirts of Cedar Rapids. "Okay, let's hurry," said Clay. Crissy and Sharon went off to buy some clothes while Clay found some jeans, shirts and underwear for himself.

By the time they'd purchased the supplies and some carryout for supper, the snowstorm had started in earnest. "We could get a lot of snow," he said. "Good thing we have this SUV."

It took about twice as much time to get back to the cabin, and they pulled up and unloaded. They went into the cabin and locked the door behind them. Clay built a fire in the pot belly stove as darkness fell around them.

"Where's the light switch?" asked Crissy.

"What light switch?" grinned Clay.

"Oh," said Crissy. "We're roughing it for real, huh?"

"Yeah, but at least we're safe for the time," he said. "We can all sleep well tonight."

The cabin had two bedrooms, one of which they assigned to Crissy. She fell asleep within moments of climbing under a massive quilt.

"She's doing a lot of sleeping, huh?" said Clay.

"I'm a little concerned, yes," said Sharon. "I don't know why she's so tired. Maybe she's throwing something off, some sort of virus. Still, other than the sleeping she seems fine."

"Uh, huh," he said, yawning. "Speaking of that—"

"You too?" she said.

"I guess," he said. "At least I'm not coughing so much."

"Uh, huh," muttered Sharon.

Chapter 9

The snow continued late into the night, but the sun came out the next day, though they had to contend with arctic cold. Crissy took Hep for a long walk and returned, again weary. She took a brief nap and arose feeling alert and active.

The cabin had stood for many long winters with only the potbelly stove for heat, and a massive wood pile behind the house kept the stove warm. Clay split some logs with an old axe he found in the shed behind the house, enjoying the physical activity.

It occurred to him to think of how, under other circumstances, this time could indeed have been an idyllic winter vacation. He noted that he and Sharon had begun falling into the behavior of a couple, losing individual identities and uniting as lovers as well as friends.

The sexual aspect of the relationship had begun as something like violence, an eruption of passion and long frustration on the part of both people. Now, however, the lovemaking had settled into something sweet, gentle, and encouraging. They had begun to exchange the murmurings of love and devotion that husband and wife might use during their intimacy.

He smiled, thinking of how much he'd missed the loving interaction of a man and woman in the comfort of marriage. Gail and he had worked hard during the day on the businesses they'd taken over, and then relaxed together at night with candlelight dinners and sex, partners at work and in love, supporting and encouraging one another.

When had that stopped?

He considered. They'd started to grow apart about the time the children came along, when he began to work away from his home and started to ignore his personal relationship with her. He'd let her raise the children, behaving with a sullen attitude when he helped with diapers and baths.

Damn, he thought, cursing himself. He missed his family, and even though Sharon had brought new and remarkable joy into his life, he still felt the void caused by his failure in his marriage.

Crissy came out. "Hey," she said.

"What's up?" he grinned.

"Let's go into town," she smiled back.

"So you want to cruise the mall, do you?"

"Well, yeah," she said. "I'd like to hit a bookstore."

"Yes?" he grinned.

"Sure," she said. "I read all the time. You don't seem to have many books in the cabin."

"Well, no, we don't," he had to admit. "We'd always use the library when I came to stay for the summer."

"I get it," she said. "You like to keep your books near to you, right?"

He had to think about that for a moment. "I don't read all that much," he said. "At least not any more."

"Why?" she asked, her tone sounding dumbfounded.

"I just work so much, so many hours every day," he muttered.

"So that you don't have time to read?" she snorted. "What's the matter with you?"

"Something serious, I'm sure," He chuckled and hugged her around the shoulder. "Let's carry in some wood," he said. "I'll get my keys and we'll go and get some books."

The group piled into the car and headed off to the Lindale Mall. They dropped Sharon at the Hy-Vee supermarket and proceeded into the mall. Crissy picked up another pair of jeans and Clay, with Crissy's expert help, bought Sharon a short jeans skirt he thought she'd look fabulous in. Then she led Clay into the bookstore.

"What are you looking for?" asked Clay.

"I'm easy," the teenager said, and walked off to shop a little. Clay looked around and found three books for her: *The Innocents Abroad* by Mark Twain, *The Varieties of Religious Experience* by William James, and *Slaughterhouse Five* by Kurt Vonnegut. Crissy looked surprised.

"What's this?" she asked.

"I guess I wanted to show you that I'm not a hopeless illiterate," he shrugged. "These are three of my favorites. Pick one or all of them, if you want."

Crissy had read *Slaughterhouse Five*, so she chose *The Innocents Abroad*, and gave Clay a couple of books she'd chosen. Clay checked them out. They made their way back to the car. They met Sharon and went to a small restaurant for lunch.

Sharon looked with approval at the books Clay and Crissy picked out. "Yes," she said. "You've done quite well." She reached across the table and patted his head with a condescending smile. All of them giggled. "And I love the denim skirt," she said. "It'll be a little tough to wear it in a blizzard, I'm sure you can understand." She and Crissy giggled together over something, and she looked away.

Clay stared for a few moments at Sharon until she looked up and met his eye. She winked at him and he grinned.

At that point, he understood that he had fallen in love. "Sharon," he said. "I've been thinking."

"Good boy," she said. "Is that unusual for you?"

"Well, not unusual," he said. "At least, I try to do it on occasion, whether I need to or not. So maybe it's not altogether noteworthy."

"Go on," she sighed. "Tell us what you're thinking."

"Would you please marry me?"

Chapter 10

A silence descended on the group. Crissy's grin brought such warmth to the table that Clay's ears felt like they were on fire.

Sharon couldn't respond. She'd been taken aback to the extent that she seemed incapable of answering him.

At last, she spoke. "Er. . ."

"See," said Clay. "I hoped for something a bit more definitive than that."

"I know," said Sharon. "I'm aware that you just paid me the greatest compliment one person can pay another. I've been so focused on what we're doing here. . ."

"Well?" said Crissy. "Come on, Sharon, answer the poor man. He's a wreck, can't you see?"

"Of course I'll marry you," Sharon managed.

"Good," said Clay. "Today?"

"No, not today," said Sharon. "Let's get Crissy settled first."

"What does that mean?" asked Crissy.

"I want you back in school, for one thing," replied Sharon. "You should be back in your college prep classes, you should go to prom, play softball, and so on."

"And when your prom date comes, I won't greet him in my undershirt," promised Clay. "Though I've got a perfect one. Sleeveless with a hole right above the navel."

Crissy giggled. "But I like being with you two," she said.

"And we love you too," asserted Sharon. "We love you too much to let that brain go to waste, uneducated and not moving forward."

"Egg salad sandwich," Clay told the waitress.

***

They ate dinner in a Japanese steakhouse in the town of Marion, northeast of Cedar Rapids, and went back to the cabin. Crissy again trooped off to bed, her nose buried in *The Innocents Abroad*.

Clay and Sharon made love before they fell into a deep, restful sleep. In the morning, he suggested they resume the activity, but Sharon pleaded that Crissy would be awake in a moment.

"Besides," she said. "We've got to confront this situation and get it over with. I love this cabin, but I want Crissy back in school, I want our house rebuilt, all that—"

"Harumph," he grumped.

"Oh, I suppose it'll be all right," she grinned. "But just once, okay?"

***

At ten o'clock, Crissy still hadn't come out. Clay and Sharon cleaned up the breakfast dishes and put them away, not being especially careful to be quiet. Sharon tiptoed to the door and peeked in.

"She's still sleeping," said Sharon, frowning.

"Ah, she's a teenager," Clay said. "Don't you think she's most likely decompressing and relaxing after months of living in fear for her life?"

"Yes, but. . ." Sharon lapsed into silence.

Clay went out with Hephzibah at his side to bring in some more wood. He heard a motor on the highway and realized a car had turned into the drive to the cabin.

What the hell? He thought. *Who knows about this place?*

He hid behind a tree and waited as the car, another SUV, made its way to the house through the snow. He saw the driver and to his relief recognized his brother...

But someone else sat next to him. Clay didn't recognize the man. He was burly, with a walrus moustache, his eyes hidden behind dark glasses.

Huh.

The vehicle stopped and the passenger climbed out. With a thrill of horror, Clay realized that the man held a pistol next to his leg. The door behind the passenger seat opened and another large oaf climbed out, also carrying a gun.

Clay moved up on the vehicle. He could see inside now. No, only the two men and Craig, who appeared to be a prisoner. Craig held his hands up.

"So you're sure they're here, right?" said Moustache.

"I think so," he said. "You saw the car tracks in the snow."

"All right, let's get going," said Moustache. He prodded Craig with the gun. "Stay here, Rollo."

Rollo? Thought Clay. *What kind of wise guy has the name Rollo?*

Clay hugged the tree line until he was five feet from the man, who kept surveying the area. He waited until Sharon screamed at the door. Rollo turned and looked at the door with a smirk.

Clay took three steps and grabbed the man in a choke hold.

The thug gave a short grunt and tried to struggle, but Clay tightened the grip around his neck. The man's eyes began to roll back up into his head and Clay grabbed the gun away from him.

Then he loosened the choke hold and the man began to gasp. Clay jammed the gun into the thug's ear. "Keep it quiet, Rollo," he said. "Or I clear your ears for you. Got it?"

The man managed to nod.

"Who the hell are you?" Clay snarled.

"We came to get the girl," Rollo said. "You got to let us take her."

"You didn't answer my question, Idiot," said Clay, rapping him on the side of the head with the gun butt.

"Ach," said the man. "Okay. The company hired us. We come out here to get the girl."

"On your knees," snapped Clay. "Do it. Now."

The man protested and Clay whipped the pistol against his temple. The man started to groan with the pain but Clay tightened the choke hold. The man knelt in a snow bank.

Clay yanked the thug's coat and belt off. He tied Rollo's wrists behind his back with his belt. He tied the man's legs together with the arms of his coat. Then he opened the SUV's door open and jammed the man face down in the well behind the front seat. Then he used the power seat controls to pin Rollo against the seat.

Rollo squirmed for a few moments. "Okay," said Clay. "I tried to be nice."

He again rapped the thug on the head. Dazed, Rollo sank into a stupor. "Back in a flash," Clay told him. "Don't go away, promise?"

Clay closed the door with a gentle shove and Rollo

presented no further threat.

What could be going on here? He wondered. *What on earth could possibly be so important about Crissy?*

Clay ran to the back of the house and pulled open the cellar door, being as quiet as he could be. He crossed to the trap door which led into the cabin. The door lay under a wing chair, but with any luck, he'd be able to see into the main room.

He lifted the door an inch or two and peered in. Crissy and Sharon, both looking terrified, sat disheveled and terrified on the couch. Sharon had her arm around Crissy and had put herself between the girl and the two men. Moustache stood right next to the couch, his gun against Sharon's temple. "I thought you said he just went out with the dog," snarled Moustache.

"He did," Sharon asserted, and hugged her daughter. "He'll be right back."

Crissy looked sideways and spotted Clay. She gave a little smile, and shut her eyes.

"We'll give him a minute or two more—" began Moustache, but stopped when he heard a scurrying noise. "What's that?" said Moustache.

"A rat," said Crissy. "Over there—"

Clay had never seen a rat anywhere near the cabin. "I hate rats," Moustache yelled but the shout turned to a grunt of pain when Clay shot him in the shoulder. The gun arm flew back and the pistol discharged into the wall.

Now Clay shoved up the trap door and climbed into the room. Craig already had crossed to the man and yanked the pistol out of his hand.

"Hi, Clay," said Craig. "God I'm sorry. They've got Gail and the girls. That's why I came."

"They what?" stammered Clay.

"Yeah," said Craig. "These guys are dead serious. They want Crissy and they say they'll kill Gail tonight if we don't give Crissy to them."

"Tonight!"

"Yeah," said Craig. "I'm so sorry. If you want, I can take the girl to them. You guys stay here where you'll be safe…"

"Craig, are you nuts?" Clay said. "I'm not going to turn Crissy over to you or them."

"If you don't give them the girl, they'll kill Gail and the girls," said Craig. "They plan to shoot the six-year-old at 9:00 tonight."

Clay turned to Crissy. "Okay," he said. "I've been willing to go along with this up until now. But the time has come for some answers. What do they want you for? What is going on?"

Crissy shook her head. "All I know is that for some reason he thinks I killed Mom. I don't have any idea why he thinks that," she said. "I don't know why Dad wants me, not at all. He just wants me dead. He has a vendetta against me."

"But Honey," said Sharon. "Clay's right. That doesn't make any sense at all. Fathers just don't set out to kill daughters. Then bring in mercenaries to help." Moustache groaned from his place on the floor.

"Craig, cover him," said Clay. He went outside and returned in a few moments with Rollo. Just before he brought him in, Clay immersed Rollo's face in a pile of snow and held it there for several moments. Then he jerked him back up and pushed him into the house.

"Okay now, Rollo?" he asked.

Rollo gave a sullen grunt and Clay punched him hard in the gut. "Oof," said Rollo.

Clay shoved him onto the couch. "All right, Rollo," he said. "You've got one chance to survive this jackpot. Answer my questions and you'll be okay. If you don't give me the answers I'm looking for, you and your buddy wind up tied up on the lake out in back, just waiting for the spring thaw. I'm going to take you out there and say goodbye. I'm pretty good at knot tying too, like a Boy Scout with a graduate degree. You can bet you won't get away and this cabin is too remote for anyone to stumble on you by accident."

Rollo blanched now, the prospect of a slow death on the ice holding little appeal to him. He hadn't been enjoying himself since he'd arrived at the cabin. He nodded. "Okay," he said.

"What's this all about?" asked Clay.

"The girl," wheezed Rollo, having a great deal of difficulty breathing. "They want the girl."

"Who wants her, Rollo?"

Rollo licked his lips. "No," said Clay. "Don't even think about lying to me."

Rollo looked around at the grim faces. He blanched again when he saw Moustache cringing in pain on the floor with Craig holding the pistol six inches from his ear.

"They hired us, see," he said. "Two grand apiece for about three days' work. See, it's like this, I been out of work for a few months…"

"I don't care about your personal history, Rollo," said Clay. "Perhaps at some time in the future I'll read your memoirs. Skip to the present time."

"Right," he said. "Well, this guy, he called me and Jayce

there and four or five other guys in."

"In where?"

"Some warehouse on the south side, abandoned," said Rollo.

"The south side of Chicago?" asked Clay.

"Yeah," said Rollo. "Yeah. Well, a couple of us, we'd worked together in the mills, and things got tough, you know? We got laid off…"

"Rollo," interrupted Clay. "I don't mean to appear insensitive to the outstanding effort you're making in this narrative, but you're boring me."

"Right, right," said Rollo. "Anyway three of the guys, they went to get some woman in Lake Geneva, see, with her kids—"

"That would be my wife and children, Rollo."

"I dint know that," said Rollo. "They dint tell us much, just what we needed to know. Me and Jayce, we went to Arlington Heights, not far from the race track, and we got this guy—" he nodded at Craig. "The man, he tole us to go get the girl. We was s'posa rough you and the woman up and bring the girl."

"They got the drop on me," said Craig. "They put a gun to my head. I thought we'd figure something out."

"Go back to my question," said Clay. "Why Crissy?"

"Who?" asked Rollo. "Oh, you mean the girl. Right, yeah. I tell you, I dunno. The man just tole us, once we bring her in, we can take off with the two large."

"Rollo," said Clay. "I'm running out of patience. Why Crissy?"

"I swear I don't know no more than I tole you," whined Rollo.

Clay reached forward, grabbed the man by his coat collar and made him lie on the floor. Then he seized Moustache/Jayce and dumped him on the couch. Jayce whimpered with pain. A similar interrogation produced a similar result.

"Look," said Jayce. "One thing I can tell you. The man told us that if the cops showed up he'd drill your wife and your kids. So no FBI, no cops, or else."

At last, Clay made Jayce give him directions to the warehouse. He wrote down the address. When he interrogated Rollo, he got the same directions.

Clay searched the men and found billfolds with a few dollars in each. He frowned.

"Any ideas?" he asked Craig.

"No," Craig shook his head. "Nothing."

Clay walked to the door. He put five dollars into each man's coat pocket. "Okay," he said. "You've got a long walk. Cedar Rapids is about ten miles that way, Mount Vernon about 8 miles that way, and you'll come to Martelle about 6 miles that way. I don't think you want to go there, since Martelle has no medical facilities. Now get going. It's going to be a cold walk."

"You can't just—" whined Jayce.

"You're no killers," said Clay. "Just a couple of stupid bozos. And you both need medical attention. I don't want to kill you, but you'd better be sure I'll drill you between the eyes if I *ever* see you again. Now hit the bricks."

"I don't—" Jayce started.

"Jayce," said Clay. "You're not listening. I'm out of time. I shot you once. I'll do it again and you'll be dead this time. Get going."

The two men stumbled out the door and started up the driveway.

"Okay," said Clay, shutting the door. "Okay, I'm going now.

Sharon and Crissy, Craig will stay with you. I'll try to end this as soon as I can. I—"

"Not a chance," said Sharon. "I'm coming with you."

Crissy shook her head with such violence that Clay worried that she might have injured herself. "You're not giving yourself up for me," she said. "Whatever's going on, I have to fight my way through it with my father."

"Don't be silly…" Clay tried.

"I'm not staying here by myself," said Craig. "Give me one of the guns. I'll meet you there and we'll get the kids and Gail out."

"I'm with you too," said Sharon. "Your children and probably Gail too have to be traumatized. I'll help."

"I'm coming too," said Crissy, defiant. "I want this over."

Clay shrugged. "Okay," he said. "Let's go."

Chapter 11

Clay drove the SUV into the Mississippi River town of Clinton, Iowa, and stopped at an Army Surplus Outlet. He and Craig went into the store and emerged wearing black outfits and stout boots. They also had watch caps and black gloves.

"What's this?" giggled Sharon. "All of a sudden I'm in a Ninja movie?"

"I don't quite know what we're facing," Clay said. "Craig and I plan to scope this place out before we take Crissy in. I'm sorry, Honey," he said to the girl, who sat in the back seat. "I know you're scared. But we have to confront this and find out what he wants or they're going to chase us all forever."

Crissy nodded. "I know," she said. "I trust you."

The group drove along I-88 until they reached the cutoff for I-90. When the SUV reached the cut-off for the Dan Ryan Expressway, Clay used the directions from the two thugs named Jayce and Rollo. Clay and his group found themselves in front of a warehouse not too many blocks from Lake Michigan and a wind blowing off the lake made the evening bone chilling cold. By now it was about 5:00 and winter dark had settled in.

Craig parked his car a block from the warehouse. He came over and climbed into the SUV, taking over the driver's seat as Clay slid over to the passenger side. "Okay," said Clay. "Give me exactly ten minutes to get up on the roof and into the building. Then pull up in front and bring the two women in. I'll bring the guns."

Craig nodded and turned off the headlights. He pulled the car into an alley as Clay opened the dome light and removed the bulb. "Any other lights go on when I open the door?" he asked Craig.

Craig shook his head. Clay turned and blew a kiss at Crissy. He gave Sharon a real kiss. "Do you think this might be good-bye for us?" Sharon murmured.

"No," he said. "We'll be okay."

"See you soon?" she whispered.

"I promise," he nodded. "'Bye, Honey," he waved to Crissy. "Be brave."

"I will," she promised.

Clay ducked out of the car and closed the door with as little racket as possible. Craig backed the car out of the alley and held up his wrist. Clay set a timer as Craig set the stop watch on his wristwatch and they started the timers at the same moment.

Clay ran back to the end of the alley and found a fire escape that led to the roof of the building. He leapt to the ladder, pulled himself up and scrambled up the ladder to the roof.

He found a trap-door and discovered that it had been padlocked. Clay pulled a bolt cutter from his tool belt and snipped away the padlock. He flipped open the hasp and pulled up the trapdoor.

The space opened before him black and uninviting. Pulling out his pocket flash, he scanned the area below him and found a catwalk. He looped the rope around a waste stack and lowered himself into the building.

His feet struck the catwalk and he reeled in the rope. He drew out the pencil light and surveyed his area. Spying a staircase, he went to it and clambered down to the next level.

He saw lights on the floor level and heard the hum of a portable generator which throbbed in the background. The lights ran off of this machine. A couple of portable toilets stood off to one side. Now he saw a cage, made with heavy gauge wire, which sat in the middle of the floor. Gail and the children sat on the floor, the two girls hugging their mom and looking terrified. The door to the makeshift cell was padlocked.

Clay had to struggle to keep his temper. The warehouse, drafty and cold, was a wretched place to hide some hostages. Still, this place spoke of some serious effort and expense on the part of Crissy's father.

"Geez," he said under his breath. "This is pretty elaborate for a hostage situation." Again that nagging question. Why was this father going to so much trouble to kill his daughter when it was clear she hadn't done anything to cause her Mom's death?

Now he spotted the guards. Three men sat at a portable table, playing cards. They had automatic rifles strapped on their backs, and sidearms that looked like .45 calibers. They also seemed to be covered by body armor.

These guys are pretty serious, he said to himself.

A door to a portable toilet opened and Clay recognized Crissy's father, the thug who had intimidated Clay near the promontory. He came into the room, squirting some hand cleaner onto his palms and rubbing them together.

"Nothing?" he said.

"Not yet, no," grunted one of the men.

Clay consulted his watch. About three minutes till Craig

brought the girls in.

He considered. He felt a strong temptation to shoot all three of the thugs and go hand to hand with Crissy's dad.

But he hesitated. These guys were just hired muscle, not involved in any direct sense. He didn't think three schmoes, out of work and desperate, deserved to die for their parts in this. They shouldn't have chosen this way to make some money, but he sort of felt sorry for them.

On the other hand, they had lethal weapons and gave every appearance of being ready to use them.

On Crissy.

On Sharon and Craig. On his ex-wife and his children.

Clay Foster made up his mind. He'd take them out if he had to.

He heard a banging, which he recognized as pounding on a metal door. One of the thugs pulled his rifle from his shoulder, glanced at Crissy's father and received a nod of approval.

He departed and returned in a few moments, following Crissy and Sharon and Craig, prodding the group with an AK47 in Crissy's back. The father grunted. "Nice work," said the father, addressing Craig. "Where are Jayce and Rollo?"

"Couldn't make it for this jackpot," said Craig. "Like I told you this morning. My brother's a lot tougher than you think. They wounded him before he killed them and I had to take him to the University of Iowa Hospital in Iowa City. He's in no condition to interfere with you."

"Hello, Daughter," said DeRosa.

"You have the nerve to call me 'Daughter'?" snarled Crissy. "After you've been trying to kill me?"

"Don't worry, I won't be trying anymore," he said. "You're

through now. So are these two." He nodded to Craig and Sharon.

"What about the children?" asked Sharon. She glanced at Gail who sat on the floor of the cage, crying with fear and impotent rage as she clutched her children to her.

"We'll let them go in a minute," said DeRosa.

Lying, thought Clay. DeRosa planned to kill Gail and the two girls as well just to cover up what he'd done. In this abandoned warehouse, their bodies might not be found for weeks, months or even years. Good grief, thought Clay. What is it with this guy?

Clay considered. The stakes in this were—had to be—a lot higher than just a teenage girl. They couldn't leave any evidence, anything that would link...

Link who?

DeRosa couldn't be the only one involved in this. Someone else had to be behind it. Making plans to murder several people ranked as barbaric.

Okay, he said. He lowered himself on the rope to the floor where Gail and the girls were being held. He had to disable a couple of the thugs with the machine guns. He couldn't just storm the scene.

"All right," began DeRosa. "Rawkins," he said, pointing at one of the men. "I want you to take the girl out to the car. Put these two—" he nodded at Sharon and Craig—"into the cage for the time being—"

"Wait," said Sharon. "This is my daughter. I'm going with her."

"*Your* daughter?" said DeRosa. "What do you mean?"

Sharon gave a brief explanation. DeRosa said nothing as

Crissy spoke up. "I want to know why you're doing this, Dad." She sneered the last word.

"You know damn well why," said DeRosa. "You're a witch."

"Are you crazy?" said Sharon. "A witch? We're not living in the fourteenth century."

"You heard me," DeRosa said. "I can't kill her with a bullet or a knife. She has to be drowned. Then she won't trouble us anymore."

"Make a sincere effort to be rational," said Sharon. "I love her. Let me take her away, out of the state or out of the country—"

"No," said DeRosa. "She's a killer and she'll kill again. She has to drown. Tonight, right now."

"Then I'll drown with her," said Sharon.

DeRosa shrugged. "Your choice. I'll give you that. Okay. Wyland, put this clown in the cage. Grab some rope. We're going back to the lake."

One of the thugs bound Sharon's hands behind her, then Crissy's. He prodded the two women with the machine gun and they started for the door. "Get them in the car," said DeRosa. "I want to make sure these clowns are secure."

"Right," said the man. He prodded Sharon with the gun and the two women turned toward the door. He led them out of the light to the open metal door and pushed them through.

Clay whacked the man on the temple with the butt of his gun. The thug collapsed to the floor.

Clay pulled the knife from his belt and cut Sharon and Crissy free. "Shhh," he whispered. "Take Crissy down the street and hide," he told Sharon. "I'll take care of this."

He turned back into the room and hid in the darkness as DeRosa walked over. He'd almost reached the door when Clay jammed the AK-47 into his back. "Hands up, mouth shut, DeRosa," he said. "It's over."

"Foster!" said DeRosa. "What are. . ." He never finished the sentence. Clay slapped the rifle across DeRosa's temple and he spun around, landing hard. Clay put a foot in his back and yanked his hands behind him. Sharon jammed a rag into the stunned man's mouth and tied DeRosa's wrists together in moments.

"What are you doing here?" Clay whispered. "I told you to take the girl—"

"No," said Sharon, a finger to her lips.

"Stay here," he said. "This time obey me." She nodded.

Clay ran back to the lighted room and stepped forward. "Hi guys," he said. "Game's up." The two thugs, startled and taken by surprise, made a belated grab for their weapons. Clay fired two bursts with the AK, shattering the table top. The two thugs threw their hands in the air.

"You. Open the cage," Clay said, pointing at the punk nearest the cage. "Want to walk again?" he asked when the thug hesitated. Clay pointed the rifle at his knee and shouldered the weapon. The thug yelled his acquiescence and opened the door. Craig ran out behind Clay, yanked the weapons away and searched the two thugs. He found a knife and a deck of cards, but nothing else.

"Gail," he said. "Get the girls out of there."

Gail appeared to be in shock from the terror of the experience, but she grabbed the children and pulled them out the door of the cage. The children ran to Clay and embraced him. "Hi, guys," said Clay. "I'm sorry. This thing is almost over, I promise. Just be brave a little longer."

Craig returned with DeRosa and the other thug. He shoved them toward the open cage door.

Gail came to him. "Hello, Clay," she said, in the voice he'd first heard when he was a senior in high school. "Thanks," she said, simply. "You were wonderful."

"Okay, you're safe," he said. He turned to De Rosa and one of the thugs. "You two. In the cage."

"Just a minute, Craig," said Gail. She nodded to the thug next to Jim DeRosa and said, "Get out of the way, please." The thug, looking puzzled, moved into the cage and Gail walked up to DeRosa, very calm and quiet.

Clay, later on, had to admit that it was one of the two or three best punches he'd ever seen thrown. Gail crouched a little with her left hand on DeRosa's chest. Then she swung from the heels and hit him below the left eye with a right cross that would have felled a fair sized steer.

DeRosa's mouth dropped open for a second, and his eyes widened. In the next second he fell backward into the cell, poleaxed by the clout. Gail stood over him, kicking and hitting him, screaming curses and epithets that Clay had never, in all their relationship, ever heard her use. Nor was he even aware that she *knew* them. He wrapped his arms around her and pulled her away. He talked to her in a gentle voice, holding her until she calmed down.

"Damn nice punch," he said, when she got herself under control.

"Beginner's luck," she nodded. "Still it helped a little. It felt good. Except I may have broken my hand." He chuckled a little.

"We'll have a doctor take a look in a little while," he promised.

The other two thugs went in the cage and Craig and Clay yanked DeRosa, still stunned by Gail's shot to his left cheek, into the cage. Sharon covered the group with an AK 47. Craig closed and locked the door behind them.

"Do you know how to use that thing?" Clay asked Sharon and took the weapon out of her hands.

"Well, no," she said. "I just assumed that you kind of point it and pull this little dangly thing, right?"

"Yep," he said. "That little dangly thing is called the trigger."

He took the gun away and turned to Craig, and the two brothers shook hands. "Please call the cops, Craig," said Clay. Then his legs wouldn't quite support him. He sank to his knees, his children holding on to him.

Chapter 12

Lieutenant Nolan came in a few moments after the first few squad cars and crossed to Clay and Gail while Sharon embraced the two girls and talked to them. "You all right, Foster?" he asked. Clay thanked him and assured him that he was. Nolan spoke to the other officers for a few moments, and then came over to Clay and Gail.

"How did DeRosa get that shiner?" he asked. "It's going to be spectacular."

"That was me, I'm afraid," said Gail. "I hit him when Clay was putting him in the cage. He's the one behind all this. He hired the men who kidnapped me and my daughters."

Nolan turned to Clay. "Huh," he grunted. "I'm sorry I missed that."

"One of the best punches I've ever seen," Clay agreed.

"What's with the guy with the concussion?" asked Lieutenant Nolan.

"One of the thugs who were holding my ex and our girls," Clay said. "I cracked him in the temple with the AK-47. I'm sorry. DeRosa had assigned him to go with him to kill Dr. Gray and Crissy."

"I don't know what he's talking about," said DeRosa. "I've never seen this man," he went on, pointing at Clay. "I knew he'd grabbed my daughter. He planned to hold her for ransom."

"Look, DeRosa," said Nolan. "It's late and I'm tired of this. Foster saved the girl from you at the Promontory and again here tonight. The question is, what am I going to do with you?"

"I hope you plan to put him in jail," snarled Crissy, looking DeRosa in the face.

Clay filled Nolan in on some more details of what had happened. DeRosa kept interjecting belligerent denials until Nolan reached the point of exasperation. "All right, DeRosa, That's enough. Evans," he said to a patrolman "Take DeRosa to a squad car." The handcuffed man turned at the door and yelled back into the room.

"She's a witch, Foster!" he bellowed. "Drown her before she kills you!"

Clay went over to Sharon and the kids. He sat down, hugging the little one and trying to calm her. Gail talked to Lieutenant Nolan and filled in the details as she knew them. As she was about to finish the story, her new husband Steve showed up.

Steve embraced Gail and the girls. Then he looked around, spotted Clay who sat on the floor with Sharon and Crissy kneeling at his side. Steve gave him a dirty look.

"You son of a bitch," he spat at Clay.

Clay stammered a few seconds, unable to speak. "What?" he managed.

"You did this," said the man. "You put my wife and children in danger."

"Steve, stop this," pleaded Gail. "Clay isn't to blame. He didn't do this. He saved us—"

"Like hell he did," snarled Steve. "You're nothing but a no-good son of a bitch—"

Before Gail could stop him, a switch flipped on in Clay's mind and he lost his temper. As quick as fire Clay exploded to his feet and grabbed Steve around the throat. Clay lifted the man off the ground and smacked him against the wall. The back of Steve's head banged hard into the cement block wall.

Clay slapped him hard and then backhanded him in the same motion. The sound of the whack resounded through the warehouse. Clay seized Steve's lapels with both hands and yelled in his face.

"You miserable bastard," Clay roared at the man who had stolen his wife. "You have the nerve to come in here—"

But now Gail grabbed his arm and tugged. "No, Clay," she pleaded. "No, please don't hit him again."

Clay's anger melted away, as it always had when this woman asked something of him. He released Steve and the man dropped to his knees, choking and dazed at the fury of the attack. He fumbled for a handkerchief and wiped blood from his mouth. He turned to Nolan. "You're a policeman, right?" he gasped at Nolan, who nodded. "Aren't you going to arrest him?"

"No, I'm not," said Nolan.

Steve rubbed his throat and choked out, "Let's get out of here," he said, his voice raspy.

"In a few moments," said Gail. "I'd like you to take the girls to the car, please, Steve. I'll be along in a second." Sharon had been sitting with the children, holding their hands and talking in gentle, calming tones to them. The children crossed over and hugged Clay. They looked shell shocked at the violence they'd witnessed over the last few hours.

When her new husband left, still rubbing his throat and looking daggers at Clay, Gail turned back to Nolan. "Do you still need me, Lieutenant?"

"Thanks, not right now," he said. "Please go home and relax, maybe have a little scotch. I've got all your information, your address and phone number. I'll be in touch."

"Thank you, Lieutenant," she said. She turned to her ex-husband. "Clay," she said. She extended her hand to him. He took it and she pulled him to her. Gail reached up, put her arms around her neck and embraced him.

The feeling of the hug startled him. It was so familiar that he didn't speak, just relished the familiar comfort of his wife pressed against him. Unbidden, a few visions of some of their sexual events in the early days of their marriage flashed into his mind, and he let himself indulge for a few moments, recalling times when they would make love with such satisfying urgency.

"Thank you," she said. "I mean it. You saved us."

"Don't mention it," he said. "Forgive me, but I'm having a hard time not being very bitter with you."

"I understand," said Gail. "Clay, we both made mistakes and we've never resolved them. I'm sorry about them. I can't and I'm not going to apologize for Steve or my life now. I know that you and I had a good marriage for a while. We can't go back to that ever. But. . ."

"Yes?" he asked.

"Maybe things aren't so final. Do you think we could start to talk from time to time?"

Clay thought for a second. "We can try it, Gail," he nodded. "I'd like to see the girls from time to time, for sure. I miss them so much..." his voice trailed off as tears formed in his eyes.

Gail squeezed his hands, and she nodded understanding of how he felt. "I've been a little cruel," she admitted. "I'll try to make it up to you." Gail extended her hand again, and he took it.

Sharon walked over now to join the conversation and Clay introduced her. "You should consider yourself fortunate to be with Clay, Dr. Gray," said Gail. "I'm sure you've seen that Clay's a wonderful man."

"Yes," said Sharon. "Yes, he certainly is." Clay could hear that Sharon's voice transmitted disapproval of Gail and dismissal.

Gail also heard the tenor in Sharon's voice. She stepped back from Clay and dropped her hand. She looked at the two of them and nodded. "Thank you, both of you," she said. "Clay, we'll speak soon, I promise." Then she turned and walked through the warehouse door.

Clay followed her to the door and watched her get into the car with her new husband and his two children. In a few moments, he watched the car drive away, carrying his two children back out of his life. He felt a tear on his cheek and brushed it away.

"Okay, Foster, we'll be in touch," said Nolan, walking up. "Nice to meet you, Dr. Gray," he said to Sharon. She nodded and smiled, and Nolan left.

"Clay?" whispered Sharon, seeing the look on Clay's face.

He turned to her. "Yeah, Honey."

"Are you okay?" she asked.

"Not quite," he said. "I'm in a fair amount of pain, as you can see."

She reached up and brushed the tear from his cheek. "We'll make it better together," she said. He nodded.

"Where's Crissy?" asked Clay.

"With Craig," said Sharon. "Over there, where she feels safe. Can we get out of this miserable warehouse now?"

"Yeah," he said. Crissy looked up, saw the two of them together and came over to them, eyes downcast. "Are you ready to go, you little punk?" Clay teased.

That brought a little smile to her lips. Crissy managed to nod. "Where are we going?"

"Why don't the three of you come to my place?" asked Craig. "We'll be comfortable there, we can have a little of that Johnny Walker Blue Label I got on the cruise last year—"

"Not tonight, I don't think, Craig," said Clay, with a glance at Sharon. She smiled, understanding how he felt, and nodded. "I'm so tired I don't think I can drive that far," Clay went on. "I just want to crash."

"Where can you go?" Craig grinned.

"Hotel," said Clay. "I'm sure the smell of smoke will be too much in the house. I'll call my cleanup guys in the morning."

"I think we've got a deal," said Craig. "I'll keep Hep with me."

***

The morning dawned over the lake, but Clay hadn't slept much. He sat in the chair by the window, the room dark. Crissy slept in one bed, looking peaceful and relaxed. Sharon's blond hair spilled on the pillow and she had a little smile on her face as well. He sighed in contentment, feeling complete and whole for the first time in ages.

So, today's the day our life really gets going. Sharon's reunited with her daughter after 17 and a half years. Sharon and I can get married, take a honeymoon, and get our lives going. I'll go over and look at the house today, get a crew in. Maybe they can get a cleanup and restoration going while we're out of town.

Then we have to get Crissy going with school again. Maybe she could just bag her high school diploma—jeez, she's sure smart enough—and go right into college...

Then, as it had all night, he saw DeRosa's face in the light of that god awful warehouse. "She's a witch! She has to die, Foster! Drown her!"

A witch?

Okay, DeRosa had to be crazy. Sure. No man in his right mind wants to kill his own daughter, adopted or not. No man would ever go to such lengths, hiring guys, risking his freedom, his soul, to murder a girl unless he was barking loony. Of course not.

He shrugged. He'd had this same conversation with himself all night long.

But DeRosa had been meticulous, thorough, careful in his plans and ideas. He'd been focused and he was convinced that he'd done the right thing.

Clay rose and went to the washroom, where he climbed into a shower that damn near scalded him. He let the hot, hot water pour over him for a long while, even though he'd showered when he'd gotten in last night about midnight.

The door to the bathroom opened and Sharon came in. "Hi," she whispered. She pulled off her robe and came into the shower with him. She embraced him, then put her hands on the sides of his head and looked into his eyes. "What's the matter with you?"

"I don't know..."

"Yes, you do," she said, her voice firm. "Everything with Crissy changed last night after the fight. You and I have progressed beyond protecting her now. We're her parents, at least in the de facto sense of the word. We have to take care of her."

"I don't know. . ."

"You do too," she said. "What's more, you're feeling guilty and you couldn't be more wrong. Listen to me. Are you listening?" Clay smiled and nodded. "Last night you did what you had to do. You had to defend me and Crissy and Craig as well as yourself against those men, you had to save your wife and children, and what's even more you know you had to do it."

"I guess so," he muttered.

"You saved my life, Crissy's, your ex-wife, your girls, Craig's, even your own," she asserted, fixing his eyes with hers. He embraced her body to his.

"You have to listen to this," he said. "What you said is true, but listen to this." He repeated what DeRosa had said.

"A witch?" scoffed Sharon.

"That's what he said," Clay said.

"Clay Foster, that's just ridiculous," she said. She pulled back a little, taking his face between her hands and staring into his eyes. "You know it is. He said the same thing to me."

"Sure, of course."

"Then why would you let it bother you? Crissy's no witch."

"You didn't see his face, Sharon," he said. "The man may be crazy, yeah. But he sure didn't look crazy. He was on a mission and he put together an intricate plot to kill the girl. Not just send her away but to kill her by drowning her in a lake as if she actually was a witch. It became his passion in life."

Sharon stroked his face. "You're in trauma, Clay," she asserted. "Things will upset you for a while that wouldn't have affected you in the slightest when you weren't under such pressure."

"Okay," he said. "Suppose I am. Suppose I'm overreacting to the farthest degree."

"You love Crissy. Like I do."

"Sure, of course I do. I'm thrilled that she's in my life."

"Yes?" she said, concern in her lovely blue eyes. "I hear a 'but' coming."

"You're right," he said. "Here it comes. But when she came into my life, she brought violence with her. I shot a man at the Promontory. The next day I disarmed him, hurt him, and chased him out of the hospital. A few days later I shot another man and sent two of them out into the elements wounded and cold. I could have killed another man."

Sharon shook her head and embraced him. She felt so good that he almost choked. "Shift your focus and look at the other perspective," she said. "You jumped into the lake to save a girl you'd never met. You saved her life on at least three different occasions. You and I met, realized we were right for one another, let ourselves fall in love, and now we're planning to be married. You broke up a dangerous plot that had several people in mortal danger, and a couple of the people got hurt but they didn't die and they'll be all right. How do you intend to look at the last several days? Positive? Negative?"

"Someone burned my house—"

"And we weren't in it. No one got hurt. You re-build houses for a living and you can fix it."

He lapsed into silence. She drew his mouth to hers. For several minutes they didn't say a great deal.

At last she sighed and smiled at him. "Making love in the shower," she said at last. "I could get to like that."

"Want to do it again?"

"Sure. But let's get this day going. We have a lot to do. We can look forward to it tonight."

"Make that a promise?"

"That's an absolute promise, Buster."

He nodded and turned off the shower. They dried and put on the robes the hotel had provided.

Crissy had left the room when they came out. Sharon looked surprised. "Huh," she said. "I didn't see her even moving when I came into the bathroom."

"Where would she go?" Clay wondered.

"I can't imagine," Sharon said.

By the time they finished dressing, Crissy still hadn't returned.

"Okay," said Sharon. "I'm starting to become alarmed."

"I don't know," shrugged Clay. "She's pretty mature, after all. She's been living on her own for a while, besides. Relax a little."

Sharon put on some makeup and fixed her hair while Clay looked at the newspaper the hotel had left at the door.

"Okay," she said. "Let's go."

They made their way to the elevator, and then down to the lobby. They looked around but didn't see Crissy in the breakfast area.

Sharon went to the front desk. "Did you see my daughter leave?" she asked the clerk.

"When?

"Within the last half hour," Sharon said.

"What does she look like?"

Sharon described the teenager. The clerk shook his head. "Attractive, you say?"

Sharon assured him of Crissy's beauty. The clerk shrugged. "No," said the clerk. "I've been right here for the last hour and a half and I didn't see her. It sounds like I'd remember her, I think."

Sharon and Clay went into the breakfast buffet and ate some fruit, a hard-boiled egg, and some coffee.

Still no Crissy. Sharon had become alarmed at this point.

"What should we do?" she asked.

"I don't have any idea," said Clay. "I think she has a room around here. Maybe she wanted to go and gather some clothes, something like that—"

"Then why not tell us?" Sharon groaned, looking miserable. "She must have known that I'd get scared, worried…"

"Well, me too, since I risked my life for her last night, too."

Sharon nodded. They lingered over coffee.

"Look," said Clay. "I want to go home and check the damage and get repairs under way, you know. . ."

"Of course," said Sharon. "I'll come with you. We'll leave a message for Crissy and tell her to call us when she returns." Clay nodded. He called a cleanup crew, who promised to meet him at the house.

The route to Hyde Park took little time and Clay parked in the street in front of his house.

"Doesn't look too bad, does it?" Sharon said.

"Well, no, but I can't really tell by looking at the outside," he shrugged.

Clay produced his key and they went in. They detected no smell of smoke permeating the house, and they saw no water damage to the carpet and floors. "Not as bad as I thought," he said.

"Doesn't look bad," said Sharon. "The place could use a good cleaning, I guess, but I don't think I see any damage."

"I intended to have it cleaned anyway," Clay agreed.

They walked into the upper floor, and Clay pulled down the stairs to the attic. "I'll go first and turn on..."

"Fine," said Sharon. "Why do you want to go up there to begin with?"

"It isn't that bad up there, Sharon," said Crissy, standing behind them. "In fact, there's a lot of room, and a floor, a skylight. . ."

Clay spun around. "Crissy!" he yelled. "How did you get up here?"

Crissy stared at him, baffled. "Er..." she said. "What are you talking about?"

"We were at the hotel," said Clay. "Sharon and I couldn't find you. I didn't know..." he broke off as he saw Sharon and Crissy staring at him in dumbfounded amazement.

A chill of dread swept over Clay. He looked back and forth between his lover and his ward, unable to speak.

"Anyhow," said Crissy. "I'm thinking, if you wouldn't mind, maybe we could finish the attic off? I mean, it doesn't have to be a top priority, but then you could let me have it as a room?"

Clay noticed that he was having a hard time speaking. He looked at Sharon.

"What the hell?" asked Clay. "What just happened?"

"Nothing," said Sharon. "We're just trying to figure out how you want to use this living space in the house, Dopey."

Clay walked into the master bedroom and scouted all around. He saw not the slightest hint of water or fire damage to the walls or carpet. He came out of the bedroom and ran downstairs. Again he saw no trace of damage anywhere in his home.

"I do love this place, Clay," said Sharon, speaking to him as she and Crissy descended the stairs to meet him. "I could live here and be very happy."

"Me too," said Crissy, grinning at him.

Clay walked into his living room and sat down.

"Did we make love this morning?" he asked Sharon.

"Clay!" said Sharon, embarrassed, with a glance at Crissy.

"Too much information! Too much information!" grinned Crissy, hands over her ears. "Can you talk this over when I'm not around?"

She hurried down the stairs and into the kitchen. She pushed on the swinging door and said, "Okay, count down from three and then talk. Ready? Go!" The door swung shut behind her.

"Yes, we made love this morning," smiled Sharon, crossing the room to him. "In the bed, twice."

"Not in the hotel?"

"Hotel?" Sharon stared at him, puzzled. "What hotel?"

Clay, by now, couldn't even speak, he was so perplexed. "Would you like some coffee?" asked Sharon. "Let me get you some."

She followed her daughter into the kitchen and the door closed behind her. A few moments later, Crissy came out holding a glass of ice-water in her hand. She looked at Clay, saw his face, and came over to him.

"Clay," she said. "You look like you've seen a whole houseful of ghosts. What's the matter with you?"

"Crissy, something has gone wrong here," he began.

She gave him a strange smile. "What do you mean?" she asked.

"I mean, you vanished from the hotel this morning," he said. "I mean Sharon and I have been worried sick. I mean, I saw my house on fire last night and now it's okay. I mean a whole bunch of stuff like that."

She sighed. "Okay," she said. "You remember. It didn't work. It almost always does."

"What didn't work?" he demanded. "What are you talking about?"

Crissy closed her eyes, opened them, and then nodded at him. "Okay," she said. "I owe you an explanation and I need to make things right with you." She crossed to him and reached out her hands. "Take my hands, Clay," said Crissy.

"What?" he asked, bewildered at her request.

"Please take my hands, Clay."

Clay reached out and took her hands. She stared into his eyes, and said, "Now please close your eyes, Clay."

He did. "Open, Clay," Crissy's voice said.

He opened his eyes.

Everything had changed. They no longer stood in his home in Hyde Park. In fact he had no idea where he was. Crissy stood with him, holding his hands.

"Where are we?" he managed.

"We've come to Salem, Massachusetts," she said. "We're

standing where we can overlook the Gibbet Hill, where they hanged witches in the 1600s."

"How did we get here?" he asked.

"I brought us, Clay," she said. "I don't come here very often. In fact, I try not to come here. It's a painful, hideous place to come. But you need to see what's going on with me, and why my dad wants to kill me. I couldn't tell you the story. You wouldn't have been able to believe it."

A crowd moved up the hill toward the gibbet. He saw that a group of large and burly men was dragging along an old woman.

"Crissy," he said. "Who is the old woman? Do they really intend to kill her?"

"Her name is Bridget Bishop. She's not really old by our standards," said Crissy with a shrug. "In her fifties. She received what passed for a fair trial, and now they're going to hang her as a witch."

In very few moments, the woman stood beneath the gibbet. Someone tied her hands behind her. The magistrate fixed the noose around her neck and tightened it with a viciousness that made Clay wince. The magistrate asked her if she wanted to confess.

"I am not a witch," she said. "I know nothing of it."

Five men, at a signal, pulled on the fatal rope and walked away. The Old woman's body lifted a few feet off the ground and her body thrashed in helpless agony. The men tied the rope off and walked away. Then, the crowd dispersed.

"What evidence did they have?" managed Clay, staggered by what he'd seen.

"They had no evidence at all," said Crissy. "At least, they

presented nothing that would be acceptable in any American court today. It was called Spectral Evidence. A couple of people testified that she had come to them as a spirit and tried to take possession of her. They raided her house, but they found no evidence that she was a witch except for a couple of little dolls they found in the cellar."

Clay's mouth dropped open. He found himself nauseous. He'd never seen an actual execution before. "Are you telling me they just hanged a woman based on that evidence?"

"This all happened centuries ago," Crissy shrugged. "They hanged a lot of women here," said Crissy. "And a couple of them were real witches, with powers, the ability to conjure, transport themselves, all manner of things."

Now it clicked in. "Women just like you, you mean?"

Crissy looked at him. "Yes," she nodded. "Just like me. And just like my mom."

Clay started to say something, stopped, and couldn't.

"I know," said Crissy. "It's a struggle to suspend your disbelief. But I assure you it's real. I have to deal with this ability all the time."

Clay considered. "What about Sharon?"

Crissy nodded. "She's on the staff at the hospital. She came to my room to work with me. I got her to talk."

"Did she have an illegitimate child out of wedlock?"

"Yes, that was true," Crissy nodded. "The child would be about my age, yes. I'm sure you've seen how much Sharon and I resemble each other, too. Also she did all the stuff she told you about. She's been looking for her child for closing in on two decades, but she hasn't had any success."

Now it clicked. "Oh boy," said Clay.

"What's that?" she asked.

"I hope I'm wrong," Clay said. "I don't even want to ask. She's married, isn't she."

"Uh, huh," said Crissy. "She has a very unhappy marriage, but yes."

"Where's her husband?"

"He went to California last week on business and stayed this week too," she said. "She thinks he'll be home day after tomorrow."

Clay felt like he'd been hit by a truck. "But..." he fumbled. "I love her."

"I know," said Crissy. "I hadn't counted on you two being so attracted to one another. I'll send her home. She won't remember anything about you, I promise.

"Swell," he said, drawing out the word. "Well that's just great. Meanwhile I think she might be the love of my life."

"I know," said Crissy. "I can see how you feel about her."

"So what do I do? How do I get by her?"

"I can fix it so you don't remember her, Clay," she said. "If that's what you want."

"But..." he mumbled, looking for a way to say what he wanted to. "Did she love me?"

"Yeah, she thought so," said Crissy. "She and her husband have been having a lot of problems. She loves children and she's desperate to have her own. He doesn't want them."

"Will they divorce, then?" he asked.

"More than likely," said Crissy. "If she signs the papers. It's a crummy marriage. They don't even sleep together any more. So sex with you, based first on mutual attraction which became devotion, struck a profound chord with her."

"She's a passionate woman," he noted. "About everything."

"Right," said Crissy. "But you proposed after knowing her for less than a week. Didn't you suspect something strange had happened?"

He thought. "So they didn't really burn my house down?"

"No," she said. "They didn't set fire to it. I just let you see that so that you'd have some more motivation."

"Motivation?" he thought. "Crissy, did any of that stuff with your father happen?"

"Yes," she said. "That part—all of it—couldn't have been more true."

"Why me?"

"Clay, my father tried to kill me several times," pleaded Crissy. "You really saved me from the lake. And at the hospital. At the house, the cabin, in the warehouse, all of it."

"But why?"

"The story about me at the tea shop, then remembering nothing until I woke up in the hospital with Sharon and the nurses standing over me—all of that was true."

"Yes?"

"You saved me," she said. "I'm not in danger at the moment—at least I don't think I am— because my father has been tossed in jail. He's been trying to kill me for five months."

"Why?"

"He blames me for Mom's death," she said. "He thinks I killed her."

"Did you?"

She didn't hesitate. "No. Clay, you have to believe me. I couldn't, anyhow. She's my mother, and I couldn't harm her at all. Even if I had wanted to kill her, I don't have enough power even now. She could have blocked any attack from me without any trouble."

"How did she die?"

"I don't know," Crissy shook her head. "I came home from school and found her. Doctors did an autopsy and found no heart disease, cancer, no toxicology, nothing obvious at all."

"Oh," said Clay, getting it now. "So your father blamed you?"

"Yes," said Crissy. "He came for me the night Mom died. I stopped him by throwing a cup of bleach at him and ran off to my grandmother's apartment. She died a month ago."

"A lot of this story holds together," he said. "Where did she live?"

"Near you," said Crissy. "Here in Hyde Park."

"Not California?"

"No, that was part of the story I gave Sharon," she said. "Grandma left me some money. When she died I stayed in her condo and struck out on my own waiting tables, like I said. My father may have seen her obituary and traced me that way."

He hesitated. "Okay, I get it," he said. "Except for one thing. Why me?"

"You said it in my hospital room," she said.

"What did I say?"

"You said you saved me because you wanted to meet someone as lonely as you."

"Oh. Yeah."

"Does that still go?"

"Of course it does."

"Then," she said, "will you help me figure out who killed my mom?"

"Sure."

"Okay, let's go back," said Crissy. "Brace yourself. This isn't going to be fun."

"All right," mumbled Clay.

Crissy smiled and in the next moment they again stood in the upstairs foyer of Clay's house.

Sharon—no, it wasn't Sharon. It was Dr. Gray—stood a few feet away. She was wearing the denim skirt he'd bought for her in Cedar Rapids.

"Mr. Foster," she smiled. "Thank you for letting me come and showing me Crissy's room. I can see you've gone to a great deal of effort to make her feel at home." She extended her hand. "Now, I really must get home," she went on.

His heart aching, Clay took her hand—for the last time? He wondered—and walked downstairs with her.

"My car," she said, looking outside.

"It's in the garage, remember?"

"Why did I pull it in the garage?" she asked, befuddled.

"I asked you to do so, if you remember," he said.

Sharon stared at him. "Don't forget your bag," said Crissy.

"My bag," repeated Sharon.

"Yes. You brought it in when you parked your car in the garage."

Sharon looked at Crissy. Crissy stared into Sharon's eyes for a moment. Then, Sharon's mind seemed to clear. "Yes, of course, I remember," said Sharon. "I feel strange."

"Would you like to sit down?" invited Clay. "Perhaps some scotch? I have a bottle of Johnny Walker Blue Label."

"That does sound wonderful," said Sharon. "My husband's been out of town for over a week, and I've done nothing but…"

her voice trailed off, and she looked puzzled again. She glanced at Crissy.

"Paperwork," said Crissy. "Tied to your desk, not looking up."

Sharon stared for a moment. Then, she again nodded.

"You'd love to stay for one drink," Crissy told her, "and then you have to say good-night."

"Okay, perhaps one drink," said Sharon. "Then, I have a long drive home."

Crissy led the way to the living room. Clay poured some scotch and watched as Sharon sat down next to Crissy, chatting about one thing and another. Sharon crossed her legs and looked down. Then she looked up, and again her face clouded with bewilderment. She looked at Clay, then at Crissy.

"Something wrong?" asked Clay.

"I don't remember where I got this skirt," she said, indicating the jeans skirt Clay bought for her in Cedar Rapids. "I never wear skirts this short. Or this sweater. I…"

"Gifts from your husband," said Crissy, looking into her eyes.

"Yes, of course, I remember," agreed Sharon, looking relieved.

"The skirt looks wonderful on you," smiled Crissy. "Very flattering."

"Thank you," said Sharon, returning the smile.

The conversation went on for several moments. Crissy prompted Sharon from time to time.

At last she finished the superb scotch, thanked Clay and complimented his taste in liquor. "Well, I really have to go," she said.

"May I walk you to your car?" said Clay. "You wouldn't call this a bad neighborhood, but..."

"Thank you, Mr. Foster," she nodded. "That would be very kind and I would be most grateful."

Clay felt like he'd swallowed a rock as he opened the front door for her, led her down the walk, and tapped in the code for the automatic garage door opener. The door slid up and he walked Sharon to the car, where he took her keys, unlocked the door, and opened it for her.

"Well, thank you for everything, Mr. Foster," she said, accepting the keys from him. "You've been wonderful to Crissy. I'm delighted that she's with such a fine..."

"Leave him," whispered Clay. "Come and be with Crissy and me. He doesn't love you. He'll never love you like you deserve or like I do."

Sharon stopped and stared at him as if he'd slapped her across the face.

"Are you referring to my husband?" she asked, and her tone was icy.

He breathed deep. "Please," he said. "Please try to remember. It's Crissy. She's done this to you so you can't remember me and the last few days and our adventures. Please..."

"I beg your pardon, Mr. Foster," her voice frost. "I have no idea..."

"I know," he said. "I understand. Crissy said you wouldn't remember."

"What is there to remember, Sir?"

"Never mind," he said. "Just thanks for all you did for Crissy. All your concern. She needs that, especially now, with her father in jail."

Her face cleared. "Oh, I see," she said, as if everything now came together. "I thought that for a second you were flirting with me, Mr. Foster. Never mind. Yes, she'll need some help and some time to get over what her father has done to her. Please tell Crissy again that I'd be delighted to meet with her—in a professional or personal sense—at any time."

"I'll tell her," said Clay, his voice hollow. He knew that the woman he'd come to love, on whom he had planned to build the rest of his life, intended to climb into her car and drive off, out of his life. "She loves you, you know," he managed.

"You are a very kind person, Mr. Foster," she said, her voice soft and elegant, as it had been last night in bed, in the shower that morning, soothing, replacing all the hurt and loneliness of the last few years with gentleness, acceptance, pride, and love.

Sharon extended her hand, and Clay took it. "You made me an absolute promise, Sharon," he said. "I won't forget it. I'll collect it if it's possible."

Her head snapped up. "Sharon?" she asked, dumbfounded. "Why would you call me..." Then her eyes clouded with bewilderment. "Clay. Why am I leaving? What..."

He grasped her arms. "Do you remember?"

Then the professional counselor, the Ph. D. in psychology returned. "Mr. Foster. I beg..."

"I'm sorry," he said. "That wasn't a pass. I thought I saw you about to stumble..."

"I see," she said. He opened the door, and struggled not to watch her short skirt ride up even more to reveal her long lovely legs. Then she put the key in the ignition, started the car and reached for the door.

"Goodnight," she smiled. "And once again thank you for your great kindness, Mr. Foster."

Then she pulled the door shut. She dropped the car into reverse, turned and backed out of the garage down the drive and into the street. Clay followed as she prepared to drive away.

He heard a squeal from the power steering unit as she straightened the wheels, pulled the shift arm into drive and stepped on the gas. He watched, standing in a cold, gray east wind as she headed down the street. She drove about half the block—And stopped.

"What is this now..." he said aloud. He saw the white backup lights go on and she backed down the street. She pulled back into the driveway, and then she threw the car into park and tossed the door open. She yanked off the seatbelt and leaped out of the car.

Sharon looked up at him. Then she looked down, clutched her hands to her temples, and shook her head.

"Clay," she cried out, and he heard fear and desperation in her voice. "Clay, help me. What happened?"

Then she ran to him and they embraced. Two lonely people, alone in the world except for each other, stood lost in the kisses of husband and wife, best friends, life partners.

Chapter 13

"Crissy," said Sharon. "You aren't evil. I know it."

"Evil?" frowned Crissy. "What do you mean?"

"Witchcraft?" said Clay. "Reading minds?"

"Come on, Clay," scoffed Crissy. "Don't be medieval."

"Look at what you did to us," said Sharon. "We were two strangers a couple of days ago. Here we are in love, and I'm in a terrible situation."

"What situation?" asked Crissy.

"Well, I'm still in a marriage, even if it's not a very good one…"

"It's worse than 'not very good'," said Crissy. "Your husband wants a divorce and you've been devastated. He's spending more time with his mistress than with you."

"How…" said Sharon. She gulped. "How would you know all that?"

"You told me," said Crissy. "In the hospital. I saw how distressed you were when you were trying to talk to me that first day. When I convinced you that you were my mother."

"Am I?" asked Sharon. "I mean, am I your mother?"

"We'd need DNA to be sure," said Crissy. "But yes, it's possible."

"You said—" began Clay.

"I don't know, okay?" said Crissy. "Even though I suspected

it from time to time, I didn't know for sure that my parents had adopted me until last night, when my father told me. They never told me. I just used a convenient memory from you, Sharon, to build your loyalty to me so you'd help Clay protect me."

"And the stress we—I mean, Sharon and I—found ourselves in drew us together even more than we would have been attracted to one another in ordinary circumstances," nodded Clay.

Crissy shrugged. "So you left out dating, candlelight dinners, and moonlight walks on the beach. So what? You can have all of that now and for the rest of your lives."

"You have an answer for everything," snapped Sharon.

Crissy turned and looked at her. "That's easy for you to say," she said. "Okay, let's play it out. Say you two didn't fall in love. Say you didn't even like each other. Then decided never to see each other. Okay. In the meantime you did something noble."

"What?" said Sharon, her anger about to erupt.

"You saved my life," said Crissy. "Both of you. Clay became a father who protected me again and again from people who wanted to murder me. Sharon, you assumed the role of my mother, a woman who comforted and supported me the way I needed her to when I found myself in the most desperate situation of my life."

Sharon and Clay turned and looked at each other. Sharon took a short sip of scotch. "But let's take a closer look at you," said Crissy. "Both of you. Sharon, your husband thinks you're a frigid, unresponsive bore, lost in her work and immune to him, no passion, no joy at all in your life."

"I beg your pardon—" began Sharon, indignant.

"Oh stop it," said Crissy. "I know. You told me, even if you didn't know you were doing it. Why do you think Clay bought you that denim skirt? He wanted to see the woman he loved in an outfit that gave him pleasure, knowing that his pleasure in you would make you feel loved and wanted."

Sharon didn't respond.

"You." She said, turning and pointing to Clay. "A flop in your marriage, alone and abandoned, working yourself to death, no meaning in life."

Clay didn't say anything. He thought he should be angry but he couldn't raise such an emotion. "And now you both have something to live for, am I right?" snapped Crissy. "I tried to take away your memory of the last couple of days, the running, the fights, gunshots, the horror of my situation. It didn't work at all with Clay, but it did with Sharon to an extent. Then when Sharon tried to leave a few moments ago, it turned out that the bonds of absolute love were too strong and those feelings overpowered the Jolt I gave you. You, both of you, couldn't forget what will be the most significant relationship in your lives. With your last breaths on earth you will say one another's names. One of you will hold the other's hand. You will know what love is about from now until the time you die."

Sharon and Clay couldn't say anything.

"You," said Crissy, pointing to Sharon. "Your marriage died before it started. You know it. From the moment he spoke the vows he had no intention of holding you as the dearest thing in the world. Am I right?"

Sharon didn't answer, just stared at the 17 year old.

"You," snapped Crissy, turning to Clay. "Look at you. You

sank a marriage so people outside of your family would like you better." She snorted. "You fixed up businesses and now houses and took care of other people so they'd think highly of you. And the people who ought to respect you the most, who ought you to love you, acted for two years as if they didn't care if they ever saw you again."

"All right, Crissy," said Sharon. "All right. Don't be cruel."

"She's not being cruel," said Clay. "She's right. She's nailed it on the head."

"But—" Sharon began.

"I know about your sex life together," interrupted Crissy. "I didn't witness it, no, didn't eavesdrop, didn't meddle or enhance it."

"What do you know?" asked Clay.

"I know enough," said Crissy. "I know that you think Sharon's a dramatic, sensual, profound lover. You haven't told her that, have you? You should. The woman you love has been wounded for months by her husband calling her names, and maligning her and calling her frigid."

"The difference is that I love you," said Sharon, taking Clay's hand. "I know how you feel, Clay."

"And I should have told you," said Clay. "I just don't know how to say…"

"You'll learn," said Crissy. "You're with the woman who can teach you."

Clay and Sharon sat together holding one another's hand. A teenaged girl, wise and perceptive beyond her years, had just given them lessons in love and marriage.

"What do you want from us?" managed Sharon.

"I need your help," said Crissy. "Clay. I need your strength, your courage, your knowledge and insight. Sharon, I need your wisdom, your love for me and your instinctive concern to protect me and support me."

"What for?" asked Clay.

"Someone killed my mother," said Crissy.

"Who?" asked Clay.

"I don't know," said Crissy. "I don't have a clue."

"Then..."

"My father, such as he is, thought I did it," said Crissy. "He convinced himself of it."

"Why would he believe such a thing of his daughter?"

"He's been afraid of me ever since he found out what I could do," sneered Crissy. "He even did research on how to kill witches. Did you know it's best if they're drowned?"

"So that's why he tried to drown you at Lake Michigan?" asked Clay.

"Of course," said Crissy. "I knew what he wanted to do almost from the beginning. I read it in his mind. That's why I hid from him. But he found me."

"How did he drug you, then?" asked Sharon.

"I'm pretty sure he paid the girl behind the counter at the bookstore," shrugged Crissy. "I've given it some thought. I think he must have bribed her to put a psychotropic of some kind into my tea. Then he took me to the Promontory, and persuaded me to jump into the ice water."

"Is that possible?" asked Clay to Sharon.

"Sure," said Sharon. "What Crissy says makes sense. I never have seen anything like depression that would lead her to commit suicide."

"This wasn't suicide, not at all," asserted Crissy. "It was

murder, plain and simple."

"Okay," said Clay. "Then your father ought to be the prime suspect in your mother's death, right?"

"I don't think so, no," said Crissy. "He was at work when Mom died. All I know for sure is that the woman I knew as my mother is ..." She choked. The emotion of the last several days finally backed up. Sharon rose to her feet and crossed to the young woman.

Sharon knelt and embraced her. Crissy hugged back and let go.

Clay stood in amazement. He'd never seen anyone so devastated as Crissy at that moment. Feeling awkward, he took his ward's hand and knelt next to her. She turned and hugged him.

"Great Christ," he said to himself. Then, "Okay," he whispered. "Relax. We'll help you."

"You will?" said Crissy between sobs.

"Of course," said Sharon.

Chapter 14

Sharon came downstairs about a half hour later and found Clay holding a glass of scotch. He leaned back on the sofa and regarded her.

"Got any more of that?" she said.

"Sure," he said. He rose to his feet and went to the kitchen. He put some ice cubes in a glass and poured a little scotch over it. He lifted the glass and started to turn, but Sharon hugged him from behind.

He stood for a while, just relishing the feel of her body against his. He thought about what Crissy had said about loving Sharon and knew what she meant.

At last she said, "Okay. We need to make some plans, Clay."

"I know," he said.

"I've been making love to you for days, haven't I?"

"Yes, you have," he agreed.

"I shouldn't have done that," she said.

"I know," he agreed. "And I never ever intended to sleep with a married woman, even if she's almost divorced."

"I'm *not* divorced, though," she said. "That's the point. I haven't signed the papers yet," more than a trace of bitterness in her voice.

"Crissy told me that," he said.

"Oh," she said, and kept hugging him. "Let me tell you,

though. I wanted to do it with you. I was never coerced. I loved every moment and I still cherish them."

"Why are you hugging me from behind?" he asked.

"Because if you turn, we're going to start kissing," she said. "You know that."

"We don't have to," he said. "Not if it will hurt or scare you, or make you sad, or…"

"It wouldn't do any of those things," she said.

"Then what…"

"Clay, I believe I love you," she said. "I don't think I can mistake these feelings."

"Yes," he said. "I feel the same way you do. But I'm devastated to learn that I've been having an affair with a married woman."

"That's how I feel," she said. "I'm perplexed, too. I never thought I'd be unfaithful to Jordan."

"I'm sorry," he mumbled. "I'm so sorry. I did this to you."

"You didn't know," she said. "You couldn't know. We didn't know each other at all. It's like we were…"

"Bewitched?"

She chuckled. "I didn't want to say that," she said.

"Okay," he agreed.

"I often work with people who are devastated in their marriage," she said. "I tell them that infidelity never heals anything. I believe that, too."

"Then what happened with you and me?" he said. "I've never been so…"

He couldn't think of the word to describe the utter surrender, the collapse of his ego into her.

"I get it," she said. "I've never been so, either." They

chuckled.

"Do you…" he began, and found he couldn't ask.

"Yes, beyond doubt," she said. "When I started to drive away, I thought about you trying not to look at my legs when I got in the car. Under normal circumstances, I'd dismiss your look and forget about it."

"Thanks a lot," he said. She laughed and gave his arm a little whack.

"But as I drove, I kept thinking that I enjoyed your attention," she said. "I liked knowing that you found me attractive and had to stifle yourself. As I drove, I got this picture of you and me in a hotel shower—"

"This morning," he said.

"Uh, huh," she said. "And I imagined you demanding that I promise a similar encounter. Then I remembered that I did promise. Then I remembered a cabin, a drive, a few sexual encounters—"

"Just a few?" he chuckled.

"Well, not as many as I'd have liked," she agreed. "And that's when I came back."

"You can't imagine how I felt watching you drive away," Clay told her.

"Yes, I can," she said. "I felt the same way when I was driving, Clay. I watched you standing there as I drove away. I almost hit a parked car. Then I came back."

"Are you planning to leave tonight?"

"I don't want to," she said. "But I know I ought to go to my home. My husband will be home tomorrow morning, I think."

"Where is he now?" he asked. "Or do you know?"

"Oh, I'm sure he's spending the night with his mistress," she sighed. "He'll tell me tomorrow he just flew into town. He'll have flight information, all that and want me to pick him up at the airport. I'm sure he came back into town today."

"Do you know where she lives?"

"Uh, huh," she said. "I even know her phone number. I guess I could call and surprise him."

"Well, yes, that would be a surprise," he agreed.

"I don't know what I'd say to them," she murmured.

"My wife had a terrific divorce lawyer, if you think you need one," he said. "I've got his card somewhere."

She stood, embracing him for a few moments. "I can't sneak around, Clay," she said. "It isn't who I am."

"I'm sure of that."

"Where's the lawyer's card?" she asked.

"Refrigerator," he nodded and pointed.

"Okay," she said after a few moments. "Here's what I want you to do. I want you to go upstairs, now. I don't want you to turn around and look at me."

"But—"

"No buts," she whispered. "Please, no ifs, no buts, no more conversation."

"Okay," he said.

"Get into the shower," she said. "If I'm not there in a few minutes, I've left. I'll call as soon as I can. I promise."

"What are you going to do?"

"That's what I'm trying to say," she said. "I don't know what I'm going to do."

"Crissy—"

"I'm not forgetting her," she said. "Not even for a moment."

"She thinks you're her mom, you know."

"And it would be the greatest honor in my life. Except knowing that you love me."

"I feel the same way," said Clay. "She needs a mom and a dad."

"Yes," said Sharon. She released him, but then put her hands on his shoulder. She guided him toward the kitchen door. He started to speak. "No," she said. "No, you promised."

He walked up the stairs, feeling like his feet were made of lead. He undressed in his room, trying not to watch the clock.

He walked into the bathroom, turned on the water in the bathtub and pulled the plunger up to turn on the shower. One of the first things he'd done when he moved into this house was replace the plumbing.

While the shower heated, he flossed and brushed his teeth. Then he shrugged, pulled back the shower curtain and climbed in. He washed his hair, shaved, and soaped up. He began to rinse, with his head under the shower.

His stomach hurt. He felt hot tears in his eyes. She'd gone home, he knew it. It had been several minutes. Well, that's okay, yeah, it is. I'll see her tomorrow, or the next day. I imagine. He reached for the shower knob. Okay, he thought. Okay. Be calm. You had no right to her to begin with, none whatever.

Sharon pulled back the curtain and climbed in behind him and embraced him. "The shower's freezing," she said.

"I nearly scalded myself," he said.

"Right," she sneered.

"Can I please turn around now?"

"Well, yes. I did promise," she agreed.

Chapter 15

The next morning, Clay reached out for Sharon, but his hand touched only the sheet. He came awake in a rush and looked around. No one had turned on the bathroom light. The door was closed.

Clay felt a moment or two of panic. He jumped out of bed and pulled on a sweatsuit, then stepped into some Crocs. He opened the door and hurried downstairs.

Sharon sat at the kitchen table, sipping at some coffee and reading the newspaper.

She looked up and giggled. "Nice hair," she teased.

He smoothed it down with a little laugh. "You scared me, that's why."

"Scared you?"

"You weren't in bed with me when I woke up," he said.

"And that scared you?"

"Well, yeah," he said. "I didn't know if you'd had a change of heart during the night…"

"Change of heart?"

"Er…yeah. You might have left."

"I confess I thought about it just now," she nodded.

"You did?"

"Yeah," she said. "You don't have any bagels in the house. Nor cream cheese. To say nothing of eggs or bacon. Or anything else, for that matter. I considered going to the store."

"Oh." He took down a cup and poured himself some coffee. He sat down opposite her.

"Good morning," she smiled.

"Yeah," he said. "Good morning."

"Look," she said. "I'm not going anywhere. Ever. I'm right next to you from now on."

"That's great," he mumbled.

"Except when I have to go to work," she conceded. They smiled together.

"I'm glad you're here, Sharon," he mumbled.

"I'm glad I'm here, too, Clay," she grinned. "I haven't slept that well in—oh, I'll bet it's been close to three years, maybe even more."

"Me, too," he said. "Even longer for me."

"'Sleep that knits up the raveled sleeve of care,'" she noted.

"Shakespeare?" he asked.

"Very good," she said, approving. "*Macbeth*, Act 2, Scene 2."

"I'd like to ask a question," he said.

"Would the question concern what I'm wearing under this robe?"

He considered. "I like the picture that statement conjures," he said. "But I must confess that wasn't it."

"Drat," she said.

"So…"

"Present your question."

"Where do we begin?"

"Might be nice to take a little vacation," she noted.

"Hmm," he said. "What did you have in mind?"

"Bring Crissy?"

"I'd like to."

"I think," said Clay, "that maybe you ought to get your divorce finished up before we leave town."

"I suppose you're right," she sighed. "In that case, I'd like to see if we could get Crissy back in school for a time."

"Look," he said. "How about if we get her into a G.E.D. program? Or let her take some classes at a community college?"

"We should talk it over with her," said Sharon.

"Yeah, of course," said Clay. "She's a lot more mature than I was at her age. She can make her own decisions."

"Agreed…" she bit her lip.

"What?"

"Clay, I'm upset that she thinks that someone murdered her mother," said Sharon.

"Yeah, me too," admitted Clay, "but what can we do? I'm a businessman, I rehab houses. I don't know anything about investigations."

"I know, I know, I'm a psychologist," she said. "But remember, her father accused her of the murder of her mother. Even if you're innocent, it's terrifying to think that someone else thinks that you're capable of such a crime."

"I don't deny that," he said. "Of course you're right. The experience has to have scarred her. But that still begs the question. I don't have even the faintest idea how to proceed."

"Still I think it might be important for her to think that we're trying to run down a satisfactory conclusion to her mother's death," Sharon shrugged.

Clay regarded her for a moment. "You know, when you talk about this girl you sound as if you're talking about a relative. Like you were her mother."

"I know," she said. "I do feel very maternal about her. A connection, you know?"

"My connection comes with pulling her out of a freezing lake and saving her life," said Clay. "Here's my point. Crissy said that you could be her mother. Shall we check it out? DNA testing, things like that?

"We could start with blood typing and simpler things than DNA," said Sharon. "We could rule it out without going to a lot of trouble if it isn't true."

"If what isn't true?" said Crissy, coming into the kitchen. Sharon rose and hugged the young woman and they exchanged good mornings.

"Crissy, Clay and I were just discussing whether I could be your mother," Sharon told her. "I think I see some physical resemblances—your eyes and mine, our height and body type, hair color, and the age would be about correct."

Crissy nodded. "Did you ever try to find your daughter?"

"No, I haven't," Sharon said, shaking her head. "No, but a day hasn't gone by that I haven't thought about her."

"I'm sure that's true," nodded Crissy. "I'm willing, Sharon."

Sharon had a tear on her cheek and she hugged Crissy. "Let's go this morning," she said. Crissy nodded.

"The other thing we need to talk about, though, regards your father and mother," said Clay.

Crissy poured some coffee and sat at the kitchen table. "Like what?"

"Honey, neither one of us have ever been investigators," Sharon noted.

"Yeah, but you aren't stupid," Crissy noted.

"Why, thank you," said Clay. Crissy giggled.

"What I mean is, I can't look at this with anything like rationality, and it's obvious my father can't either," said Crissy.

Clay spoke up. "Okay," he said. "Tell us all you know."

Sharon poured them a little more coffee as Crissy tapped a finger on the table.

"I came home from school," she said. "The bus broke down on the way home, though, and I walked in about an hour late.

"The front door stood ajar, just a little. That jarred me a little, I remember. Mom parked her car in the driveway but she'd left the driver's door open."

"Wide open?"

"No, no, just a crack," Crissy said. "I opened the door and saw that the seatbelt had fallen into the opening and kept the door from closing all the way." Sharon and Clay nodded.

"Did you notice the dome light on?"

Crissy considered. "It was, yes. Do you think that's important?"

"Dunno yet," Clay said. "Keep going."

"Anyhow, I walked in and called out, as I always did, you know, 'Mom, I'm home,'" Crissy went on. "She didn't answer. That didn't surprise me, because we had a huge house, and sometimes she'd be in her bedroom or in the lower level and she wouldn't hear."

"I understand," said Sharon.

"I went into the kitchen and grabbed an apple," Crissy said. "I walked down and got the mail. I glanced through the mail, but found nothing for me."

"Then what happened?" murmured Sharon.

"I thought I should check my e-mail and phone messages, so I went up to my room…"

"Did you have your own line?" Clay asked.

"No," Crissy shook her head. "A cell phone, but the school wouldn't let us bring them in."

"Why?"

"They said they didn't want drug dealers making calls."

Sharon and Clay exchanged glances. "What if a parent really needed to reach a child?" Sharon asked.

"They could call the school office, I guess," shrugged Crissy. "Anyhow, I called out to Mom but she didn't answer. So I went into my room, changed into some jeans and came back out. I walked down to her room and found her on the floor in the spare bedroom..." Crissy's voice wavered and Sharon embraced her.

A few moments later Crissy resumed the narrative. "She wore an ivory negligee," she said. Clay saw Sharon's eyes open wide for a few moments. "One that I'd never seen, one that she'd never worn to my knowledge."

"Why would you know about that?" asked Sharon.

"Oh, we were shopping partners," shrugged Crissy. "I went with her for clothes and so on. We were about the same size, so I always made suggestions in case I'd want to wear things."

"Okay," said Sharon. "But she could have bought this without your knowledge?"

"Well, I suppose, or maybe it could have been a gift..." Crissy trailed off. "But that would seem strange, because Dad gave her gifts...I mean, I always saw the gifts he gave her. Anyhow I thought I did."

"Why did you think this was important?" asked Clay.

"I don't know that it was important," said Crissy. "But it did seem kind of strange that she had a negligee on in the afternoon.

I mean, she'd gone out to work early—"

"Where did she work?"

"At the same company as my Dad," said Crissy. "Northland Chemical. She did some research but on a part-time basis only."

"Huh," said Clay. "Isn't that unusual? A part time researcher?"

"I don't know," said Crissy. "She stayed home with me from when I was born until I went to school. Then she went back to work, but took working hours so that she'd be home when I arrived home from school."

"She must have been pretty good, to be allowed to set her own hours like that," muttered Sharon.

"Yes, people from their company often told me that they regarded Mom as brilliant. Well, they said the same thing about Dad, too. She graduated from the University of Illinois with a bachelor's and master's in biochemistry. She was a James scholar there, too..."

"I take it that's real good, huh?" asked Clay.

"The best," confirmed Sharon. "I got my bachelor's degree there also."

"Uh, huh," nodded Clay. "Do you know what they had her working on?"

Crissy shook her head. "No, they never discussed their work with me," he said. "I don't know what they did. They met in grad school, fell in love and got married after they finished their master's degrees."

"Come back to that afternoon you found her," said Clay.

"Okay."

"Think, now," Clay urged. "Are you sure the dome light was on in the car when you shut it?"

"Yes, it was a dismal afternoon and I noticed the driver's door open because I could see the light. It went off when I shut the door."

Clay thought. "Did anyone use the car after that?"

"Uh huh," said Crissy. "Dad pulled it in the garage later."

"Do you remember that it started up okay?"

Crissy looked puzzled. "Yeah, I think so. I don't remember him needing—what do they call those things? Jumper cables?"

"Yeah, I use them all the time on the truck," he said. "Okay. How old was the car?"

"Oh I don't know if I can be exact," said Crissy. "A couple of years at the most…"

"Right," said Clay.

"What does that mean?" asked Sharon.

"Gives a little bit of a time frame," said Clay. "The battery would've gone dead in a certain number of hours. We could check and set some limits."

Crissy shrugged. "Well, I became hysterical," she said. "I tried some CPR—"

"Where did you learn CPR?" asked Sharon.

"School," Crissy said. "I took a class in it."

"Okay," said Sharon.

"—anyhow, it didn't do any good," said Crissy. "She'd been gone too long."

"That must have been horrible for you," murmured Sharon. "I'm so sorry, honey. What a terrible memory."

Crissy didn't speak for a few seconds and Sharon embraced her. "I called the police in moments," the young woman said. "They came with an ambulance, but Mom was gone."

"Yeah," said Clay.

"Then Dad came home. He drove over to the hospital, but of course he couldn't do any good," said Crissy. "I just sat in the living room. I called Grandma Walden—"

"Your mother's mom," said Sharon.

"Uh, huh," said Crissy. "Well, she lived about ten minutes away at that time and she said she'd be right over. I decided to do some wash—"

"What?" laughed Clay.

"Laundry was one of my chores," she shrugged, looking a bit sheepish. "I know it sounds strange, but I don't think I could be accused of firing on all cylinders."

"Of course not," said Sharon.

"Anyhow, Grandma came in as I was working. I set the machine to fill, and measured out the soap and bleach. Then I lost it. I hugged Grandma and began to cry."

"Uh, huh," murmured Sharon, embracing her shoulders.

"And Dad came in," Crissy shuddered. "He came into the laundry room, screaming. He said I'd killed Mom, he knew it, and he was going to get me."

"You must have been terrified," said Clay.

"Yeah, I was, but I grabbed the first thing that came to hand, the cup of bleach," said Crissy. "I warned him, but he kept coming. He kept yelling that he was going to kill me.

"Grandma screamed at him to calm down. He turned to her and told her to shut up. As he turned, I threw the bleach into his face."

"My God," said Sharon.

"He went crazy and ran to the shower at the end of the hall. I grabbed my purse and phone and a jacket and ran out of the house."

"Grandma came out right behind me and we drove off," said Crissy. "I haven't been to that house since. Grandma took an apartment here in Hyde Park, where she hid me for a couple of months, but then she died."

"A sudden death?" asked Clay.

"I guess so," she said. "She had a heart attack, and I found myself on my own. A day or so before she died, she wrote a check to me for five thousand dollars."

"Why?" asked Sharon.

"She said it was an advance on my mother's estate. I guess Mom made me a beneficiary of her life insurance policy, but I can't collect on it until my eighteenth birthday. Grandma made me the beneficiary of her will, also. I was about to start to pursue it when Dad attacked me."

"I see," said Clay. "I take it it's significant?"

"To say the least," Crissy said.

"Good for you," smiled Sharon.

"And so I had a little money when she died," said Crissy. "I couldn't go back to school, so I kept Grandma's condo and took a job waiting tables."

"And so your father continues to hold you responsible for your mother's death," nodded Sharon. "That's why he tried to murder you?"

"I don't know," said Crissy. "I think that's what he wants, but…"

"Could he have another motivation?" asked Clay. "I mean, losing your cool over a sudden death seems—well, not normal, but at least a bit more understandable than anything else, I guess."

"Well, does it make sense to you? It sure doesn't to me," said

Crissy. "I thought he'd forgotten about me until—"

"Until the lake," nodded Clay.

"Right," Crissy said.

"Okay," said Sharon. "Why don't Clay and I go to the jail and try to interview him? You don't have to come. Maybe we can...I don't know...talk some sense into him."

Crissy considered. "That's a very nice offer," she said. "Maybe it'd work, I don't know."

"I'm pretty good at interviews," added Sharon. "Maybe he'll respond. Of course, maybe he won't even see us."

"Tell him I didn't do it, will you?" Crissy asked, a note of pleading in her voice.

"That's one of the primary reasons we're going to see him," said Sharon. "I want to know why he's been so intent on killing you."

"You're pretty good at asking questions," said Crissy. "If anyone can get it out of him, I think it's you."

"Meantime, let's talk about getting you back in school, okay?" said Clay. Crissy smiled.

***

Crissy left a few moments later to go up to her room. Sharon hadn't spoken much, to Clay's puzzlement.

"What's up?" he asked when Crissy left the room.

Sharon shushed him. "Clay, go and see if she's out of earshot."

Clay stood and walked to the stairs. "Yeah, she's closed the door," he said. "Is something up?"

"This situation seems to go a lot deeper than I thought at first," said Sharon. "It sounds like Grace was having an affair."

Clay did a double take. "Huh?"

"Clay, let me ask you," said Sharon. "Did your wife own negligees like the one that Grace was wearing?"

Clay shrugged. "Sure," he said. "I gave her a few for gifts."

"This is important," she said. "Do you remember that she ever wore one to lounge around the house after work?"

He smiled a little at that. "Well, no—"

"Of course not," Sharon said. "No woman would wear something like that with her teenage daughter coming home from school. She'd change into jeans, or something just as casual like a sweat suit."

Clay thought. "Well, does that of necessity mean she'd had an affair?"

"Give me another explanation," said Sharon.

Clay stammered. "Well, okay," he said at last. "I can't think of one."

Sharon nodded. "I have to make a few phone calls and confirm some stuff Crissy said," she said. "Then let's go to the jail."

***

"Have you been here before?" asked Clay, as they parked at the Cook County Jail, a grim edifice located at 26th and California on the south side of Chicago.

Sharon nodded. "I have to come here every once in a while when the hospital gets a drug overdose, a suicide, a murder, something like that."

"Yech. What a miserable place," said Clay.

"You have no idea," nodded Sharon. "They used to hang people in the basement. Then, it was one of three sites in Illinois where they electrocuted people. I read that between 1928 and 1962 they killed 67 people at the jail in the electric chair."

In the jail, Sharon used her professional credentials to gain access to DeRosa. They were shown to an interview room and Crissy's father entered on the other side of the protective screen. He snarled when he saw them.

"What do you want, Foster?"

"I want to talk about your daughter, DeRosa," said Clay. "We're thinking that it's quite possible that this woman—" he nodded at Sharon—"is Crissy's birth mother."

DeRosa looked like he'd been slapped in the face. "What?"

Sharon told the bare facts of her story, how she'd missed her daughter for more than 17 years, and pointed out the physical resemblances between her and Crissy. DeRosa peered at her.

"She was born on July 17," said Sharon.

"Yeah," he said, his entire posture reflecting a grudging and resentful attitude. "I guess it could be. Clarisse came to us a few days after the day you mentioned. We always called July 22 her birthday since that's the day we got her."

"Did you ever forgive her for being adopted?" asked Sharon.

DeRosa gave her a dirty look. "What do you mean by that?" snapped DeRosa.

"You didn't want her, did you?" Sharon asked, her voice calm, her posture unruffled.

They could see DeRosa gathering himself to deliver a blistering retort. Then he saw Sharon's calm and professional demeanor, her neutral expression, and the bluster retreated.

"Okay, so I didn't really want her," said DeRosa.

"Uh, huh," said Sharon. "I'm not judging you. I gave my daughter up and sent her away, so I'm not in a position to criticize you."

"I tried to love her," admitted DeRosa. "She never knew that I opposed her adoption. At that time, Grace and I were making—"

"—A lot of money," nodded Clay. "I can guess some of this," he went on. "You saw your life as your job, your wife, skiing, golf, snorkeling, all that, right?"

DeRosa stared for a few moments. "Okay, okay," he said. "But I went along with it. I did try to make the best of it."

"But you still felt some resentment anyhow," said Sharon.

DeRosa shrugged. "I guess I snapped when she killed Grace."

"What makes you think she killed him?" asked Sharon, in professional mode, the trained psychologist extracting answers from a reluctant client. Clay looked at her posture, her calm expression, and decided she was the best one to handle questions.

"I came home, she was there, she was the only one who'd been there at the time Grace died."

"What time did she die?" asked Sharon.

"Sometime between 2:00 and 4:00 P. M.," shrugged DeRosa. "She got out of school at 3:00. She always got home off the bus at the latest by 3:30. Something happened, and she went in and killed Grace."

"Did you find a weapon?" Sharon asked, not rising to the accusation.

"No," admitted DeRosa. "But she didn't really need one, did she?"

Clay saw that the question took Sharon by surprise. "What do you mean?" she asked.

DeRosa snickered. "You've been with her," he shrugged. "You know what she's capable of. She yanked Grace's soul right out of her."

"What about the affair?" asked Sharon.

Clay had to struggle to keep from gasping. Quiet, he told himself. Let her handle it.

DeRosa started to speak. "I…" he managed.

"Your wife was having an affair, wasn't she," said Sharon.

"Look, you can't…" DeRosa choked out.

"The whole thing doesn't add up unless she'd become involved with someone," said Sharon. "You know this. You must see it's the truth."

"What do you mean, lady?" demanded DeRosa, his face deep red with fury.

"That's the only way it makes sense," said Sharon. "She'd gone to her job that morning, which means a shower, makeup, clean clothes. Then she went to work and came home. There she changed out of her suit and heels and put on that negligee when she got home. No woman lounges around in a sexy negligee after coming home from work, particularly with her teenage daughter coming home in minutes."

"I don't know—" stammered DeRosa. Clay could see that Sharon had baffled him.

"You may not want to face it," said Sharon. "But it's true nonetheless, isn't it."

"What if I gave her that negligee?" said DeRosa.

"But you didn't," said Sharon. "Crissy always went with you to shop for clothes for Grace. She had never seen that negligee. The best explanation is that Grace wore it that day because a lover came over, isn't that right?"

DeRosa looked like he'd been clubbed. All the bluster had departed. "I don't know," he stammered again.

"Did you know your wife had a lover, DeRosa?" asked Clay.

"The doctor found no evidence that she'd had sex that day," said DeRosa. "We didn't have intercourse that morning. I left for work early. She came into the office an hour later, after she made sure Crissy got off to school."

"Did she always do that?" asked Clay.

"Yes," DeRosa said. "Grace stayed home with our daughter until Crissy went into first grade. Then she always left work so she'd be home when Crissy got there."

"Was Crissy in any activities at school?" asked Sharon.

"Yeah, she was a good little athlete," admitted DeRosa, looking like it pained him to say it. "She played softball and volleyball. Plus she was in student council, drama, all that."

Clay sprung the trap. "Did you know the bus arrived late that day, DeRosa?" asked Clay.

DeRosa started to speak. Then he asked, "What?"

"The bus broke down," said Clay, and Sharon nodded. "She got home late, not until 4:30."

DeRosa stared at them for a moment. His mouth worked as he tried to digest this information. "So she—"

"—couldn't have killed your wife, right," said Sharon.

DeRosa still couldn't frame a statement. "So if that's true..."

"It means you've been wrong and you've alienated Crissy and gotten yourself thrown in the clink for nothing," said Clay.

"No," said DeRosa. "She had to have done it."

"Crissy found your wife on the floor, dead," said Sharon. "She tried to administer CPR but wasn't successful."

DeRosa recovered a little. "No," he said, shaking his head.

"She's bewitched you. You don't even know it. She's twisted the truth, twisted your minds. You don't know what you're involved with here."

"We know quite a bit of it," said Sharon. "Yes, she worked it on us. She's very good at her mind tricks."

"She's a witch, Dr. Gray," asserted DeRosa. "She's been altered so that she can construct these hideous realities so that you don't know what is true and false, you can't tell right from wrong."

"I know," said Sharon. "We've been victimized by it." Clay nodded.

"Then you know that you can't believe anything she says," argued DeRosa.

"I won't agree, nor will I disagree," said Sharon. "But we've verified everything we just told you. We called the bus company. I talked to the medical examiner. Everything rings true, Mr. DeRosa."

DeRosa stood and began to pace back and forth. "This can't be," he said. "It can't."

"We verified the time Crissy got home. We know your wife was dead by then. Crissy had been at school all day long," said Clay. "No, she may have extraordinary abilities, but this is true. The police have never considered her a suspect."

"But..." DeRosa stammered.

"Look," said Clay. "We could withdraw our complaint. We might be able to get you out of here. Not that you deserve it. But we'll offer you a carrot."

"What's that?" asked DeRosa, his eyes narrowing.

"Crissy wants to know who killed her mother," said Clay. "Just like you do."

"She cares, huh," grunted DeRosa, rolling his eyes.

"You have to reframe your thinking, Mr. DeRosa," said Sharon. "You've let hatred and fear overcome you, take you captive. You can't imagine how you've harmed yourself since your wife died."

"Even if Crissy had done it," said Clay, "and I don't think even for a moment that she did, you still need to be her father in this situation, not her executioner, her Torquemada."

DeRosa sat in silence for some time. "I don't know if I can be," he said.

"You can re-train yourself," said Sharon. "You don't have to hate her."

"I'll consider it," DeRosa agreed.

"Okay," said Clay. "Crissy shares something with you. She wants to know who killed her mom as much as you do. She wants justice for the person who killed her mom, too."

DeRosa shrugged. "I don't have a clue if she didn't do it," he said.

"Go back to the idea of an affair," said Sharon. "I'm sorry if that hurts, Mr. DeRosa. I mean that. I know you're still in the process of grieving for Grace. But consider the look of things. She came home early from work, leaving her job at lunch time. She knew Crissy would be home around 3:30."

"Okay," said DeRosa. Clay was surprised to see tears in his eyes.

"She doesn't change into jeans, or a sweat suit," said Sharon. "Instead she puts on a negligee, one that neither you nor Crissy had ever seen."

"Not only that," said Clay. "She must have been in a big hurry to enter the house."

"Why do you say that?" said DeRosa.

"Crissy saw that she'd shut the buckle of the seat belt into the door," Clay nodded, and DeRosa looked surprised. "Your wife hadn't gone back to check. Crissy noticed the dome light hadn't gone out."

"Could that have been an accident?" asked Sharon.

DeRosa considered. "I doubt it," he said. "Grace did everything with such exquisite precision. Her meticulous attention to detail made her a superb researcher."

"Hmm," said Sharon. "Then it seems obvious that she had something on her mind."

"Could it have been an assignation, DeRosa?" asked Clay.

"I've never thought about it," said DeRosa. "I just..."

"You couldn't imagine it?" ventured Sharon.

A tear started down DeRosa's cheek. He mumbled a profanity. "My whole life," he said. "Shot in the keester."

"What do you mean?

"My wife, gone," he said. "My job. My daughter hates me."

"Why did you go after Crissy?" said Sharon.

DeRosa considered. He brushed at his cheek. "Well, dammit, healthy women don't just die!" he yelled.

"Take it easy," cautioned Clay. "This interview could come to a screeching halt."

DeRosa made a visible effort to calm down. He nodded.

"Help us," said Sharon, in that soothing voice of the trained professional. "We'll try to run down who did it."

"You really think someone murdered Grace, like I do?" said DeRosa.

Sharon gave a non-committal shrug. "Crissy thinks it too," she noted. "But the police and the medical examiner didn't feel that way. They found no evidence of murder, of rape, no violence at all."

"But you didn't know Grace," said DeRosa. "She ran several miles five times a week or worked out on the exercise bike. She worked out with weights. We ate a terrific diet. Crissy almost never even tasted fast food, and we used pizza as a rare treat. Grace had a physical and one of those heart scan things last summer. No disease anywhere, heart, lungs, all that fine."

"I want to ask you something," said Clay. "I'm sorry, Mr. DeRosa, I don't want to pry. Had you noticed a change in your sex life?"

Clay saw that DeRosa had to struggle to maintain his composure, not to lash out at the question.

"Well, yes," he said. "The last six months weren't great."

"Without being graphic," said Sharon, "could you be any more specific?"

DeRosa thought. "Until Crissy came along, everything went along like they were supposed to, except—"

"—except you couldn't conceive," asked Sharon.

"Yeah, there was that," agreed DeRosa. "Then, I guess like all couples, we had rough going for a while with the newborn up at all hours, and that."

"I understand," said Clay.

"Other couples have told me much the same thing," nodded Sharon. "I don't have any children," she added.

DeRosa nodded. "Then we settled into a routine, you know, couple times a week."

"Do you know why you couldn't have children?" ventured Sharon.

DeRosa hesitated. "I don't like talking about this," said the man. "I feel like I'm like betraying Grace's confidence."

"I'm a professional counselor," said Sharon. "I deal with this all the time. I have professional ethics about confidentiality. Clay is trustworthy, but if you'd rather he leave..."

DeRosa shook his head. "Nah, stay," he said. "Grace never could conceive. We tried everything, shots, procedures, all that. It bothered her for her whole life."

"I understand," said Sharon.

"So one day she asked what I'd think about adopting, we talked it over, I said okay, we got Crissy."

"Yeah," said Clay. "But she still wanted her own children, huh?"

"Yeah, we kept trying."

Clay shrugged. "All right," he said. "Let's talk about Crissy. When did you notice that she had this...what? This ability, I'd guess we could say?"

"About three months before Grace died," said DeRosa. "That was strange how we found out. We were at dinner. Crissy said she had a date that weekend, just a movie. She was dating a guy I couldn't stand."

Sharon smiled. "Why didn't you like him?"

"I called him 'The Circle'," DeRosa said. "He wore this stupid baseball hat all the time, with the bill bent into a shape so that to this day I couldn't tell you the color of his eyes."

"So you didn't trust him?" said Sharon.

"Not for a moment," said DeRosa. "Besides his whole family raised lizards."

"What?" laughed Sharon, and Clay chuckled.

"Yeah, you've never seen anything like that house," said DeRosa. "I had to go over there to pick Crissy up once and they invited me in. Jeez, they had aquariums all over the place, they kept the house temperature at about 85 degrees all the time…"

"I get the picture," said Clay.

"Yeah," said DeRosa. "Anyhow for her Homecoming dance last fall, we bought her a beautiful dress, she had her hair done…"

"I imagine she looked lovely," nodded Sharon.

"Yeah, well, The Circle showed up in ripped jeans and a sweatshirt with profanity on it," said DeRosa. "Didn't even bring her a flower. He stank of liquor, too."

"You didn't let her go with him, did you?" said Sharon.

"Hell no," said DeRosa. "I grabbed him by the back of the shirt, threw him out of the house, booted his ass down the front step. She went to the dance with a group of her friends. Well anyway, a few weeks later we were at dinner, and she told us she was going out with The Circle on Friday. I kept my head down, but I thought to myself, 'maybe we'll get lucky and he'll flip his car over before he gets here.'"

Clay smiled. "I'd probably feel the same way," he noted.

"Yeah," said DeRosa. "But then Crissy said, 'That's a terrible thing to say, Dad.'"

"Well, she was right," sniffed Sharon.

"You didn't listen to what I said just now," said DeRosa. "I mean, I didn't speak aloud."

Sharon stared at him a few moments. "Oh," she said. "She heard you think it, didn't she."

"Yes," said DeRosa.

"All right," said Clay. "When did she acquire this ability?"

"That was the first time I saw her do it," shrugged DeRosa. "I don't know when she learned it or how. You know, she could have screwed up her brains with drugs, she ran around with that creep—"

"I've never seen any indication of drug usage in all the time I've been with her," said Sharon. "For that matter I've never heard of someone acquiring the abilities she had through drug usage. Not ever, nothing even close. Drugs don't sharpen senses."

DeRosa didn't look at them for several moments. "Okay," he said. "I guess you deserve to know."

Clay and Sharon exchanged glances. "What do you mean?" asked Sharon.

"Grace could do much the same thing," said DeRosa.

"You mean—" said Clay. "—read minds?"

"Yeah," said DeRosa. "That's what I mean."

"I'd say that's silly, except I've seen what Crissy can do," shrugged Sharon. "Could she always do it?"

"No, no," said DeRosa. "This started not too long after Grace took that trip out East."

Sharon leaned back and shook her head. "I've never heard of anything even resembling this."

"I know," said DeRosa. "But it happened, just like I'm telling you. One day Grace could do it."

"How did you find out?" asked Sharon.

"Grace didn't know she could do it," said DeRosa. "It showed up during sex one night. I don't want to give details…"

"No, I understand," said Sharon.

"But all of a sudden our sex life became better than it had ever been before. Much better. I only had to think of something and she'd do it for me."

"Did you ask her about it?"

"Not at first," said DeRosa. "I didn't really even think about it for several nights. About—well, I guess it was a month later— I said something. 'How did you know what I wanted you to do?' I asked. 'You said it,' she replied. She looked surprised. 'No, I didn't,' I said. "I didn't say anything." She sat up in the bed and looked down at me.

"'What do you mean you didn't say anything?' she managed at last. I repeated what I said. She looked baffled. 'No,' she said. 'No, I heard you.'

"Well, we talked for quite a while. It turned out that the passion of the—well, you know—got her started."

"Sexual intercourse is the most intense communication possible between two people, yes," said Sharon. When DeRosa looked away, she gave Clay's hand a quick squeeze.

"It turned out that the ability increased with usage," said DeRosa. "I mean, in a short time, a couple of weeks maybe, she could hear my thoughts. Then she began to create mental pictures."

"And she and Crissy acquired this ability at about the same time?" asked Clay, wrenching his thoughts away from making love to Sharon. Good grief, he thought. How much more intense could it get?

"I think so," DeRosa said. "We realized what Crissy could do. It became evident that she began to notice things that her creep of her boyfriend thought as they—er—well, as they made out."

"You don't mean sex, I hope," said Sharon.

"No, I'm confident that didn't become involved," said DeRosa. "She began to realize that this guy only had that on his mind. She told us that she'd realized how, well, dumb the guy was. She came to realize that he didn't have the same intellect as she."

"I hope she wasn't unkind to him," said Sharon.

"Nah, I don't think so," said DeRosa. "But she felt creepy when she'd be with him. She broke it off."

"Happened to me, several times," shrugged Clay.

"Anyhow, same deal," said DeRosa. "The ability increased with use. She got better at it as she went along."

"You mean," said Clay, "you thought Crissy scared her to death?"

"Well, I guess something like that," said DeRosa. "I mean, no marks on her body, no evidence of heart failure, no stroke, anything. The Medical Examiner couldn't figure out why she died. He had no idea. He said it seemed like she just...had..." he hesitated. "Like she had her soul yanked out of her."

Clay felt a shiver of dread pass through him. "What could do that?" he asked.

"Now you see why I thought it had to be Crissy," said DeRosa. "I have no idea what her power has gotten to be."

"We've seen that she can create alternate realities," said Clay. "She gave me a vision of my house burning down, took me to Salem, Massachusetts in 1692 or so, and simulated a mouse running across the floor for one of your thugs."

"That's when you shot him?" said DeRosa. Clay nodded.

"Well, that's more than she could do last time I saw her," nodded DeRosa. "So I guess she hasn't reached her limits yet."

"Good grief," said Sharon.

"Yeah," said DeRosa.

Clay thought for a second. "Look, you said your wife conducted research, right?"

"Yeah, that was her job at the lab," nodded DeRosa. "She'd been working on..." he paused.

"Working on?" asked Sharon.

DeRosa sat without moving for a while. "Okay, she was doing medical research. She'd been working on genetic alterations using stem cells from adults."

"Just adults?" asked Sharon.

DeRosa nodded. "I'm pretty sure," he shrugged. "Embryonic stem cells can be pretty tough to get hold of."

"Could she have stumbled on something like this?" asked Sharon. "I mean while she was doing research?"

"I don't know what she was doing," said DeRosa. "I guess it's possible, but I don't have any knowledge of it."

"What about her notes? Records?"

"I don't know," said DeRosa.

"Did they clean out her stuff at work?" said Sharon.

"I'm sure they boxed it up," said DeRosa. "The stuff would be intact, I'd guess. Grace's meticulous attention to detail was legendary."

"What about at home?" asked Clay. "Did she keep any records there?"

"Yeah, some," said DeRosa. "I haven't looked."

"But you're a researcher," said Sharon, looking flabbergasted. "Didn't you suspect—"

"No," said DeRosa. "I don't know what happened to her stuff, what it contains, or even exactly what she was working on. I really have no idea."

Clay and Sharon said they would be in touch, but they had no idea why they were being nice to this man. He'd tried to kill Crissy, a couple of times; intimidated Craig; kidnapped and frightened Clay's ex-wife and her children...

"What now," asked Sharon as they left the jail.

"We're getting into stuff I don't understand at all," said Clay. "We're talking about two people whose entire mental chemistry seems to have been altered."

"Yes," said Sharon. "I resent what Crissy did to us, though the result has been fine. I don't think you invade someone else's mind like she did with impunity."

"Agreed," nodded Clay.

"I've never believed that the end justifies the means," shrugged Sharon. "We have to talk to Crissy about responsibility with this enormous power."

"Uh huh," nodded Clay.

A silence set in on them. "Want to tell me?" he asked her.

"I don't..." then tears rose in her eyes. She fumbled in her purse for a Kleenex and dabbed at her eyes.

"Let me guess," Clay said "The call to your husband didn't go well."

"No, it was awful," said Sharon. "It was humiliating, hurtful, and antagonistic. I want to start on some counseling, Clay," she added a few moments later.

"Sounds like a plan to me," he nodded. "I needed about a year with a counselor, then I worked in a group setting, you know, divorce recovery group, interventions, all that. But the hurt is still there. The other night at the warehouse my gut ached at seeing Gail again."

"I know," she said. "When you give your heart to someone you can't imagine that it could wind up the way my marriage has. Here I am, skilled in counseling, embarrassed at what my husband did, my own failures in the marriage—" She broke off.

"I'm sorry," she said. "You don't need to hear my problems."

"That's what I'm here for," he said. "But I'm glad I saw a counselor."

"I may need that," said Sharon. "I think I'm just feeling, well, relieved to get rid of him, if you understand."

"Yes," said Clay. "I suppose I do understand."

"But more than that," she said. "I thought that if my marriage ended, I'd be free to do what I pleased with my life. I'd like to live on my own, answer to no one, come and go as I please, you know."

"Uh, huh."

"But I don't feel that way now," she said. "I want to be with you and watch Crissy grow up."

"That suits me fine," he said. She took his hand and held it most of the way home. He just let her grieve.

Chapter 17

When they walked into the house, they found Crissy lying curled up on the couch, snuggling with Hephzibah.

"Hi," she said as her guardians came through the door. She couldn't muster her customary smile. On the contrary, she looked terrified.

"Relax, Honey," said Clay.

"Yes," said Sharon, smiling. "Everything will be okay, I promise."

"What did you find out?"

They related the details of their interview. Crissy looked surprised in several places.

"So they noticed Mom's ability for the first time during their intimacy?" she asked.

"Yes," said Sharon.

"Why would that be the case?" Crissy began. "What made that so special?"

"The most intense communication possible between two people occurs during sex, Honey," said Sharon.

The teenager considered this statement. "Now that you mention it," Crissy mused, "I began noticing my ability when I made out with my boyfriend."

"What was that you said about 'too much information' a

while ago?" asked Clay.

"It never got beyond the basics," said Crissy. "My dad hated him, and I didn't blame Dad once I heard Alex's thoughts."

"Is this too much information again?" asked Clay.

"Oh he made me sick," said Crissy, "once I knew what he wanted from me. Yech."

Sharon and Clay chuckled. "When did your mind reading start?"

"Last October, if I remember it right," said Crissy. "It's gotten more and more powerful over the last few months as I've used it more and more."

"Well, that's kind of strange," said Clay.

"No, I don't think it is," said Crissy. "Like when I was on the track team at the high school. They had me work on the high jump. At first I was awful at it, but then I began to improve as I practiced it."

Sharon nodded. "Did you ever discuss this with your mom?" she asked.

"Yes," said Crissy. "We talked it over a lot, in fact. One of the first things we had to learn was how to block the thoughts of other people."

"So can you do that?" asked Sharon.

"Yes," said Crissy. "Except for Mom. I don't have to hear someone else's thoughts if I don't want to. I couldn't block her, though. And she couldn't block me either. But—" she hestitated.

"What?" asked Sharon.

"Well, with Mom, I never knew when she was doing it to me," said Crissy. "But she claimed she always could tell when I was doing it to her."

"So what did you do?" asked Clay.

"I guess we just made an agreement that we wouldn't do it to one another," Crissy shrugged.

"Okay," said Clay. "I take it you both got this ability at about the same time, huh?"

"Yeah," said Crissy. "Anyway, pretty close to the same time. Last fall, I think."

"Do you have any idea why?" asked Sharon.

"Well, Mom did take that trip out east to Massachusetts," said Crissy. "She said she wanted to check something out in the town of Salem, you know, as in the Witch Trials, like I told you, Clay." She paused, and grew silent.

"Yes?" said Sharon.

"I don't know," said Crissy. "She had been doing some reading about the history of the area, you know. . ."

"Why?" asked Clay.

Crissy shrugged. "I guess we'll never know," she said. "Unless..."

"Yeah?" Clay asked.

"Now that I think of it," said Crissy, "Mom kept a diary. I don't know what happened to it. Dad may have destroyed it, of course."

"You mean a personal diary or professional diary?" asked Sharon.

"Both combined in one, I think," nodded Crissy.

"Could we find out?" asked Clay.

"Sure," said Crissy. "I know where she kept the diaries. She wrote in it every day."

"Could we go there and check?" asked Sharon.

"Of course," said Crissy. "I have a key, after all."

"Should we get permission from your father?" asked Sharon.

"I don't think he knows anything about the diaries," said Crissy. "She had a private office that he never went into and she stored the diaries in a private closet."

"So how do you know about it?" asked Clay.

"She took me in there every day of my life when I was little, of course," said Crissy. "I had a play pen when I was little, and then a toybox and coloring books when I was a little older. I know where she put her diaries."

"I think I'd feel creepy reading someone else's diary," said Sharon.

"But you're a psychologist," said Clay. "People entrust you with intimate secrets, every day."

"Yes, of course that's true," agreed Sharon, "but they do it with the knowledge of my absolute confidentiality. They also give me permission to enter their lives, Clay."

"But Crissy's mom is dead," said Clay. "She can't give you permission. She didn't know she'd be murdered. This might help us figure out who did it."

Sharon thought. "Maybe," she said. "And her closest living relative, other than her husband, did give us permission…"

"Let's go," said Crissy.

The drive to the DeRosa home took a little while, but the house impressed both Sharon and Clay. A two story mansion with six bedrooms and four full baths, the brick and stone exterior was beautiful. The gated driveway was paved with brick, and the doors were dark, burnished oak. When they entered, they found that the floor of the entranceway was marble. Oak floors gleamed in the living room and dining room.

Lavish leather furniture decorated the living areas.

"Where do we go, Crissy?" asked Sharon, trying to recover from being impressed with the most beautiful home she'd ever entered.

"Mom's office is downstairs," said Crissy.

They entered a finished basement which glowed with sunlight in the afternoon sun. A set of French doors opened onto a large backyard with a vestigial swing set. "Yours, I presume," smiled Sharon.

"Yes," said Crissy. "Mom and Dad wanted to keep it in anticipation of grandchildren. Everything changed, though, of course..."

Tears came to Crissy's eyes, now. Sharon enfolded her and murmured some comfort. Of course, thought Clay. "This place has a lot of memories for you, I'm sure," he said.

Crissy nodded. "The Christmas tree always stood down here, and I looked for Easter eggs in the yard, and learned to ride my bike..." she choked a little.

"I bet the gardens are beautiful in the summer, huh?" asked Clay.

"Yeah, they sure are," said Crissy. "It was Mom's favorite pastime, taking care of the gardens. I used to cut the grass when I got to be old enough."

Sharon hugged the girl's shoulders. "Okay, Honey. Come on, let's get this over with."

Crissy nodded, and pointed down a hallway toward a double French door. "That's Mom's office," she said. "They always made it out of bounds for me. For that matter I couldn't go into Dad's office, either. Mom stayed out of his office, and he stayed out of hers."

Clay chuckled. "That's a novel arrangement."

Crissy shrugged. "They seemed to be okay with keeping certain parts of their lives distinct from one another. I never thought much about it."

"Do you think it's important?" asked Sharon.

"Probably not," said Clay. "Come on, let's get it done."

They walked down a hallway to the office door and Crissy opened it.

"Over here," she said. She walked across the room to a strange, almost grotesque picture on the wall. She lifted the picture and revealed a small door in a recessed opening, perhaps a foot square, which had been padlocked.

"Do you have the key?" asked Sharon.

Crissy nodded. She turned the picture over and bent down a corner of the backing paper. Taped to the cardboard they saw a small brass key with a round head. Crissy pulled back the tape which secured the key to the cardboard and inserted the key in the lock.

She opened the door and removed a tiny hard drive.

"An external hard drive," nodded Sharon. "A lot better than paper, for sure."

Clay nodded. "Holds a ton of information. Smart woman," he noted.

"You have no idea," said Crissy. "My mother was one of the smartest women I've ever known. Straight A's at the U of I, both bachelor's and master's degrees."

"You mean your father never knew about this little safe?" marveled Sharon.

"Yeah," said Crissy. "Mom had it installed while he was at work, then hid it behind the picture. He knew about her other locations in the office at work, but never this."

"How did you know?" asked Clay.

"She worked in here all the time when I was little," said Crissy. "She did her computer research in here. I came in here when the carpenter installed it."

"And you could read her mind," smiled Clay.

"Well, yeah," said Crissy. By now she'd plugged the hard drive into the Dell Computer tower which stood next to the desk. She pressed the circular button and the computer came to life.

After the boot procedures, Crissy accessed the external hard drive. The screen requested a password. Crissy thought for a second, and then typed some letters. The screen cleared and presented a lengthy catalog.

"How did you know the password?" asked Sharon.

"Mom never thought much about them," shrugged Crissy. "She tended to use the same one over and over."

"Oh," said Sharon.

"My birthday," smiled Crissy. "Here," she said, pointing to the screen.

Clay and Sharon dragged up folding chairs and looked over Crissy's shoulder. In the list of files, they found one labeled "Crissy."

"The date is October 26 of last year," said Crissy. "One day before she died."

Now the screen went to Microsoft Word, and they waited as the program loaded. At last they saw a blank screen. Crissy went to the file menu and clicked on Open.

At least twenty files appeared in the catalog. Crissy clicked the most recent entry, saved the day before her mother died.

Sharon took Clay's hand. "Honey," she said to Crissy. "I think Clay and I ought to step into the other room and give you some privacy."

Crissy hesitated. "You think it may be bad?" she blinked. Clay realized what a strain this adventure had caused Crissy. She hadn't spoken to her mother in months, and now she was almost ready to peer into the last communication her mother had left for her.

Clay embraced the girl. "Do you want us to stay?" he said.

Crissy stared at the screen. "Why don't you read it to me?" she asked.

"Me?" said Clay. Crissy nodded. Sharon moved up next to the girl and embraced her as Clay turned the flat panel screen to him and slid his chair up.

He began. "Hi, Honey," he read. "By now I imagine that the worst has happened, since you're reading this. I'm so sorry I'm not going to be there. I know what's about to happen."

"What on earth," said Crissy. "What could. . ."

"I need to tell you some things," read Clay. "I know they want me, and they plan to kill me. They've been after me since I found the secret."

"The secret?" said Crissy. "What's that?"

"Last fall, you know, both you and I changed. I did it to you," Clay read. "I did it without thinking it all the way through, without realizing what would happen. I didn't know that you'd be altered the way I was when I gave you the injection of the serum."

Crissy gasped. The uncharacteristic sound surprised both Clay and Sharon and they glanced up.

The teenager sat with her hand over her mouth, her face the

color of paste.

Sharon moved to her and embraced her. "Crissy?" she asked, baffled at the devastation in the girl's face.

Crissy couldn't talk for a few moments. At last she managed to say, "Mom—my mother—she injected me with something."

"You didn't know that?" said Clay, baffled. "How could you not know you'd been given a shot?"

"I don't know," said Crissy. "When I had to get a shot when I was little, I'd scream like a banshee. I still hate them. Shots, I mean. Not banshees."

"To the point of terror?" asked Sharon, looking worried.

"Oh yes," said Crissy.

Clay and Sharon exchanged looks, eyebrows lifted.

"Crissy," said Clay. "Have you ever had memory blackouts?"

"I don't remember them if I did," said Crissy, after some consideration.

"But you don't remember jumping in the lake, either," noted Sharon. "Could you have blocked your memory of this injection? Or maybe your mom blocked it?"

"Or, maybe, her mother slipped her a Mickey and then injected her," Clay suggested.

Sharon giggled. "'Slipped her a Mickey?'" she said. "Have I suddenly stepped into a 1940s film noir?"

"That's what I thought it was called," said Clay, his face reddening.

"I think you mean 'a sedative'," Sharon told him.

"Let's go on," said Crissy, assuming the role of the adult.

Crissy shrugged, and the phone rang behind her. Crissy looked puzzled, and looked at her guardians. "Should I answer it?"

Clay shrugged. "I guess so," he said. Crissy picked up the phone and spoke into it.

"Hello?" said the girl. In a moment she turned to Sharon and Clay. She looked at their eyes.

Chapter 18

Sharon moved, her body smooth and warm against him. Clay woke up and opened his eyes, smiling to find her next to him in his bed. "Hi," he whispered. "Good Morning."

Sharon opened her eyes, gave him one of her beautiful smiles, and embraced him. She lifted her lips for a good morning kiss...

And they stopped. They looked around. "What the hell?" said Clay. "What happened?" They were in the bedroom of the Hyde Park house, snuggled in exquisite comfort.

Sharon also looked bewildered. "How did we get here?" she asked. "We were just—"

"Where?" asked Clay. "I have no memory of us going to bed, do you?"

Sharon's bewilderment didn't ease either. She moved her body against him, and she felt terrific, as always, but Clay couldn't respond.

He leaned over and snapped on the radio, a morning talk show featuring a husband and wife. "It's morning?" said Clay.

Sharon looked as puzzled as he felt. She rose and donned a robe while Clay put on a sweat suit and they trooped down stairs.

Crissy sat at the kitchen table, reading *The Innocents Abroad*. "So," she said, looking up. "You two finally decided to get up?

About time! It's almost eight o'clock."

Clay and Sharon looked at one another, and then back at their ward. "Honey, what day is this?" asked Sharon.

"Friday, of course," said Crissy, looking surprised.

"Friday?" asked Sharon.

"Of course," said Crissy. "What's the matter with you two this morning?"

Clay spoke up. "Honey, the last thing we remember is being at your mom's house, in her office."

"What office?" asked Crissy.

"In the basement of your parents' home," said Sharon. "You took us to Winnetka, took us into the house, and you were showing us your mom's office."

"Mom didn't have an office in the basement," said Crissy. "Her office was off the bedroom upstairs."

Clay and Sharon stared at the girl. She stared back, mouth open in amazement. "And what were we doing at Mom's house?" asked Crissy. She looked into Sharon's eyes.

"I don't know," said Sharon. "Now I can't remember."

Crissy turned to Clay. She looked at his eyes…

"Stop it!" he screamed. "Get out of my mind!"

Everything stopped. "What?" said Crissy.

"What happened?" said Sharon.

"Crissy just tried to bewitch me," said Clay. "I think she did it to you." Both Sharon and Clay turned to her.

"Crissy?" asked Sharon. "Are you doing something to us?"

"Doing something to you?" said Crissy. "I don't know what you mean…"

"We were talking about your Mom's office," said Clay. "The office in the basement in the house in Winnetka."

"We were?" said Sharon.

"Yes," asserted Clay. "Let's go back to the house, now."

"Why?" said Crissy. "Why would you want to go back there? We didn't find anything."

"We found your mom's diary," said Clay. "In her basement office."

Crissy's seemed to be getting more and more nervous. "I don't understand," she said. "What are you talking about?"

"Clay, are you sure we didn't dream something?" asked Sharon, looking a bit dazed.

"Yes, I'm sure," said Clay. "We didn't have parallel dreams. Crissy's enchantment stuff doesn't always work on me, for some reason. Yesterday it did. Today it didn't."

"What do you mean?" asked Sharon.

"I knew that she meant to enchant me, or whatever the hell it is that she does," said Clay. "She got you, but not me this time. She got both of us yesterday."

"What do you mean?" asked Crissy. "I didn't try to. . ." Her face clouded. "Wait a second," she said. "I showed you where we used to put the Christmas tree, didn't I?"

"Uh, huh," said Clay.

"Oh, brother," said Crissy. She looked frightened and puzzled.

"What?" asked Sharon.

"I think someone is enchanting me," she said. "I only have vague pictures of being at the house."

"Yes," said Clay. "I remember the phone rang, you answered. The next thing I remember is waking up next to Sharon. About 16 hours are missing from my life."

Sharon shook her head. "I don't remember anything since

we were in the office yesterday," she asserted. "Until I woke up a few moments ago."

Crissy looked scared. "Wait a second," she said. "Do you guys think I..."

"You just did it to Sharon," Clay pointed out. "And you tried to do it to me."

Crissy again put a hand to her mouth. "I did, didn't I?"

"Who could be doing that to you?" asked Sharon. "And even more to the point, why would you do that to us? We've done our best to take care of you and protect you."

Crissy looked a little embarrassed. "I can't guess," she said. "I don't remember meeting anyone who could do what we do other than me or Mom."

"Uh, huh," said Clay.

Two hours later, they again pulled into the driveway of the huge home owned by Crissy's parents. She led them inside and at Clay's insistence down the steps to the basement. "You pointed there," he told Crissy, indicating the area by the French doors, "and said that's where you put the family Christmas trees."

Crissy gave a slow nod. "And down the hall is Crissy's Mom's office," said Clay. He pointed to a hallway.

The group walked down the hallway and opened the door...

They found nothing in the room except a strange, eerie picture on the wall. No desk, no chair, no phone: "What happened to everything?" said Sharon.

"I don't get it," said Crissy.

"What about the safe?" said Sharon. Both Clay and Crissy turned to her in surprise.

"You mean a wall safe?" said Clay.

"Yes," said Sharon. "I have a flash of memory on that spot there," she said, pointing to wall above where a desk should have been. A picture did hang there.

"That picture's always been there," said Crissy.

"And I remember that there's a safe behind it," nodded Clay.

Crissy looked bewildered. "Okay…" she said. She tugged on the picture and pulled it away from the hook. They stared at a blank wall. "What the…" began Sharon. "I could have sworn…"

Clay nodded. "Me too," he said. He walked to the spot and inspected it closely. Now he ran his fingers over the wall. "Hmm," he said, tapping his finger against the wall. "Right," he said, and smacked the wall with his fist. The wall collapsed and Crissy gave a little cry.

Clay pulled the broken pieces of wallboard away. Some pinkish insulation came out and the group saw the door of a safe. "Uh, huh," he said. "Whoever did this tried hard but they weren't contractors. They used the wrong type of wallboard. The paint didn't quite match. The original wallboard is waterproof green board and they used a standard gray to cover up the safe."

"Do you know where the key is?" Sharon said to Crissy.

Crissy stared. "Yes," she said. "Behind that picture in the top right corner." Clay nodded and peeled back the backing paper. He found the small gold key and inserted it in the lock. The safe opened and they found the hard drive inside.

"Let's get out of here," he said, urgency in his voice. "They may be watching."

"Where do we go?" asked Sharon.

"I've got an idea," said Clay. "Do you need anything else, Crissy?"

"Nothing urgent," she said. "But I—" The phone rang in the next room. "I'll get it," said Crissy.

Something struck Clay. "No," he said. "No, Crissy. You mustn't." She looked puzzled at the urgency in his voice.

He grabbed the girl. "Let's go," he said. "Now."

"No, Clay!" she asserted. "I have to—" Now he got it. Her eyes were glazed over. She didn't quite hear his fear. He grabbed her, spun her around and lifted her. She began to scream and Clay ran.

"Sharon," he yelled. "Get the back door. Now." But Sharon had caught on. She sprinted to the back door and threw open the locks. She struggled for a moment with the door but then it gave way and opened.

They shot across the backyard, Crissy struggling. "No," she said. "You don't understand. Please let me—"

"There they go!" yelled a voice. "Shoot them!"

Crissy's eyes focused. "Clay! I'm all right!"

Clay set her down as they sprinted across the yard. Three gunshots rang out and splinters erupted from the trees around them. Then they burst into the neighbor's yard and crossed at a dead run.

"I thought this might happen," said Clay. "Head for the other side of the street."

Clay had again parked Sharon's car down the street and they ran to it. Sharon tossed Clay the keys and he opened the passenger side door. Sharon and Crissy piled in and Sharon yanked up the lock on the driver's side.

In the next instant Clay piled in and started the car. He backed it into the nearest driveway, then spun the wheel and slammed the car into drive.

Tires screamed as he saw three men burst from between the houses. One of them gestured and the others ran into the street. Then Clay turned the corner and gunned the car, turned again and headed toward Route 294. He took the south bound exit and accelerated.

"Did we lose them?" he snapped at Crissy.

"I think so," she said.

"Okay," he said. "So we have to find a hideout."

"Where?" said Sharon. "If these people can read minds, what chance do we have of escaping?"

"I'm sort of hoping we might glean something from this hard drive," said Clay. "She might know something that would help."

"I don't see how," said Sharon. "Grace couldn't help herself, so why could she suggest something for us?"

"A little positive thinking, okay?" said Clay. "We can't give up. These guys are killers, remember?"

"And that doesn't make any sense," said Sharon. "Crissy ought to be invaluable to anyone, not a threat."

"Unless they're a threat to each other as well," said Clay.

Crissy hadn't spoken for a few moments. Clay looked at her in the rear view mirror.

"She's asleep, I think," he whispered.

"What the. . ." said Sharon. She turned, concern on her face. She reached for Crissy's wrist and felt her pulse.

"Okay, that's really strange," she said.

"What's strange?" said Clay.

"My heart is still pounding a mile a minute," said Sharon. "Are you on overload too?"

"I'm sure I'm still fired up too," he said. "Why?"

"Crissy's pulse. It can't be more than fifty beats a minute."

"Well, so what? Mine's fifty—" He got it. "My God. You mean she calmed down that fast?"

Sharon nodded, chewing a little on her lower lip. She turned back to face the front. Then she shrugged. "Where are you headed?"

"Elgin," he said. "We need a computer."

"Why don't we just go—" then she understood. "You think that group has staked out our places, right?"

He nodded. "I don't know where to head once I get the computer, though."

"I'm thinking," she agreed.

About an hour later he turned onto Route 31 and headed south into Elgin, stopping behind a warehouse. Crissy woke up. "Where are we?" she asked.

Clay told her. "I know the guys here," he said. "The company is named MRK. They sell used computers. I want to buy something and then head out for parts unknown."

They walked into the large warehouse where a receptionist summoned the sales manager whose name was Chick. He shook hands with Clay and nodded greetings to Sharon and Crissy. "Need something for school?" Chick grinned, smiling at Crissy.

"No, we're looking for a good laptop if you've got one," said Clay, amused at the way the workers in the warehouse had stopped work to gaze at his beautiful young ward.

"Oh, this is for you?" asked Chick, looking a little disappointed. "Yeah, let's go into the warehouse."

Fifteen minutes later they'd found a good used Toshiba unit and while a technician put an operating system on the machine,

Chick found Clay a good used printer/fax/copier. A few of the workers came close to a fist fight in their eagerness to help Crissy load the gear into their car.

After Clay used a Visa card to pay for the computer gear, they headed south. They took Route 20 to Randall Road, where Clay stopped at a Best Buy electronics store. He bought some word processing software and other materials.

An hour later, they stopped at a shopping center near a large hospital and got some sandwiches for lunch at a bakery restaurant. Now Clay addressed his two charges.

"Okay," he said. "We need a place to hide and re-group."

"My mother lives in Pontiac," said Sharon. "But I don't think I want to see her, if you understand."

"Yeah, I can imagine," said Clay. "Also, we may put your parents in danger if we arrive, you know."

"How about if we rent a motor home?" suggested Crissy. Clay considered her suggestion.

"No," he said at last. "It's not a bad idea, but I think this group could find us if we did that. I tell you what. Let's find someplace where we can examine that hard drive. I gather that this group can find us no matter where we go. If we have any hope at all, it has to be on that hard drive."

"What do you mean, hope?" asked Sharon.

"You saw. They plan to kill us, Sharon. Then drown Crissy," asserted Clay. "And as far as I can see, we have only limited immunity to this group's mental powers."

Sharon nodded. "They seem to be able to affect you, too," she said to Crissy. "You managed to short circuit us yesterday after someone called you. I don't know why they didn't try to kill us yesterday."

Crissy thought. "I can't kill you," she said. "And even though I robbed your memory of about 12 hours, you still were functioning. You talked to each other, we went out to dinner, and when we got home we went to bed. You just forgot everything."

"Did we do anything wrong?" asked Clay. "Break any laws?"

"No, I don't think you can do anything you wouldn't do when you were in complete control," said Crissy.

"But they got you to try to kill yourself," said Sharon.

"Yes, but they used drugs, too," said Crissy. Sharon nodded.

Now Clay stopped the car in a Hotel entranceway. He went inside and got two adjoining rooms with a connecting door.

The group made their way to the rooms, intending to start right away on the hard drive. "Wait a minute," said Clay. "Let's sleep a little."

"What?" said Sharon.

"We've been intense for hours," he said. "We should rest."

Sharon and Crissy considered, and then agreed. "I don't think I'll be able to sleep," said Sharon. "But if you want to relax, then. . ."

The group lay down for a bit, and Sharon fell asleep within thirty seconds, followed by Crissy and then Clay, who waited to make sure the women were comfortable.

Clay awoke first, checked his watch, and found that two hours had passed. He went to the window and watched the sun set over a shopping center to the west of the hotel. Darkness settled in with some surprising speed. He called a local pizzeria, that agreed to deliver what was known as the Fiesta Size, with cheese and sausage and green peppers and onions.

Sharon came awake with a slow ease. "Did I fall asleep?" she asked. Clay chuckled and nodded as Crissy stirred.

"What time is it?" she asked.

"Almost seven," answered Clay. "I just called for a pizza, and I may run across and get us some wine and soda."

Sharon nodded and indicated that she'd enjoy a soda. Clay drove over to a Meijer store and picked up a few necessities. By the time he got back, he saw that Sharon had climbed into the shower and freshened up. Crissy had set out the laptop and attached the hard drive...

But they weren't there.

Huh.

He walked into Crissy's suite. Called out. No answer.

Now, he began to worry.

At that moment he heard a knock at the door. A peek through the knothole revealed a young man holding a pizza box.

Clay opened the door. The delivery man presented the bill and Clay paid him, including a generous tip.

He walked back into the room, puzzled and worried. But the rooms showed no signs of a struggle.

Could they be hiding?

He picked up the phone and called the front desk. He asked if anyone had called the room. "A pizza guy showed up a few moments ago. We just sent him up."

"That's fine," he said. "I meant ten minutes or so ago."

"No," the clerk said, with a little hesitation. "We haven't gotten any calls for anyone in the building in the last half hour or so."

Clay thanked him and hung up the phone. He shrugged.

Well, maybe they went to the pool, he thought.

He opened the box of pizza and ate a couple of pieces. Sensational, he thought. He opened a bottle of a fine merlot and poured himself a glass, using a tumbler that the motel provided in the room.

He took his time, but he couldn't shake the fear.

Where could they have gone?

He turned on the room television. A logo for the hotel appeared, talking about how the hotel provided wi-fi service.

Of course.

Crissy would have left him a note. On the computer. Where the creeps wouldn't know or think of looking at.

He poked at the hard drive and the screen presented him a logo, then asked for a password, He typed in Crissy's password and hit return. At once the screen displayed a list of the files on the hard drive.

He loaded Microsoft Word and asked the program to open a file called Cal*yMichigan. In a matter of moments the screen displayed a message written in all capitals.

CLAY THEY WANT ME AND THEY'RE GOING TO GET US. I CAN'T STOP THEM. I THINK THEY'LL TAKE ME TO THE RIVER IN GENEVA AND THROW ME IN. TRY TO BE BRAVE. THANKS FOR EVERYTHING.

I LOVE YOU. YOU'VE BEEN WONDERFUL. I WISH YOU HAD REALLY BEEN MY FATHER. LOVE CRIS....

Clay sat staring at the screen for several moments, not sure what to do. Would they kill Sharon too? Yes, of course they would. They'd have killed him if he'd been there.

His stomach aching, he rose and went to the window. They'd drawn the curtains, but he opened them and looked out at the vast array of stores and shops that lined Randall Road. He didn't register much.

His mind numb, he went back to the computer. The pizza box stood open and the half-drunk bottle of wine rested next to it.

God save me, he thought. Everyone who comes into my life. They leave, destroyed, and glad to be away from me.

He slumped onto the couch and tried to focus.

The hallway door opened. He jumped to his feet.

A tall blond woman stood there, smiling at him.

"Excuse me?" he said.

"Mr. Foster, I think," said the woman.

"Yes," Clay said. "Who the hell are you?"

She walked into the room and left the door open behind her.

"Would you share your pizza with me?" she asked.

"What the hell do you mean, share my pizza?" he snarled.

"No sense letting Aurelio's pizza go to waste," she smiled.

She sat down, picked up a napkin and took a piece of pizza. She bit into it, waved her hand in front of her mouth, chewed for a moment and swallowed. "Hot," she said.

"Who are you?" Clay repeated.

"My name is Charlotte Bishop," she said. "Feel better now?"

"No," he said. "Your name means nothing to me."

"Think for a moment," said Charlotte.

Clay did. He noticed, now, that something about this woman looked familiar. Like they'd met before.

Then it came to him. A vision of a 1690s village of the Massachusetts colony. An old woman. "You look like a woman I saw executed in Salem," he said.

"The girl took you there," Charlotte Bishop nodded. "You

saw the woman choked to death at the end of a humiliating rope in Salem," said the woman.

"Bridget Bishop," he remembered now.

"Right," said Charlotte.

"Her descendant?" asked Clay.

"Yes," said Charlotte, reaching for another piece of pizza. "Would you please pour us some wine? And sit down?"

"I'm afraid we need to insist, Mr. Foster," said a voice from the door. He whirled to look. Now three more people stood there.

And Clay felt fear.

***

Clay watched as the three people joined Charlotte. One of them held another pizza, which he opened. The group set to eating. Another handed over a bottle of fine wine, a magnificent Cabernet Sauvignon. "Goes well with pizza, Mr. Foster," said the man, who now pulled a corkscrew out of his pocket. He cut away the seal, twisted in the corkscrew and opened the cobwebby, dusty bottle. Clay realized this bottle had been in a private collection. The man poured him a glass.

Clay stood with his back against the window, trying to figure out how to get away.

"You're witches, aren't you," he said.

They shrugged. "Yes," said Charlotte, with a glance at the others, who nodded. "At least, in a manner of speaking."

"Not like Margaret Hamilton," said one of the men.

"Who?" said Clay.

"The Wicked Witch of the West," said Charlotte, smiling. "From *The Wizard of Oz*, MGM, 1939."

"Oh, brother," he said, not sure what to do now.

"I understand that you are afraid, and also I understand your fear, Mr. Foster," said the man who had produced the wine. "But if we had any intention of harming you we would have moved already, wouldn't we."

The others nodded. "No, Mr. Foster," said another of the women. "We haven't the slightest interest in harming you. Rather the opposite."

"What do you mean?" he asked.

"We came to save you," said Charlotte. "That is, to save you from the two women who've enchanted you."

"Crissy and Sharon?" he said. "Enchanted me?"

"Yes," said Charlotte, the only one whose name he knew.

"Why should I believe you?" he asked.

"Mr. Foster, you need to understand something. You've been enchanted for several days now," said the man. "You've been the victim of that girl. However, you won't need to worry about her any more. She's at the bottom of the Fox River now."

"What!" yelled Clay. "You killed Crissy—"

"In a way, yes," said Charlotte, smiling.

"Is she dead?" Clay demanded.

"Oh yes. She's joined her mother, thank goodness, at last," said one of the women.

"And you say Sharon is also dead?" Clay asked, tears starting in his eyes.

"Yes, Sharon," said the man, taking another piece of pizza. "She mentioned that was her name." He spoke as if giving the score of a meaningless baseball game.

Clay hesitated, not wanting to know the answer. "You killed her, too?"

The group nodded almost as if moving in choreography. As they did, Charlotte took a bite of pizza and sipped at a small glass of wine.

Now Clay began to cry. The tears coursed down his cheeks and he felt shame, embarrassed at crying in front of a coven of witches.

"Mr. Foster," said the man. "I can see you're distraught. But you mustn't be. Those two wouldn't have been satisfied until you were dead. They were evil beyond expression."

"Evil?" gasped Clay. "Sharon and Crissy evil?"

"Oh yes," said Charlotte. "Please eat some pizza, Mr. Foster." She handed him a piece.

Clay, numb, took the piece of pizza. He ate without thinking, bewildered by the assertions of this strange group.

"Am I dreaming?" he asked.

"No, not now," said Charlotte. "This is real. We're real." She poured him some wine. He sipped, trying to clear a loud roaring in his ears.

"We intend to put things right," said the man. "My name is Oakshott," he said in reply to Clay's question. "We've been watching you right along."

"Why didn't you stop her father?" asked Clay. "Why did I have. . ."

"He did what we wanted him to," smiled Charlotte. "But you interfered. It was brave and noble. But let me ask you something. How do you feel?"

He checked himself out. "I feel fine, except I'm very sleepy," he said, and felt some surprise. "That's odd. I'm not tired. . ."

Then it clicked in. "You drugged me," he said.

The coven nodded. "Go to sleep, Mr. Fowler," said Charlotte.

"I don't seem to have a choice. . ." Clay began. Then, everything went black.

Clay Foster woke up in a hospital bed. For a moment, he lay there, jarred and disoriented, trying to get his bearings. *Why am I in the hospital?* He wondered.

He heard a knock at his door. "Come on in," he said, trying to clear the sleep away.

A policeman opened the door and came in. "Mr. Foster," he said. "My name is Nolan. I'm here to talk to you about what happened earlier today."

"Okay," said Clay. "Let me warn you. I'm feeling a little groggy, but I'll do what I can."

"Did you know the girl before all this?"

"You mean the girl at the lake?"

"Yes, that's what I mean, Sir."

"No, I've never laid eyes on her," said Clay. He explained what had happened. He'd gone running with his dog, and he'd seen a pretty girl standing on the rocks at the Promontory. She collapsed into the waves before he could get to her.

"Then you went in for her," nodded Nolan.

"Yes, I did," he nodded.

"You pulled her out, then," said Nolan.

"Yeah, then I tried CPR," Clay said. "I thought maybe I'd brought her back."

"Was she alive when you got her out?" asked Nolan.

"Why?" asked Clay. "Isn't she. . ." He understood now where the cop was going with these questions. "Oh, Jeez," he said.

"Yeah," said the cop with a nod. "Yeah, she's gone. I'm afraid she died here at the hospital a little bit ago."

"Damn," said Clay. "That's terrible news. I thought I'd gotten to her in time."

"I know how you feel," said Nolan. "She looked to be a real pretty girl, too."

"What makes a girl do that?" mused Clay.

"Lots of stuff," shrugged Nolan. "I. . ." A knock at the door interrupted him.

"Come on in," hollered Clay. A tall blond woman pushed open the door and walked into the room.

"Hello," said Clay.

"Mr.—" she consulted a clipboard "—Foster, correct?" He nodded. "I'm Dr. Sharon Gray," she said. "I'm one of the consulting psychologists here at the hospital."

"Nice to meet you," said Clay. He took her outstretched hand and felt an almost electric charge surge through him. Sharon Gray was quite beautiful, to say the least.

They stared into one another's eyes for a moment, but then Sharon broke the charm. "Lieutenant, if you're busy with Mr. Foster, I can certainly come back later—" she began with a glance at Lt. Nolan.

"No, please stay," said Nolan. "You don't have to leave. I just wanted to meet Mr. Foster. He's quite a hero, despite the girl's death. We don't by any means consider him a suspect in the girl's death." He turned to Clay and handed him a card. Clay thanked the policeman, who took his exit.

"How are you doing?" asked Sharon.

"Should I call you Dr. Gray?" he asked.

"Sharon would do very well," said Sharon. "I wanted to give you an opportunity to talk."

"Talk about what?" asked Clay.

"Well, the primary thing would be the girl's death," said Sharon, glancing up. He smiled at her, but he thought that she'd probably be a joyless, humorless spike, about as much fun as a serious cold.

"Okay," he said.

"Did you ever go through the process of grieving before?" she asked. For the next several minutes she asked him question after question. At first he answered with brief one or two word responses. Then, rather to his surprise, he found himself warming to this woman.

She'd struck him as attractive at first. Now though as she sat next to his bed, her legs crossed, smiling a gentle smile, her eyes sparkling, he thought that he'd never seen a more striking woman. Not just beautiful, but with engaging warmth, kindness, outstanding listening skills and grace.

She spent almost two hours with him and as she began to excuse herself, he cleared his throat. "Excuse me," he said.

She turned and smiled at him.

"Yes," she said, one eyebrow cocked.

"I know your husband's out of town," he said. "Please excuse me for being forward. I'll be out of here a little later. I'd appreciate it if you'd consider having dinner with me."

She stared at him, thunderstruck. Her mouth moved for a few moments but nothing came out.

"I'm sorry," he said. "I guess that must sound way out of line. I imagine you have professional ethics—" he stopped when he saw her waving her hand.

"That's not it," she said. "How did you know my husband is out of town? Or that I'm married? I don't wear a ring."

Now he couldn't speak. At last he managed, "I don't know

how I know. I just do. Maybe you told me?"

"No," she said, shaking her head. "I never said anything at all about being married or my personal life."

"Oh," he said, feeling himself reddening. "I see...uh...none of my business, you know—"

"Mr. Foster," she began.

"Please," he said. "Let me apologize. I want to assure you that I'm not as rude as I must have—"

"Mr. Foster!" she interrupted. "Please stop and listen to me. I'd love to have dinner with you. I just..." She paused.

"Okay," he said, when she didn't go on. "I'd like to go home and change. May I meet you here?"

"That would be fine."

Clay checked out of the hospital and walked across the lobby toward a revolving door. He saw an elderly gentleman about to walk through the doors—

He hurried forward as the old gentleman lost his balance and fell backward. Clay caught him and held him upright.

"My goodness," said the man. "Thank you so much. I just don't know what. . ." The thanks continued for a few moments until Clay assured him that things were okay. Then he went and retrieved the antique Sting Ray from the garage.

Wait a minute, He thought, coming to a halt next to it and looking around. *How did the Corvette get here? I left it at the Promontory.* He puzzled for several moments and made a mental note to ask the Police Lieutenant about it. He'll have an explanation—

Yeah, but how did I know where it was parked here at the hospital? I walked right to it—

Clay climbed behind the wheel of the 'Vette, lowered the

window and breathed deep, filling his lungs with cold air blowing off nearby Lake Michigan. Then he drove home and climbed into a shower.

He stood under the hot, hot water and enjoyed an erotic memory of taking a shower with—

With whom? He found that the remembrance of a shower with a woman stirred him to a remarkable extent.

As he toweled off, he kept thinking that he knew the woman well. That he'd asked her to marry him, even. They had enjoyed a sexual relationship that had been powerful, dramatic and satisfying beyond expression.

With no little effort, he forced his mind to focus on his date for the evening. This would be his first date, he thought, in months. He let his mind wander to the beautiful Dr. Gray, her lovely legs and attractive figure, her kind voice…

Clay couldn't stop thinking that he'd had this sex with her. He kept trying to get over the memory, but he couldn't get by it. Dr. Gray. Sharon. Grandma and Papa's cabin in Iowa. A shower. His bedroom at the townhouse.

No, he told himself again and again. *That can't be. I just met her.*

He changed into his best suit with a cream-colored silk shirt and a silk tie with a quiet muted pattern. As he knotted the tie, he had a strange feeling that he'd never seen the tie before. Nor the shirt, nor even the suit. He buffed his good black shoes and splashed on expensive cologne—

"Where did I get this cologne?" he asked aloud. Why were so many things wrong here?

Clay drove back toward the hospital and stopped at a car wash. The old Corvette gleamed as he pulled up in front of the vast hospital complex at 7:00 on the dot.

To his relief, Sharon Gray came out through the revolving door almost at once. He climbed out of the Corvette and walked around to her side. He opened and held the door for her, struggling not to stare at her lovely legs as she climbed in. She grinned and thanked him as he got back behind the wheel.

"Nice 'Vette," she grinned, settling into the black leather passenger seat.

"Yeah, thanks," he said. "As you can imagine it's my pride and joy. I bought it when I was about twenty-three, not long before I married Gail. I've had it rebuilt twice from the lug nuts up."

"What kind of engine?" she asked.

"Small V-8," he smiled.

"283?" she asked.

Now he felt amazed but managed to nod. "Four barrel carb, though," he said. "Not a deuce."

"Nice," She said, and nodded with approval.

"You know cars?" he asked.

"Well, I know a little about Corvettes ," she said. "My dad had three of these things: A '58, a fuel injected '64 Stingray, and a '98 with a 413."

"Did he let you drive them?" he asked.

"Once in a while I drove the 413," she smiled. "The others were long gone by the time I was old enough to drive. We were really good friends, Dad and me." She turned to look out at the lake front as they stopped at a traffic light. This gave him an opportunity to admire her beautiful legs. His eyes roved up to her lovely bust line…

Wait a minute. Sharon has no relationship with her parents.

They've been alienated since she was 15 or so—

How did I know that?

"You'd better go," she said. "The guy behind you has honked once. He might start shooting, you know."

Clay laughed and headed off down Lake Shore Drive, heading north. He took Sharon to a steak house on the near north side where the waiters knew him. He introduced Sharon as a good friend and the wait staff treated her with more than ordinary deference.

"Are you famous?" grinned Sharon.

"Hardly," he smiled. "I'm just in this area a fair bit and like to stop here when I can."

"What do I want to order?"

Clay recommended that they split a 24 ounce porterhouse, and she accepted. They each had a cocktail—Clay a martini, Sharon a cosmopolitan.

After about ten minutes of chit chat about nothing much, Clay said, "It's really too bad about Clarisse," he said. "Such a pretty young girl. What would have driven her to commit suicide?"

"I don't know," said Sharon. "I've struggled with that question too many times with suicidal youngsters. I just. . ." She broke off and looked at him.

"What?" he said, concerned at the expression on her face.

"How did you know her name?"

"I beg your pardon?"

"The hospital hasn't released her name pending notification of next of kin."

"That would be her father," he nodded.

"How did you know that?" she asked again.

"Her mother's dead," said Clay.

"Yes," said Sharon. "Again: how do you know that, Mr. Foster?"

"Well, I. . ." he began. Then he stopped. "I don't know. Someone must have told me…"

"No one from the hospital told you, Mr. Foster," she said. "I just found this out an hour ago."

"The cop, then. The one who took my dog to my neighbor."

"No," said Sharon. "He didn't know those details when he spoke to you. He only figured out the other stuff—her name, her parents—when you had been discharged and had left the hospital."

"Am I incorrect?" he asked.

"No, you're right on every count, including her name, Clarisse."

"Crissy, she likes to be called."

"I didn't know that," said Sharon. "No, wait. I did know that."

"How would you know?" asked Clay.

"Well…" she stammered.

"Did you have a child when you were fourteen years old?"

She stared at him for a few moments. Then, "Yes," said Sharon. "Well, fifteen. And you live in Hyde Park in a big duplex you've been rehabbing."

Clay could only nod. "Have we met before?"

"I don't think that's possible," she said. "I know I'd never seen you before this afternoon."

The waiter appeared as Sharon and Clay sat staring at one another. Clay ordered the steak and another round of drinks.

"What's happened?" Sharon asked.

"I can't begin to imagine," said Clay. "I keep having flashes of memory about you, about Crissy, several other things."

"Like what?"

"I think her father tried to kill her," he said. "I think he succeeded now. He hates her..." He broke off the conversation.

Several moments later she asked, "Why'd you stop?"

"I can't quite remember," he said. "He blamed her for—"

"Her mother's death," finished Sharon.

"Yeah," he said. He sat staring at her for several moments. "Er. . .is this a massive coincidence?" he asked.

"No such thing," she said.

"I know," he said.

"Clay," she said.

"Sharon," he said. "I love you, don't I."

"I'm pretty sure I love you," she said.

"What's happened?" he asked her.

"I can't imagine," she said, shaking her head. "I'm having a terrible time with this disorientation, this dizziness. It came on when we started to talk about Crissy."

"Is she dead?" said Clay. "I mean, are you sure?"

"I think so," said Sharon. "I saw her body in the hospital. Still I remember talking to her, hugging her. . ."

"I know," he said. "She thinks. . ." he paused. "No. She thought we were her parents. Or the next thing to it."

Sharon didn't say anything.

"Sharon," he said. She looked up. "Please tell me the absolute truth. Are you a witch?"

Sharon's mouth dropped open. "Who told you that?"

"Answer the question," he said. "Are you?"

She didn't speak for several moments. "I'm sorry, Clay," she said. "I can't answer you."

"Why?"

"Because someone told me *you* were a witch," she said. "In the motel room."

"What motel—" he started. Then he remembered. "In Geneva. We were hiding with Crissy."

"They tried to enchant us," said Sharon. "They may have succeeded. They may have forced us to go back and re-live something in order to change it. They didn't think we'd remember as much as we did."

"What do we do now?" said Clay.

"I think we should eat a good dinner. Then let's go to your townhouse."

"Why?"

"Somehow that's the center of all this. The townhouse is the key."

"Key to what?" he asked, now becoming exasperated. "What has happened?"

Sharon framed an answer. "If they're witches, as I suspect," she noted, "then we've stumbled into something dark and dangerous. They want Crissy dead, but they can't kill her. No witch can kill another. They have to rely on an outside agency."

"So do you know who killed Crissy's mother?"

Sharon thought. "I think I do. I think I know. The thing is, can we restore Crissy?"

"How?" he asked. "Isn't she dead?"

"Well," she frowned. "Maybe she is. Maybe she isn't."

"What the hell does *that* mean?"

Sharon drained her Cosmopolitan. She put it down and looked him in the eye. "Okay," she said. "I need to tell you the truth." He felt a chill of terror.

Their meals arrived and they ate in silence except for comments about their outstanding dinner. "One of the best steaks I've ever had," Sharon said.

"Uh, huh," he mumbled.

They eschewed dessert and Clay paid the tab. He retrieved the Corvette from the parking garage and they headed south on the Outer Drive.

"Well?" he said.

"Wait," said Sharon. "Wait until we get to the townhouse. Something's going to happen."

"What's going to happen?"

"I don't know," she said.

He sat for a few moments as they headed toward the Field Museum. "Sharon," he said. "Are you a witch?"

She didn't answer.

"If I'm in the car with a witch," he said, "I have a right to know. Is my immortal soul in danger?"

"Shh," she said. "Relax."

He drove in silence until they reached the house. He opened the door for her and they walked to the front door. Clay had his key out, but the door opened as they reached for it.

Clay saw that the interior of the house was dark. The shades were drawn. Sharon said, "Let me go first."

"Are you sure?" said Clay.

"Oh yes," said Sharon.

They walked in and Sharon led him up the steps. They stopped at one of the smaller bedrooms, where the door was shut. Sharon knocked.

"Yes?" said a girl's voice from inside.

"Can I come in?" asked Sharon.

"Of course," said the girl.

Sharon opened the door and walked in. She turned and motioned Clay to enter behind her.

"Hi, Clay," said Crissy.

Clay couldn't speak for a few moments. "Crissy," he said. "Can it be you?"

"Sure," grinned the girl. "Thanks for protecting me."

"What do you mean?"

"You've been jerked back and forth all day," she said. "But you really did save me, twice, three times. So they couldn't really harm you."

"Will someone please explain what's happening here?" Clay asked.

Sharon and Crissy looked back and forth at one another, and then both grinned at Clay. "What do you think is happening?" asked Sharon.

"Somehow, I'm being stretched out between two worlds," he said.

"Sharon and I love you, though," said Crissy.

"Uh, huh?" asked Clay. "Then let me try something. Crissy: what book did I give you in Cedar Rapids?"

"Book?" said Crissy, looking dumbfounded.

"Sharon: what part of your body do I like the most?"

"That's a silly question," Sharon replied after a few moments. "How would I know?"

Clay drew himself up, and then walked into his living room. He crossed to a painting on the wall and removed it, exposing a wall safe. He spun the dial a few times and pulled on the handle.

Clay removed his Glock 19 and several rounds of

ammunition. He loaded it with six rounds. Then he turned back and confronted the two women who had just entered the room.

"Okay," he said. "People tell me that you can't be killed except by drowning. Can you be wounded, though?"

"What is this, Clay?" gasped Sharon. "You aren't going to shoot me?"

"Let's call it a science experiment," smiled Clay, a passive and neutral grin. "Can witches be hurt by a bullet, same as everybody else?"

"Clay," said Sharon. "You can't think..."

"Where are Sharon and Crissy?" demanded Clay. "You've got a ten count, and then I shoot your shoulder, Sharon, or whoever you are. One. Two.

"Clay, you can't shoot us—"

"Oh, I don't know," shrugged Clay. "I shot your father, O-wicked-witch-who-looks-like-Crissy. Winged him right on the arm. Then I shot Jayce, the thug at the Iowa cabin. Remember? They wanted to hurt me, or the people I've come to love. Five. Six."

"What do you want?" pleaded Sharon. "Please don't shoot. We can—"

"Eight. Nine." Continued Clay. "Last chance—"

The room dissolved and Clay found himself lying on the bed in a motel. He recognized the room at once. The motel in Geneva where they'd taken refuge. He jerked upright.

"Sharon!" he said, and the woman next to him on the bed stirred.

"Hmmm?" she drowsed. "What's up?"

Clay crossed to the bedroom door and looked in to find Crissy asleep on her bed.

"Sharon?" he asked, turning back to the woman who smiled at him from the bed.

"Still here," she said.

"What part of your body do I like the most?" he demanded.

Sharon stared at him with a blank, stunned expression. "I don't know," she said at last. "I think my legs, though."

Now Crissy stirred. "What's going on?"

"Crissy," he shouted. "What book did I buy you in Iowa?"

"Is this a test?" she chuckled.

"Now," he shouted.

"*The Innocents Abroad*, of course," said Crissy.

"Okay," he said, relieved. He crossed to Sharon, embraced her and kissed her.

"Thank you," she said, still puzzled. Crissy had come into the room and he embraced her.

"What happened, Clay?" asked Crissy, looking befuddled.

"Somehow, they came for me," said Clay. "They told me you were dead, that they'd killed you, thrown you both into the river."

"Who?" said Sharon.

"I'll explain later," he said. "Let's get back to the townhouse, now."

Clay grabbed the computer and hustled the two women to the car. He pulled out of the lot and squealed the tires into the traffic on Randall Road.

"Clay, what happened?" asked Sharon.

"We have to get back to the townhouse, and I have to get the dog from Craig."

"Can we get something to eat soon?" asked Crissy. "We haven't eaten since early this morning."

"Sure," said Clay. He pulled into a fast food restaurant and ordered cheeseburgers for all at the drive-up window.

As he drove north toward I-90, he explained about the way time had been twisted by the group of witches.

"They can manage time?" asked Sharon.

"I don't know. They may have invaded my mind and shown me fantasies. They stripped away my memory of you, Sharon. For a while I didn't remember much about Crissy, whom, they assured me, had died in the lake accident."

"So what do we do now?"

Clay thought. At last he said, "They told me that my house is the key to this whole thing. I don't think that's true. I think the key is your house, Crissy."

***

Sometime later the car stopped in front of Crissy's parents' home. Crissy went to the door and opened it.

"Hello?" she yelled. "Anyone here?"

No answer. Crissy turned and nodded to them, and the group went inside. "Let's go to my room," she said.

In the room, Crissy started up her computer and plugged in the hard drive. Clay sat on the bed with Sharon, trying to bring her up to speed.

"Guys," said Crissy. They turned and looked as Crissy indicated the screen. "Mom wrote this note the day before the last one. It seems she sensed the danger she'd fallen into."

"Hmm," said Clay. He looked at the screen. Crissy pointed to a line and told him to start reading aloud.

"'I began reading about the Salem Witch Trials of the 1690's,'" he quoted. "'One aspect struck me in particular.

Several of the women were convicted on the basis of what was called 'Spectral Evidence'. That meant that the witnesses testified that the women came to them as Spectres and talked to them, trying to steal their souls from them.' "

"'However, one of the leaders of the colony ruled that Spectral Evidence had to be inadmissible. He noted that the witness standard was two or three witnesses to the same act.' "

Clay adjusted the screen a little and continued to read. "'But it struck me that this seemed to be a consistent testimony. Several people talked about these Spectral visitations. I wondered about it.'"

"'So I said to myself, "what if they weren't lying? What if this had happened? That the women really did come to them as specters?"'"

"What on earth?" said Sharon.

"Sometimes it helps to think the unthinkable," shrugged Clay. "This guy Increase Mather—"

"Who?" said Sharon.

"The father of Cotton Mather, who helped found Harvard," said Clay. "Just about as famous as his son and sincere in his faith."

He resumed reading. "'It struck me to ask: Why do we have to assume that these witnesses were lying?'"

"'These people, after all, were committed Christians. The Massachusetts colony had been founded on the basis of a profound belief in Christ and of exercising religious freedom. People have always assumed that the witnesses were lying about many things, including the Spectral Evidence. Why would they make such an assumption?'"

Clay sat back in the chair. "Oh my gosh," he said. "What a

mind. Of course she would question something like that."

"Uh, huh," said Crissy. "She never accepted conventional wisdom in anything. She always asked penetrating questions to get at the truth. I never could get away with much."

Clay smiled as he turned back. He laid his right hand on the mouse. To his delight, he felt Sharon take his other hand and give it a gentle squeeze. He turned and smiled at her and received a warm smile in return.

"Uh," said Crissy. "Can we get back to business?"

"Right," said Clay as he adjusted the screen. "'So I went to Salem and toured the village. I didn't know what I was looking for, to be frank. I set about to walk out of town—I don't think I want to relate the direction—and walked until I was far out of the village. I found a small spring in a cave, a freshwater creek, and took a sample of the waters. I found several other rivulets over the next several days.'"

"Springs of water?" said Crissy.

"Sounds like it," nodded Sharon.

"'I have to emphasize how remote and off the beaten path these springs were,'" the letter resumed. "'I must have visited several dozen. I kept a lot of the samples and took them back to the lab here in Chicago where I could do analysis on the water.

"'It took several weeks, but I did find that the water of one tiny creek was different from all the others. I found an element in the water I couldn't identify. It was neither carbon, nor silicone, but somewhere in between. I believed for a little that I'd found a new element, but I decided that somehow the soil of the area transmuted a few common elements into a highly complex molecule. If I have the chance, I'll write a paper describing the compound. It could be revolutionary—'"

"To say the least," muttered Sharon. Clay nodded.

"'I injected myself with a dose of the water,'" said Clay. "'Nothing seemed to happen at all. I felt a little nausea for a day or so, but other than that I didn't think much about it. Then, about a week later, I began hearing Jim speaking to me during the height of our romantic episodes. I responded as he asked, to his intense delight.'"

"DeRosa told us this story," muttered Clay. Sharon thought for a moment and agreed.

"I remember him saying that when we questioned him," she said. "That's very interesting."

"Oh brother," sighed Crissy in that tone of voice that said 'too much information'. Clay chuckled and went back into the letter.

"'When I realized what had happened, I decided that I needed to correlate it. I found a way to inject Crissy while she slept. She never knew what I did. I had to do it that way. . .'"

"She used her daughter for a science experiment?" asked Sharon, aghast.

"'Anyone who reads this,'" continued Clay, "'That decision will haunt me forever. Perhaps I can mitigate it by saying that I thought that the water would give her a big advantage in her life. That this ability would heighten her senses and allow her to see things other people have never seen, or felt or experienced.'"

Clay stopped reading. He shook his head. "'I'm so sorry,'" he read. "'I've never made such a terrible decision. I took her life into my hands. I know better. Crissy, I hope you can come to the point of forgiving me, please. I think that the water blurred my sense of right and wrong. I'm sorry. That must sound like an excuse and I can't make an excuse.'

"Unbelievable," said Sharon.

"No, I think I understand," said Crissy. "I'll explain later. Let's just keep going."

"'Then they came for me,'" Clay went on. "'A group of very ordinary looking people. They would show up at odd times. I'd be aware of someone watching me, standing just out of my range of vision, just beyond my periphery. This went on for several weeks, as Crissy learned to exercise her ability. I tried to guide her with it, and help her understand, but my heart had hardened somehow. I no longer saw things as black and white. Instead I saw right as what I decided was right, and wrong as anything which opposed me.

"'Vanity, yes, vain hideous narcissism,'" the letter went on. "'I thought of myself as somehow superior to others. After all, I could do something that no one else could. Just by thinking I could change someone else's behavior. I could get them to do things they would never do. Sleep with someone besides their husband or wife; skip paying for lunch at a restaurant; think vile thoughts about others. I don't remember inspiring someone to do something good, however.

"'When I realized what I had done, I began to get scared. I wasn't using the gift for good, but for—I hate to say it—for evil. I became Richard the Third.'"

Clay stopped reading. He turned to his ward and asked: "Honey. Do you find yourself going that way too?"

Crissy leaned back in the armchair and drummed her fingers on the armrest, thinking. "I don't know," she admitted at last. "I want to say no, that the gift has only brought good. But I did twist you two. I put you both in harm's way to protect me. I don't know if that was evil or not."

"It's the opposite of what we ought to do," said Sharon. "To live a happy life we ought to see ourselves as the servants of others."

"Is that what you two do?" asked the girl.

"Not always," admitted Clay. "You've already discussed how I destroyed my marriage working for others. But really, what I was doing was working to satisfy myself. I see that now. I didn't want to be a father, I guess. So I injured Gail, wounded my girls. . ."

"But you jumped in the lake in March to save me," said Crissy.

"Well, that's true—"

"Of course it is," said Sharon. "What episode in your recent life gives you the most pleasure?"

"You're right," Clay nodded. "Besides meeting you, it has to be saving Crissy as well as serving as a father to her."

"Let's go on," urged Crissy.

"'Then they came for me,'" Clay went on. "'They knew what I'd done, that I'd found the secret spring that gives them their ability. It's been a secret in this group for centuries. They've used the power to enhance their lives, to take shortcuts. They have a strict code of silence about it.'"

"So how did she get to the water?" asked Crissy. "If they guarded it that closely, surely they must have—"

"'They got careless over the years,'" the diary continued. "They want, I'm sure, to kill me and stop everything here. Then they can go back to their own lives, coming out only to steal thoughts and make money when they need it.'"

"'How would they do that? Simple. Imagine that you could

bewitch someone as they can. They set up sexual liaisons, exciting fantasies for corporate leaders, steal secrets about business from them. Then they sell the secrets to competitors in the business realm. It's the ultimate insider trading scheme."

"'But they also locate rich people with no heirs to their estate and convince them to will them everything. Never do the people comprehend that they've been manipulated.'"

"'One of the men approached me a few months ago,'" Clay continued. "'They'd felt my ability growing. Yes. It seems that the skill grows as it is used. They call themselves The Coven of the Spring. They don't think of themselves as witches, but they are, of course—they have powers both as individuals and as a group that make me look feeble by comparison.'"

"'This man said that they wanted Crissy,'" Clay read. He sat back, fear almost choking him. "Oh my God," he said. "That's what they were after. You could become one of this group. You could be a sexual slave for them, stealing secrets from men's minds.'"

Sharon hugged Crissy and murmured comfort. "They won't do it, I promise," said Sharon. "We'll stop them somehow."

Crissy stared into space, ashen.

"'Now I saw the truth,'" said Clay, reading again. "'They wanted me to give you to them. I refused. They said they'd steal my husband's mind, my mind, then take Crissy anyway.'"

"So I proposed a deal,'" Clay read. "'I asked them to let me take Crissy's place as the Coven's sex slave. I pointed out that I could be valuable to them and that many older men would find me attractive.'"

"They rejected the idea at first. Then I told them that my abilities at sex would preclude any age compromise. One of the men said he'd try me out. He's coming tomorrow to the house in the early afternoon.'"

"'So I have to die, I know it,'" said Clay, his voice a whisper. "'I'm going to implant my husband with the thought that Crissy has murdered me and that he has to avenge me. He'll never know what I've done. I can fix it so that he'll think it's the right thing to do.'"

"'And if Crissy dies, then I'll have her with me in death,'" Clay read. "'Oh God. I can't face this alone. I'm so scared. They'll rip my soul out of me and come for her. He has to succeed. I'm so sorry. I just can't think of any other way to save her than to pull away her soul before they can pollute it. She's my angel of light, the comfort of my life, the joy of my existence. Oh God, please forgive me for what I have to do to my little girl. I can't face it. But I can't see another choice.'"

"'Whoever reads this: Jim isn't to blame. He loves Crissy as much as I do, I know. Please don't hold him responsible. Please. Let Crissy's death be on my soul.'"

"'Dear Crissy: If somehow you read this, please believe that I love you. I have always loved you. I became too smart, I think. I opened up a door that I shouldn't have. I saw what I thought was a chance to help mankind, by expanding our powers and mental abilities. I thought that I would use this discovery to take mankind to the next level.'"

"'Please forgive me.'"

"That's all," Clay said.

***

"So what happened?" asked Crissy, tears streaming down her face.

"I think this man came to her house," said Clay.

"Yes," nodded Sharon.

"He came in, they went to the bedroom," said Clay. "Or rather, a bedroom. I don't think she'd have used the bed she shared with your father. Then he went for her mind and destroyed it. You saw her body lying on the floor a little while after he killed her. She may have managed to shield what she'd done to your father."

"That does seem probable," said Sharon. "If she hadn't, they would have been waiting for you at the house."

"When you say destroyed her mind. . ." asked Crissy.

"He yanked her soul right out of her body," said Clay.

"Clay!" said Sharon. "Don't be cruel to her. . ."

"I don't mean to be, Honey," said Clay, taking Crissy in his arms. "I never want to hurt you. But what's going on here transcends murder. These people have given way to anything that approaches morality."

"But why?" asked Crissy.

Sharon spoke up. "You see this sometimes with celebrities, or famous people like movie stars or music heroes. When those people make exceptional amounts of money, or receive extraordinary adulation, they begin to feel that they are somehow more equal than others."

"Is that why you here sometimes about sexual scandals among the wealthy or the famous?" asked Clay.

"Yes, somewhat," said Sharon. "But more often the sexual

misconduct has to do with stress relief."

"Yes?" said Crissy.

Sharon nodded. "I still don't see how this helps us," she said. "This group still wants Crissy, that should be obvious."

"I guess I don't see why they want me," said Crissy slowly. "Why would I be important? I mean, couldn't they convince any girl to do what they want? I didn't seem to have much problem getting you going with each other."

"That's different," said Clay.

"Yes," agreed Sharon. "What happened with us had to do with the stress we found ourselves under, loneliness, mutual attraction. . ."

"So you really wanted to be with one another," said Crissy. "All I did was reduce the barriers."

"Uh, huh," said Sharon.

"In any case, it looks like they still want you, Crissy," said Clay. "You'd be invaluable, at least for a while."

"What do you mean?"

"Not everybody can live as they want you to for long," said Sharon. "Despite what you see in the media, being a prostitute can have terrible ramifications."

"Like what?" asked Crissy.

"Health issues of course, such as venereal disease and AIDS, but a psychological toll as well. Diminished self concept, all sorts of things like narcotics abuse, alcohol problems and serious depression almost always go with the job."

"Well, I sure don't want any part of it," sniffed Crissy.

"No, of course not," Sharon nodded.

"So how could we handle these people?" asked Clay. "They seem to be amoral, not just immoral."

"As you say," Sharon shrugged. "I hoped that we might see something we could do about them in Grace's letters."

"We haven't read them all," Clay noted.

"Still she couldn't seem to help herself, could she," Crissy sighed.

Sharon shrugged. "Or is it possible she didn't want to?"

Clay turned. "What do you mean?"

"Maybe she gave herself up for Crissy," said Sharon. "Maybe it was an attempt to protect her."

"She planned to kill Crissy," said Clay. "We just read it."

"But she had a much more potent link to these people than you or I do," said Sharon. "Think about it. Sometimes Crissy has success in influencing you and sometimes she doesn't, right?"

"You too," said Clay. Sharon nodded. He turned to Crissy. "Is she right? Can we block them?"

Crissy thought. "I think so," she said. "I don't know if I can."

"What do you mean?"

"Every time the phone rings, I have an insane desire to answer. Even if it's your cell phones or your house phones or the one in my house, I feel this compulsion."

"Yes," said Sharon. "I remember we saw that yesterday."

"Uh, huh," muttered Crissy. "Once we were out of the house and I couldn't hear the phone ring, I didn't feel the urge. You remember. The sound of a phone ringing seems to bewitch me."

"Do they say something to you?" asked Sharon.

"They must, but I can't remember it." Crissy chewed at her lip. She thought for a few moments. "They must have some sort of a trigger that shuts down an area of my mind and then they can make a command. That's what I do, I think. I find an area in the brain, shut it down, and give a command."

"But it doesn't work all the time," said Clay.

"No, I know it," said Crissy, resuming chewing her lip.

"What would they be frightened of?" asked Sharon.

"Huh?" murmured Crissy. "I don't know."

"Are you afraid of anything?" Clay asked.

"No, I. . ." the girl began. "Well, yes. I find that every time we cross over water, or go near the lake, I'm terrified."

"What do you mean?" puzzled Sharon.

"You asked me to go with you for a swim at the hotel," said Crissy. Sharon nodded. "Two years ago, I would have jumped at the chance. We'd have gone to buy swim suits and played in the pool all afternoon. But when you suggested it, I went numb with fear."

"Strange," said Clay. "So the thing that starts this is a compound from a remote spring. Then you live your life in fear of drowning."

"Uh, huh," said Crissy. "When we went to the motel on the interstate, we had to cross over the Fox River. I was asleep, you remember. When we crossed over the river I woke up, scared to desperation."

"Does that affect them, too?" asked Sharon.

"I don't know," shrugged Crissy. "I imagine it would."

"Is there a way we could check it out?" asked Clay.

"I'm afraid to get near them," Crissy said. "I think we ought to stay as far away from them as we can."

"No doubt we should," Clay agreed, "if we could be sure that ignoring or evading them would make them go away."

"Yes," said Sharon.

"But I don't like to hide from problems now," said Clay. "I

distinguished myself in my marriage by avoiding responsibility and refusing to confront personal fears and doubts. Rather than deal with Gail and our problems, I just worked harder and longer hours."

"So the situation fell apart before your eyes," said Crissy. "Oh brother."

"Me too," said Sharon. "My marriage fell apart in front of my eyes from the beginning. I never insisted on my husband following the vows he'd made. I know better, but I just kept thinking that if I ignored the behavior, it'd get better."

"Right," said Crissy. The group lapsed into silence. "What can we do?"

"For one thing we need to find out how the group can control Crissy's mind," Sharon said.

"Yeah, but when they call, Crissy loses control," Clay noted. "How can we prevent that? Last time she stole something like twelve or thirteen hours from us and we didn't know she did it."

Sharon nodded. "Could we set up a recording to answer in her name?"

"You know, Craig could, now you mention it," said Clay.

"Your brother?" asked Sharon. "How?"

"He works as a sound technician at a TV station," said Clay. "He's also recorded professional singers."

"How do we get to him?" asked Sharon. "I'm sure the group has him staked out."

"I could call his cell and have him meet us somewhere," suggested Clay.

"No good," said Crissy. "They'd follow him."

"Could he do a recording over the phone, I wonder?"

suggested Clay.

Crissy shrugged. "We could try," she said.

The group went back to Sharon's car and drove toward Lake Michigan. Clay couldn't reach Craig on the cell phone with repeated efforts. "Strange," said Clay.

"Did you try his work phone?" asked Sharon.

"Yeah, but they said he isn't in today," Clay replied.

"Should we chance it and go to his house?" asked Crissy.

"My first reaction would be no," said Sharon. 'We could put him in further danger. Are you worried about your dog?"

Clay shook his head. "No, I'm sure Craig made arrangements for her."

"Where then?" said Sharon. "We can't keep driving eternally, stopping off here and there."

"No, of course not," said Clay. "What if we'd go where they'd be afraid to go?"

"Where would that be?" asked Crissy. "I mean, the only thing they'd fear is the ocean, right? Or some large body of water. . ." she broke off. Sharon turned to look at her and Clay glanced at her in the rear view mirror.

Crissy had gone dead white. "What's wrong?" asked Sharon.

"Just thinking of water made me think about Lake Michigan, and how scared I was, cold, miserable and lonely," said Crissy. "Now I'm wondering if my life will ever be anything but that. Do you think I'm always going to have to be on the run from these people?"

"Not if I can help it," asserted Clay with a grim set to his jaw.

"What do you think, Sharon?" Crissy asked.

"Clay's right," Sharon said, taking Crissy's hand. "We'll protect you however we can."

"No," said Crissy. "You have no reason to do that."

"We love you, honey," said Sharon.

"Yes, we do," said Clay.

"But why?" said Crissy. "Why would you risk your life for me?"

"What's a better thing to do with a life?" said Clay.

"Huh?" said Crissy.

"The boy who impregnated me," said Sharon. "He stole from me what I ought to have been allowed to give to the man I love. I gave up his baby so I'd have my life free ahead of me."

"And look at the success you've become," said Crissy. "When you gave up the baby, your life opened before you."

"Certain things about my life opened up, I agree," said Sharon. "But I certainly didn't ever feel freedom, complete freedom I mean, from the day I conceived the baby. I got rid of my responsibility, but not the depth of pain, the heartache, and the profound loneliness of not having that baby with me."

Crissy sat in silence, staring out the window. "So why," she began at last. "Why would you help someone you don't even know?"

"I know you, honey," said Sharon. "You're every lonely or frightened person I've ever known or worked with. You're one girl, to be sure, but everyone I deal with is pursued by his own demons."

"Me too," agreed Clay. "The key, I think, is that I can help you, or at least try to help you. I'm not afraid to die. But let's try to save you. You're precious."

"What do you suggest?" asked Sharon.

"I'm thinking that we ought to get out to sea," said Clay.

Crissy blanched, appalled at the idea of going out on the ocean. "What will that accomplish?" she asked.

"For one thing it'd get us away from the Coven and give us some time to recuperate, right?" shrugged Clay.

"Also you could eat and rest, honey," said Sharon. "I'm worried about you because of the stress you've been under. On a cruise the most dramatic decision you have to make is what you are going to have for dinner."

"But I'm scared of water," said Crissy. "Terrified, in fact."

"Is it something I could help you with?" asked Sharon.

Crissy considered, and then shrugged. "I just don't know," she said. "I don't know whether this is a permanent trauma or something that might be treatable. I used to be able to swim very well."

"These guys have guns," said Clay. "Straight up I don't mind going hand to hand with any of them and if they go on a ship they can't bring pistols."

"That's true," admitted Crissy. "Can we get seasick pills?" Sharon and Clay laughed and agreed. Sharon suggested the seasick patches placed behind the ear.

Clay rented another SUV in the next town and the group headed east toward New York.

Chapter 19

Sharon worked with Crissy almost non-stop, even when the girl took a turn driving. Clay sat amazed at Sharon's penetration, her gift for asking questions and probing just enough to unpack the deep troubles and fears of Crissy's soul.

An explosion of anger lit up the car as the group crossed into Pennsylvania. Crissy had been talking about her mother and the curiosity her mother had, something that seemed to dominate her soul. Crissy had to confront the rage about her mother inoculating her with a substance that changed her forever. "She did this just to see what would happen!" she yelled.

When the rage hit, the girl screamed with fury. She beat on the seat and cried with anger. Sharon held her and spoke to her with gentle, loving kindness.

When the storm passed, Crissy leaned against Sharon and dozed off.

"She's still sleeping a great deal," said Sharon. "I don't know if we did any good here, but she's going to need a great deal of work for the next several days."

Clay nodded. "Know something?"

"What?" said Sharon.

"I wish I'd worked with you to get over what I dealt with when Gail moved out," he said, a pain in his chest noticeable for the first time in some months.

Sharon smiled and took his hand. "Thank you," she said. "I need to do something like this myself. This catharsis that Crissy just went through will help a lot in the days to come."

"Catharsis?" asked Clay.

"Yes," said Sharon. "It's a Greek word and it means a cleansing of emotion. The Greeks used it to discuss the theory of dramatic tragedy."

"You mean like *Oedipus Rex*, and like that?" asked Clay.

"Just exactly like that," she nodded. "The master works of Sophocles, Euripides and Aeschylus. Great tragedy has a purifying effect on the soul."

"Did you just do that?" asked Clay.

Sharon nodded. "Imagine that you had an inner tube that needed fixing. The only way to do it is to let all the air out of the tube and then put a patch on. That's what I tried to do with Crissy."

"Looks like it worked," Clay smiled.

"Without meaning to make it sound like a lecture hall," she smiled, "the Greeks were big on the idea of balance in your life. For example, picture a window divided into four parts, each frame the same size."

"Sure," said Clay.

"Let one of the parts represent your physical nature, another be your spiritual, another mental, and the last one emotional aspects."

"Okay," said Clay.

"Now imagine that one of those frames gets to be too big. What happens to the others?"

"They get smaller, right?"

"That's it exactly," she nodded. "Even to the point of losing touch with one of those aspects. I remember my grandparents. They never once exercised or did anything physical, except maybe mowing the lawn or going up and down the steps. They died way too early, of course. They were pretty badly out of condition. Their hearts just gave out from lack of use."

Clay changed the subject. "Do you like my idea of a cruise?" he asked with a grin.

"It'll probably be pretty expensive," she agreed. "But it sure sounds like fun. Also, as I say, we can sleep and relax and eat good food. I've never been on a cruise."

"Yeah," he said. "We'll have to get some clothes. Wal-mart okay with you?"

"Well, I'd prefer Macey's, but any old port in a storm, right?"

"Yeah," he said. "But as you know, every cloud has a silver lining, right?"

"You can make book on it," she grinned, enjoying the game. "We've had our nose to the grindstone far too long. Your turn."

"Welcome to the Sharon Gray Cliché Festival," he said in an announcer's voice. "I'm just as happy as a lark to be here, you bet your bottom dollar."

"Yes, well, that's what you get for wearing your heart on your sleeve, you know," she agreed.

"Well, I certainly hope we aren't robbing Peter to pay Paul," he nodded.

Now they laughed together.

While Sharon took a turn driving, Clay used his cell phone to locate a cruise that would take them to Bermuda for the week. He'd reserved a suite with a king-size bed in one bedroom and a fold out couch in the living room. The cost staggered him, but he decided that he would never enjoy himself more than he would with these two people.

He shrugged and smiled. The danger seemed to have subsided—

"Clay," said Crissy.

"Hey Sleepyhead," he responded.

"They're coming."

"What?" Clay asked.

"They're trying to reach me," she said. "Turn off the cell phones."

"Why?" asked Sharon.

"They're going to call and triangulate where we are," said Crissy.

"How do—" began Clay. He shut up at once when a Ford F-350 pickup cut in front of his car, missing them by inches. "What the. . ." Clay shouted. Then he got it. "Oh brother," he said.

He heard a horn honking behind him. He saw a Cadillac tailgating him. Four people sat in the car but he couldn't see their faces.

"Pull over, Mr. Foster," said a voice.

"What—who spoke to me?" Clay said.

"I heard it too," said Sharon. Crissy nodded.

"They want me," said Crissy. "They've combined their strength. We've got to get away."

"Mr. Foster," said the voice. Now he realized that the voice sounded like a compilation of five or more voices. "Yes," said the voice. "You have no choice against us..."

Clay yanked the wheel to the left and moved across to the median strip. "This is going to get rough, I'm afraid," he said.

He braked hard and the Cadillac shot by. The passengers turned to look, but Clay had driven the SUV into the ditch which separated the east-bound lanes of the super highway from the west-bound lanes.

He jerked the wheel to the left, hoping the rental SUV's suspension would hold out. The car teetered, but then came back straight. Clay completed the U-turn and fired the car toward the west bound lanes.

Sharon and Crissy, he realized, had been screaming as he negotiated this u-turn.

He yelled at them to hold on to the ceiling grips. Now the SUV, tires screaming, shot up onto the shoulder. The car shuddered with the strain, but the tires gripped. Clay floored the accelerator.

The SUV shot along the shoulder of the road as it picked up speed. Clay heard the honking of several horns, the drivers indignant at what they perceived as idiotic driving. He merged into traffic and headed toward the closest exit.

"Clay, my God," screamed Sharon.

"Easy," he said. "We're getting away. What's that exit up there?"

Clay swerved through the traffic and rushed up the ramp. He spotted a gas station several hundred yards down the two lane highway.

He pulled in and got out to pump some gas. He managed to get the nozzle into the car's tank before the shakes hit.

Chapter 20

Several minutes later, Clay finished a can of coke and took a deep breath. "Good God," he said. Sharon's fury at him had subsided almost at once and now she embraced him.

"I know," she said. "You must have been terrified."

"I'll say," he agreed.

"Where did you learn to drive like that?"

"I didn't," he smiled. "I just made it up as I went along."

Crissy came over. "I don't have any sense of them anywhere," she said. "They must be several miles off, or they're not trying hard now."

"Crissy," said Clay. "What can we do to block them? To keep them from tracking us, from using mind tricks to follow us?"

"I'm thinking," she said. "I don't know offhand."

"What about an electrical pulse?" said Sharon.

Clay and Crissy turned to look at her. "Huh?" they said in unison.

"Aren't there machines that generate—what do they call it —white noise?" Sharon asked.

"Yeah," said Clay. "But how about just a portable radio? Set to static?"

Crissy bit her lip. "Let's try it," she said. They climbed into the car and Clay set the radio to a hum. "Okay," he nodded.

Crissy concentrated for a few moments. "No," she said. "I can't read anything at all in either one of you."

"Won't we be driven crazy by that static?" said Sharon.

"Well, maybe not," said Clay. Fifteen minutes later the group found a Wal-Mart, where Clay bought a boom box and several dollars-worth of batteries.

They conversed by sign language the rest of the day. Following the directions the mechanic at the service station had given them, they sped along back roads toward Norfolk, Virginia.

The group hid in a motel that night well off the road. Their dinner consisted of Slim-Jims, potato chips and onion dip, as well as vegetable juice. "Gack," said Sharon as they pulled the covers over them.

"Never mind," said Clay. "We eat like royalty beginning tomorrow."

"Do we get ice cream?" asked Crissy from the next bed.

"All you can eat," he assured her. "Pounds and pounds of it."

In the morning they resumed the trip. Arriving at Norfolk, they bought some clothing at a local store. When they found the pier they made their way onto the ship.

Sharon and Crissy did some laundry and then shopped in the ship's store for swim suits and other necessities.

As the great ship sailed, Clay turned to Crissy who stood next to him at the rail. "Are you okay?"

"Yes," she said. "But look." The ship passed a park. Clay saw ten or twelve people wearing sunglasses standing in a large group, staring up at them.

"They're telling me to have a nice time," said Crissy, her

eyes hollow. "They say they'll be waiting."

"What a bunch of creeps," he sneered. "Losers, every one of them. I feel like I need a shower."

Chapter 21

Sharon and Crissy went to the ship's boutique and each bought a dress for the formal nights. Dinner found them placed with two delightful couples, one from Virginia and the other from Maryland.

Crissy's nervousness and upset from the departure began to ease as the dinner proceeded. Clay smiled at her as she joked and laughed with the others, enjoying the girl's lovely laughter and grace.

Sharon had looked wan and scared for most of the last few days but a cocktail and some food relaxed her. She took his hand under the table and held it when the opportunity presented itself.

Meanwhile Clay couldn't help but think ahead to the return trip. He didn't doubt even in the slightest that the group would indeed be waiting for them. He felt sure they wouldn't allow Sharon and him to live. Crissy would, if they had their way, be forced into prostitution for the community.

There had to be a way out of this, he told himself. He began to consider settling in Bermuda, starting a new life there with Sharon and Crissy.

I could do a lot worse, he thought. If not Bermuda, maybe just continue on to the United Kingdom, or Italy perhaps.

"You there?" asked Sharon, touching his elbow.

"Yeah," he said. "Sorry. Did you say something?"

"Several people have tried chatting with you," she said, a tone of reproach.

He apologized to the table and muttered an excuse about problems on the mainland. One of the men reminded him that this was a vacation and should be regarded as fun. He grinned and nodded, and made an effort to participate in the conversation.

What am I missing? He thought.

Then he realized what had been bothering him.

Why hadn't the group hung around Crissy's house after they killed her mother?

If they wanted Crissy, why not just wait until she got home and take her then?

It couldn't have been more than an hour to wait. And even if her father had come home, he had no possible way to defend her, nor would he want to.

Damn. What is wrong?

He saw two possibilities. One might be that the group feared Crissy.

He glanced at the girl. She looked lovely in a casual blouse and skirt. Several of the young men on the ship had been gazing at her in open admiration.

Why would the group be afraid of her, though?

Another possibility might be that they really didn't want Crissy. Maybe they just wanted to kill her so that no one outside their clique would be able to spread the secrets of the cult. They liked being exclusive, a tiny confraternity of wretched, self-absorbed demons. Yes, it bordered on supernatural evil. He couldn't think of another word.

Crissy's mom and the girl seemed to be the only ones outside the cult who had the gift.

Dinner concluded and Clay took the two women to a dance lounge. Crissy made friends with some other teenagers and went off with them to the teen disco. She told them not to wait up for her, promising to be quiet when she returned to the room.

Clay invited Sharon to dance. Sharon looked first surprised that he knew how to dance, and then delighted to spend the time in his arms. Clay made a conscious effort not to worry and to enjoy the evening with Sharon, but the worries about the return to the mainland haunted him, nattering about at the edges of his consciousness.

Sharon took Clay's arm and led him to the deck, where they strolled and chatted together.

At last she said, "You just can't relax, can you."

"I'm struggling," he said, shaking his head. "Still I think we're safe for the time. But when we go back. . ." his voice trailed off.

"I know," she said. "I've been thinking about that too."

"Do you see a way out of this mess?"

"No," said Sharon. "But something has been troubling me."

"Yes?"

"I don't get it," she frowned. "Why did this cult kill Crissy's mom? Why not just go along with letting Grace take Crissy's place as the whore?"

Clay stopped at a table near an open air bar and they sat, enjoying the ocean air and a pleasant breeze. "Not a bad night," he noted.

She nodded.

"I've been troubled by the way that they didn't hang around to steal Crissy," he related.

"Yeah, there's that too," said Sharon. "What are you coming up with?"

"They must have some agenda that we aren't thinking of," Clay said.

Sharon bit at a thumbnail in preoccupied thought. "What if they are scared?" she asked at last. "Scared by Crissy, scared by what happened with her mother?"

"Why would they be scared of her?" Clay puzzled.

"I think you'd agree that Crissy has, and her mom probably had, strong personalities," Sharon tried. "When you belong to a cult like this, you have to have a cultic mindset. I don't know who the leader of this group is, or if they even have a leader."

"Not tracking," said Clay.

Sharon took a deep breath, let it out and paused. "What if they fear authority?" she said. "What if they can't stand a woman with Grace's intelligence?"

"Why?"

"Because if someone with her abilities and intellectual prowess came into a group like that, they wouldn't be able to maintain their little status quo," shrugged Sharon. "She must have been a competent, forceful person, from what we've seen and from what Crissy's told us."

"Yeah," said Clay.

"So if Grace comes into the cult," said Sharon, "don't you think she would be running the show in no time? That's what happened in every job she ever went into, right?"

"That's what Crissy says," he agreed.

"And look at Crissy," said Sharon. "Do you find her to be

immoral?"

He thought. "She lied to us once or twice, affected us when we didn't know what was happening," he said. "But she's intelligent, she's not a druggie, she's brave –"

"To say the least," she agreed.

"—and she's committed to being a moral person," he concluded. "She wouldn't sleep with her boyfriend, for example."

"Okay," said Sharon. "So what would happen if they brought these two into the cult?"

"I suspect they'd change it," he said, nodding at her point. "The group has been going along just as they like for more than three centuries. There has to be quite a bit of inbreeding in a small group like that. So you think they'd be intimidated by those two, do you?"

"Makes sense," said Sharon. "Those two women could alter the whole direction of the cult. You know, they could get the people to rethink the way they've run the whole thing, to start to use the gift in a responsible way—"

"Yeah," said Clay. "Changing years of thought can be daunting."

"But the things they could accomplish," mused Sharon. "The positive aspects of the gift—"

"I haven't seen any yet," he noted. "Every time someone used it on us, it's been for less than noble purposes."

"Agreed," Sharon said. "Still, consider Crissy and how remarkable we find her."

"Yeah," he shrugged.

"With proper parenting, guiding, couldn't she become invaluable?"

Clay nodded agreement. "She has enormous talent without the Charm, don't you think?"

The conversation continued into the cabin, where they changed into swim suits and made their way to the hot tub on the top deck. An hour or so later, they returned to the cabin. Crissy hadn't come in before they went to bed.

***

Clay woke up when he heard Crissy come into the cabin and pressed the illumination button on his watch. 5:30 A. M. He chuckled to himself. He'd have a chat with her later in the morning, he decided.

Well, perhaps the afternoon. She'd need to sleep a while, he imagined.

"What the. . ." muttered Sharon.

"Nothing," he whispered. "Go back to sleep."

"Did you hear Crissy come in?" she asked.

"Uh, huh."

"What time?" she managed.

"Early," he whispered. "Get some more sleep."

She took his arm and pulled it between her breasts. They snuggled together, her back to his front. In a few moments he heard her breathing settle into a deep rhythm.

Clay's mind, though, didn't unplug, and he knew he awakened for the day. He had a little headache but overall he couldn't have felt better—at least in a physical sense, he thought.

Damn. There had to be a way out of this. Had to be. These creeps with the Coven had shown no creativity, no deep thought, no introspection at all. They'd resorted to absurd and even brutish methods to rid themselves of the two whom they counted as enemies, Sharon and Crissy.

They'd come to rely on shortcuts in everything. They'd seen no need to develop beyond a certain level of accomplishment.

Eat, sleep, have sex, steal and lie. That had become their pattern.

What a life, mused Clay. All shortcuts, all pleasure. No efforts. No growth. No achievement. All selfishness and self-gratification.

What would happen if he took all that away? If he found some way to counteract the effects of the spring, what would these people do?

Then he decided that thinking didn't take them anywhere. If he could defeat the coven, he had to do it.

They were murderers.

Being as gentle as he could, he extricated himself from the embrace with Sharon. He looked out the porthole and saw the sun beginning to rise.

He put on a sweat suit and his jogging shoes and let himself out of the bedroom. He went up to the exercise room and when he saw that the area hadn't opened, he jogged around the top deck and lifted weights.

At about 7:00, Sharon joined him and they did an aerobics class together, and then went to the aft deck for breakfast.

"You seem pre-occupied," she smiled over a coffee rim.

He nodded. He leaned back and related what he'd been thinking.

"Yes," she said. "One of my neighbors taught school for many years. He told me that once he'd spoken to a student about his lack of achievement. The boy couldn't read, couldn't do math, and had none of the skills that you would expect from a junior in high school. 'What are you going to do with your life?'" he asked.

"The boy replied that he had skill as a guitarist, and he planned to form a group and record music until he made it big. My neighbor told him that the chances of that happening weren't good. The boy shrugged and said, 'Well, maybe I'll win the Lotto.'"

Clay snorted. "Amazing what lack of long range vision can do to you, isn't it."

She smiled and changed the subject. "Thank you for last night," she said, her voice soft. "And for everything on this whole trip. Not just the cruise, but all of your faithfulness, kindness, grace—all you've meant to me and to Crissy."

"We do pretty well together, don't we," he grinned back.

"Better than I would have believed possible," she agreed. "It's so wonderful to make love—I mean that in the real sense, not as a synonym for sex. My life with Jordan always felt like he wanted nothing but the physical aspect." She gave his hand a squeeze.

He squeezed back. Then he asked, "So how do we survive this?"

Sharon thought. "As brilliant as Grace must have been," she began, "there has to be a reason they killed her that we aren't seeing. They must have sensed something they saw or felt in her mind."

"Why?"

"Think about it," she said. "We know that Grace had a stunning figure and that she worked on her body with fanaticism. She was also gorgeous with breathtaking intelligence."

"Seems right," he agreed.

"Yet when the man came to the house, he didn't have sex with her," said Sharon. "Instead, it appears, he just went ahead and murdered her. How many men would come into that house, find her in a bedroom wearing that negligee, and not take some advantage of the situation?"

Clay considered. "You have a point," he said. "But look at something else. We found nothing remarkable on the hard drive where she kept her diary."

Grace chewed her lower lip. "Maybe she hid it too well?"

"So that Crissy couldn't even find it?" he looked up.

Sharon went silent. "Let's finish breakfast and then go take a look at that computer hard drive again."

He shrugged. "I work with computers a lot, but I'm no pro," he admitted.

At that moment, a bleary-eyed Crissy appeared carrying a tray filled with fruit and other goodies. She slumped into a chair and rubbed at her eyes.

"Did you have fun last night?" asked Sharon with a wink at Clay.

"To say the least," she said. "I've met a nice bunch of guys and girls here. Some from the states, several from Canada, my age or around it. It has been fun," she concluded with a wide yawn.

"I'm glad you're enjoying yourself," grinned Clay.

"You guys having fun too?" she asked.

"Of course," said Clay. "We were out dancing until – how late, Sharon?"

"Oh boy," said Sharon. "I know it was late. I bet my head

didn't hit the pillow until 9:30."

"And even then we were just reeking of lemonade and chocolate fondue," he added.

Crissy giggled. "That's what you get for getting old and senile," she noted.

Clay affected a large sigh. "Can we chat for a few moments?" he asked.

"Sure," said Crissy, looking bewildered that he thought he needed to ask permission.

"We've been talking," he said. He related the substance of the conversation that had taken place before the young woman joined them. Sharon emphasized a few points. Crissy listened, rapt with interest, and nodded.

When the two older adults had concluded, Crissy sat in silence, chewing at the fruit she'd brought out with her.

At last she nodded. "So you think they're afraid of me?"

"I don't know," said Clay. "I keep trying out all kinds of scenarios and this seems to be the best guess I've got, honey."

"But why wouldn't they just do to me what they did to Mom?" Crissy asked. "Why not just wait and steal my mind too?"

"Again, I think they may have wanted—may still want—for you to sleep with people to bring money into the coven," said Grace.

"I suppose that's possible," Crissy nodded. "Maybe they think they can bully me into doing what they want?"

"Well, if they'd wanted us dead, they could have killed us before," said Sharon. "I think it's significant that they didn't." Clay nodded agreement.

"Any ideas how we can fight them?" asked Crissy.

"No, not at all," said Sharon. "But something has always struck me."

"Yes?" said Crissy.

"No sex," said Sharon. "And from what you've said your mother, especially wearing that ivory negligee, would tempt any man."

"Yeah," said Crissy. "What does that tell you?"

"Could be several things, of course," said Clay. "But one possibility is that she scared them. She might have fought back. If she had discovered how to defeat them—"

"Yeah," said Crissy. "But how did she do it?"

"Crissy," said Sharon. "Is there any chance that she left a note for you on that hard drive?"

"I've been reading her messages," said Crissy. "They're pretty mundane."

"Yeah," said Clay, "but what about the possibility that she hid a message for you? That she didn't name it as she did the other diary entries?"

"Hmm," said Crissy. "How would she do that?"

Clay shrugged. "What about if she typed in a message and saved it with all control letters?"

"What do you mean?" asked Sharon.

"She types in a message the regular way," explained Clay. "But then, when she goes to save it, she only types invisible letters? To hide in case the Coven found the hard drive?"

"Uh, huh," said Crissy. "There are a couple of messages I can't open," she said after a few moments of reflection. "But they didn't concern me because they were older, well before she took the potion."

"Uh, huh," said Clay.

"I tell you what," said Crissy. "I'm meeting a bunch of guys in about fifteen minutes and we're going to ride and walk around the island. I'll be back at about 3, grab a late lunch, and take a brief nap, if I can."

"Sure," said Sharon.

"Let me think this through, okay?" said Crissy. "Mom wouldn't have left something obvious, that's for sure."

"Right," said Clay, and the conversation drifted into other channels.

The ship docked later that afternoon, and Clay and Sharon stood on deck to watch the great ship come to rest. The lovely air of Bermuda wafted across the dock, masking the ocean smell and the shore breeze. "Good grief," said Sharon.

"Paradise, right?" smiled Clay.

"Have you been here before?"

"No," he said. "I'm anxious to see what it looks like tomorrow."

At six o'clock that evening, Clay and Sharon were changing for cocktails and dinner. They intended to meet some friends in the martini bar before going into dinner at 8:30.

Sharon came out of the bathroom wearing a formal black sheath dress with a slit on the right side well above her knee. She'd treated herself to an appointment in the beauty salon, and with her hair done, makeup perfect, and the lovely smile that accompanied the outfit, Clay felt his knees go weak.

"Thank you so much," she gave him a little smile.

"For what?" Clay managed.

"For looking at me like that," she said. "It means a lot."

He grinned wider. "Not at all," he said. "A well deserved tribute to a beautiful woman."

Sharon embraced him and they kissed. Things began to progress, but at that moment Sharon said, "Clay."

"Mm-hmm?" he said, moving to kiss her neck.

"Someone's knocking," she whispered.

Clay released Sharon and turned to the door. Crissy stood there, not speaking.

"You haven't dressed for dinner," began Sharon.

"No," said Crissy. "You have to see this."

Sharon and Clay exchanged puzzled glances as they followed Crissy into the cabin's drawing room. "I found it," she said.

"Found what?" asked Clay, then he got it.

"A letter from your mom?" asked Sharon.

"Yeah," murmured Crissy. "You were right, Clay. I went to the File Menu in Word, then Open, and Typed in my birthday holding down the control key. This opened," she said with a nod to the computer.

Clay and Sharon saw text on the screen and sat on the couch. "Did you read it yet?"

"Just the first few lines," Crissy said.

"Oh boy," said Clay.

"Yeah," said Crissy. "It looks like what we wanted."

Clay sat back against the couch. "Do we read it now?" he asked.

"Not by my advice," Sharon shook her head. "Let's save this file with a different code and lock the hard drive into the room safe until we can spend enough time with it."

"Crissy?" asked Clay.

"Yeah, okay," said Crissy with a detached tone.

"Look," said Clay. "This'll keep. We can't do anything about it tonight."

"True," said Crissy.

They saved the file under a new name, erased the old copy from the hard drive and tucked it into the room safe. A few moments later, Clay and Sharon left, with Crissy promising to join them in the cocktail lounge a bit later.

Clay sipped at a Beefeater Martini and smacked his lips in appreciation. "Yummy," he said to a distracted Sharon.

She came to and looked up. Then she nodded. "A lot of bartenders just don't use enough vermouth," she said, and nibbled at an olive stuffed with bleu cheese. "This is delightful."

"So?" he said. "What are you thinking?"

"I don't want this time on the ship to end," she said with a rueful smile.

He took her hand and grinned back. They tapped their glasses together.

"Why does it have to end?" he asked.

"Because we're going to have to go home soon," she said.

"Not necessarily," he shrugged.

"What do you mean?"

"Well, I've been thinking," he said. "We could stay here in Bermuda. Or, we could go on to England, or some other country..."

"No," said Sharon. "Crissy has a terrific secret. Someone will find out."

"Maybe you're right," he said. "And they'd try to exploit her."

"Exactly," she said.

"You think Crissy's mom is the one who discovered the secret?" he asked.

"I think it's quite possible," she agreed.

Crissy came over. Clay remembered the first time he'd seen her in the hospital room when she'd showered and done her hair. She wore an outfit that Sharon had bought for her on the island that day, a short dress with high heels.

"Wowee," he said. Crissy gave him a mind blowing smile and introduced several of her friends, most of whom seemed to be following in her wake. The group chatted with the two adults for a few moments.

"Sharon, Clay," she said. "We're going to have dinner on the deck tonight, okay?"

"Sure," he said and Sharon nodded. Crissy moved off, her arms linked in those of a couple of delighted young men.

"Nice, isn't it," said Sharon.

"Huh?"

"Nice to see her so happy," Sharon smiled.

"Yeah," he agreed. Some of the people they'd met on the ship joined them. They found themselves engaged in other conversation.

They didn't hear Crissy come in that night. They began to become alarmed sometime around dawn.

***

"Clay," said Sharon at about 6:00 A. M.

"Mmm?" he managed.

"Did you hear Crissy come in last night?" she whispered.

"No," he said, coming awake. He tiptoed to the door and peeked out.

"She's not in bed," he reported.

Sharon gave a little groan and climbed out of bed. She

grabbed a robe from the end of the bed and went into the washroom. She emerged a few moments later wearing shorts and a tee shirt. "Come on," she said.

Clay climbed into some clothes and they went out. They searched the decks, the pool area, the buffet and breakfast area. No Crissy.

"Okay," said Clay. "Let's be logical. She has to be on the boat, right?"

"Why? What if she went ashore last night?"

"Well, let's see," he agreed.

They located the assistant cruise director just getting into his office. He made a few calls, and then turned to them.

"Crissy went ashore at about 2:00 A. M.," he said. "She hasn't returned."

"Oh dear," muttered Sharon.

"Now I urge you not to worry," said the assistant. "We'll check and see whom she went ashore with, okay?"

Sharon nodded. Clay and Sharon went to breakfast and then to a dance class, but still had no word of Crissy.

"What do we do?" asked Sharon, now worried to near distraction.

"Let's check with the cruise director," he said. "Maybe there's some word, huh?"

But Crissy had not returned. They did find the names of the people she had gone ashore with and made their way to their cabins. In each case, the young people were in their cabins, not yet awake from the late night activities. Still they said that Yes, Crissy had gone ashore with them, but hadn't returned after a stop at an island disco. No, they had no idea where she could be.

Clay and Sharon went ashore, keeping an eye out for any sign of Crissy. Noon came and passed. Three o'clock. Dinner time. Sharon was so worried that she couldn't talk well.

"Clay," said Crissy's voice as he stood under the shower.

"Crissy!" he yelled. He leapt from the shower, pulled on a bathrobe and went into the cabin. The girl was nowhere to be seen.

"What?" asked Sharon, bewildered.

"Crissy just spoke to me," he said.

"She couldn't have," Sharon gasped.

"I think she thought to me," he said. "For some reason she didn't—"

"Clay," said the voice. "Sharon." Now Sharon nodded. She heard it too.

"Crissy," he said. "Where are you?"

"I'm hiding until the sun goes down," she said.

"But why?" he asked.

"Because somebody's after me," she said. "I'm hiding where they can't find me, not a chance."

"How. . ." Sharon began.

"Look, I'm okay," she said. "And I know what to do. Trust me. I'll be on board after dark, but I have to be pretty secretive. They'll have everything staked out."

"So how. . ." Sharon asked.

"Look, just don't worry," she said. "I'll take care of it."

"Let me come and get you, please," said Clay.

"No, it'd be too dangerous for you," said Crissy. "I'm sorry, but I just couldn't contact you before."

"Okay—" said Clay, but the communication ended with the abruptness with which it began.

Clay and Sharon stared at one another for a few moments. "What do we do?"

"Let's go on with life," she shrugged.

Two hours later they had just been served their entrée at dinner. "Hi," said Crissy.

Clay and Sharon jumped to their feet. Sharon seized the girl and hugged her. Crissy looked bedraggled and haggard from lack of sleep, but unharmed.

"Are you all right, Honey?" asked Clay.

"Yeah," she said. "Let me get some food and some sleep, and we'll talk in the morning. I know the secret," she said.

"I'm not leaving you alone now," said Sharon.

"Okay," Crissy agreed. "I'd appreciate it."

Clay apologized to the waiter, who looked scandalized that they were not going to eat in the dining room. Then the three of them made their way to a deli restaurant and took a table away from everyone else.

After ordering some food, Clay couldn't take it anymore. "What happened to you?"

Crissy nodded. "I felt my mind being probed last night in a club we'd gone to," she said. "I couldn't identify who was doing it at first. All I knew was that several of the Coven had come to Bermuda to find me."

"So what did you do?" Clay asked.

"I ran out the back of the club and found a cab," she said. "I had him take me to the dock, but I saw several Coven members waiting by the entrance to the dock. I knew I couldn't get past them and I had the driver take me to a hotel. I got a room and hid myself, locking the door."

"Yes?" Sharon said, urging the girl to go on.

"Well, I turned on the television to jam their thoughts," said Crissy. "Then, I tried to get some sleep. It isn't easy with a lot of static on the TV, you know."

"Right," Sharon nodded, rolling her hand to get the young woman to talk.

"I managed some sleep, then turned off the radio long enough to talk to you," Crissy went on. "I had the manager call a cab to meet me at the back entrance to the hotel, and we sped back here."

"I thought they couldn't cross water," said Sharon.

"They must have flown under some sort of tranquilizing drug or suggestion," Clay guessed.

"Okay," said Sharon. "This means they're beginning to figure out our dodges, I guess."

"Right," said Crissy. "So what do we do?"

"They can't get on the ship, can they?" asked Sharon.

"It'd be hard," Clay admitted. "But I'm not ready to put anything past their capabilities."

"When do we sail?" Crissy asked.

"One o'clock tomorrow," said Clay. "And they'll be waiting in Norfolk when we go ashore, I'm sure."

"So we need some sort of a plan, right?" said Sharon.

"Any ideas, Crissy?" asked Clay.

"None whatever," said Crissy.

"What if we fly back?" said Clay.

"How would that help?" asked Sharon.

"We could go to Salem and try to find the spring," said Clay. "Fly into Boston, then it isn't far from there."

"And then?" said Crissy.

"Then, we destroy the spring," said Clay.

The three stood in silence for a few seconds.

"Wait," said Sharon. "We're forgetting your mom's letter."

"I don't see how. . ." said Crissy.

"Perhaps she has an answer to the problem," shrugged Clay.

Crissy nodded. She crossed to the wall safe and touched in the numbers. Then, extracting the hard drive, she plugged it into the computer.

A few moments later the text appeared.

"Hi, honey," Clay read, and Sharon embraced Crissy whose eyes had welled with tears. "If you're reading this, I think you must be okay."

"Oh, my good God," murmured Crissy.

"Please forgive me, my darling girl," read Clay. "You are the light of my life, the hope of all that I am. I love you so much. But I'm afraid that the water of the spring warped me, honey, and I'm very much afraid it will do so to you if you are not careful."

"Warped?" asked Crissy, dumbfounded.

Clay went on. "I've tried so hard to find a way out of this predicament I'm in. If I don't perform some sexual acts for the Coven, they've threatened to steal you and force you into prostitution to serve their desires. They're coming now. I think I'll just have time to write what to do.

"Honey, when I was driving home today, something happened. I pulled out of the plant and drove along Route 41, the route I always take. I came to a cross street and I had the right-of-way, so I didn't slow.

"However, a woman in a minivan pulled out in front of me," Clay continued. "I had to slam on my brakes and the car swerved. I only just missed her."

"'The way the water affects me is terrifying,'" said Clay.

"I've developed a temper that terrifies me at times. It has almost wrecked my marriage with your father, Honey. I'm ashamed of it once the spasm passes. It's like a monster living inside of me, and sometimes I let it out."

"Does that happen to you, Crissy?" asked Sharon.

"Hasn't so far," Crissy shrugged. "I mean, I can get mad, but nothing as extreme as what she describes."

"Maybe the water affects different people different ways?" Sharon guessed.

"Yeah," said Crissy. "After all, Mom and I don't have—or didn't have—similar body chemistries. I'm not her biological daughter."

"Right," said Sharon.

"Look, I'll watch it, okay?" smiled Crissy.

"I know you will," Sharon nodded.

"So," said Clay, going back to reading, "in a fit of rage I decided to let the woman have it. I focused on her mind and gave her an impulse to drive into a ditch."

"Oh, no," gasped Crissy. "She couldn't. . ."

"But it didn't happen," said Clay. "She didn't respond, didn't alter her path at all. I was dumbfounded. I began to wonder if I'd lost the gift. So I pulled into a gas station."

"The attendant was helping the mechanic in the garage, and didn't seem to be at all interested in helping me, despite the fact that I'd pulled up to a full service pump. So I smacked him. His head jerked up at once and he turned to look at me, with something like terror in his eyes. He almost ran over to the car, apologizing."

"So what was different, Mom?" pleaded Crissy. "Please tell us."

"When I got home, I changed into a provocative outfit, set up a bedroom, did my makeup and so on. But I couldn't stop thinking about what had happened. I'd never really had the jolt fail. What was different, I kept asking myself."

"Then I remembered the samples of the water. When the water came out of the ground, it had one chemistry. Ten yards down the stream, where it hit sunlight, the chemistry changed."

"Like a photosynthesis?" asked Crissy.

"Must be," agreed Sharon.

"I thought about what happened," resumed Clay. "The women who cut me off did so in bright, vivid sunlight. When I went into the gas station, I parked out of the sunlight. It occurred to me to remember that I have never tried to jolt someone in bright light."

"Honey, I don't have time to test this, I don't. I'm going to try to set something up. If I succeed, you'll never need to read this."

"I only have a few more moments. Yes, Honey, we did adopt you. You were a few days old when we did so. You aren't mine in a biological sense, maybe. But no one has ever loved a daughter more than I love you. Be at peace."

"Love, Mom."

Chapter 22

Crissy cried for several moments, leaning against Sharon while Clay held her hand.

"I can't believe it," she said. "They stole Mom's soul right out of her."

"It sounds that way," Clay agreed. "I wonder what her plan was. More than that, I wonder why it didn't work."

Sharon bit at a thumbnail. "What if it did?"

"Huh?"

"Well, remember, we were talking about why they left," said Sharon. "It doesn't seem to make sense. Why not stay and just conscript Crissy?"

"You mean—" said Clay. "You think it worked?"

"Yeah, I do," said Sharon.

Crissy blew her nose and wiped at her eyes. "Then she didn't survive anyway."

Clay thought for a second or two. He and Sharon exchanged glances. Sharon nodded, as if she knew what he was thinking.

"Maybe she did," Clay said.

Crissy stared at him. She couldn't say anything for a few moments.

"No, Clay," she said. "No. She was dead. I saw her. The ambulance took her away."

"The ambulance took someone away," said Clay. He

thought for a second. "Maybe."

Crissy stared. "But…" said Crissy.

"Look, we've been pretty lucky right along, Crissy," Clay noted.

"Lucky!"

"Yeah," he said. "Why did I show up to save you?"

"Don't you run along the lake as a matter of routine?" asked Sharon.

"In the summer, yes," he agreed. "Well into the fall and on nice days in the Spring. But that day was awful, windy, freezing cold."

"I remember," said Sharon. "I couldn't imagine why you went over there."

"I have been thinking about it," said Clay. "I have a route that I run in the neighborhood on real windy days. I didn't need to go to the lake."

"Then why did you go?"

"I don't know," he said. "I went to work on the house that morning and worked until about noon. Then I put on my jogging suit, intending to take Hep through the neighborhood."

"Then what?" asked Crissy.

Clay thought. "At noon, I went outside with Hep on her leash. I remember thinking it was a good idea that I go over to the Lake that day. So I went back in, got my wallet and keys, put Hep in the car and went over to the lake."

"And found me there," said Crissy.

"Let me try a long shot," said Sharon. "Did you know her mother?"

"I don't think so," Clay said. "I don't know anyone in Winnetka."

"Where did you go to high school?" asked Crissy.

"I grew up in Flossmoor, on the south side, so I went to Homewood-Flossmoor High School."

"So did Mom," said Crissy.

"What was her name then?" he asked.

"Grace Whitfield," said Crissy. "When did you graduate?"

Clay named the year. Crissy nodded. "That's the same year as Mom," she said. "Did you know her then?"

Clay thought. "I suppose that's possible," he admitted. "If I saw a picture of her, maybe..."

"I can take care of that," said Crissy. Grabbing her room key, she hurried out the door and let it slam behind her.

"Well, well," smiled Sharon. "The thick plottens."

"Where did Crissy go?" asked Clay.

"I'm going to guess," Sharon mused. "I think she went to use the on-board computers, then to see if she could find a picture of her Mom on-line."

"But what good would that do?" asked Clay. "Even if I knew her, how would that help?"

"I see what Crissy's thinking," said Sharon.

"What?" asked Clay, bewildered.

"Were you a lifeguard in high school, maybe?"

"Well, yeah," he said. "I played football, swam on the swim team, earned good but not sensational grades, kind of stayed to myself in terms of social settings. . ."

"Yes?"

"Well, I did work during the summer as a lifeguard at the high school pool, taught swimming. . ." he broke off.

"Hello?" grinned Sharon at last.

"You can't be thinking that Grace is still alive," he scoffed.

"The coroner passed on her autopsy, remember?"

"She might have done an autopsy on someone, Clay," said Sharon. "Consider what we know about Crissy's skill. Her mom was even better, right?"

"So. . .?"

"So maybe she planted the vision of herself dead in Crissy's mind, huh?"

"How would she arrange the deal with the bus being late, though?"

"Think about it," Sharon said. "What if she planted the idea in the driver's mind that something was wrong with the bus?"

"So let me see if I understand," said Clay. "You and Crissy think that Grace faked her death, told the bus driver that the bus was bad, then convinced her daughter that she was dead, and on and on, huh?"

"What was the defining characteristic of Grace?"

"Her intelligence, I guess," said Clay.

"Sure, that's true," said Sharon. "But Crissy also thought she was beautiful, with a splendid figure, and whip-smart on top of it all."

At that moment they heard a key snick the lock open. Crissy came in holding a piece of paper.

"Look, Clay," said the young woman.

Clay stared at a high school yearbook picture of a young woman. She had mousy hair, thick glasses, and a rather poor complexion.

"I remember seeing her at school," said Clay, surprised. "She may have been in some of my classes, I don't know. This is your Mom?"

"As a senior in high school, yes," said Crissy. "I accessed the high school web site and managed to find this picture in their yearbook on-line file."

"I thought you said she was beautiful," said Clay.

"She was," said Crissy. "She must've changed a lot when she went to college."

"Looking at this picture, and the expression, and the dumpy clothes, I don't think this young woman had much of a self-concept." Sharon frowned at the picture.

"I'm sure I never dated her," said Clay. "But she might have known about me, I guess. If I go back to Homewood, once in a while someone will remember me."

"Do you remember what happened that morning?" Grace asked.

"I came out to go running at about noon," said Clay. "The weather was windy, crazy cold for March."

"Yes, it was," nodded Sharon.

"I changed into some warm sweats, then grabbed the leash and hooked up Hep," he said, "and then went out the door. I got to the bottom of the step and realized I didn't want to run in the neighborhood. I wanted to breathe the air off the lake."

"Did that seem strange at the time?" asked Sharon.

"A little, I think," said Clay. "But I've never been a person who works from a script, so it didn't bother me. I went back into the house and grabbed my wallet and keys, then drove over to the lakefront. I remember wondering why I was going over there, I mean, to the lake front."

"Okay," said Sharon. "And you'd been running for how long when you saw Crissy?"

"Only a couple of minutes," he shrugged. "I remember thinking that it was really wretched out there and I was freezing. Then I saw Crissy, and went in after her."

"This can't be a coincidence," said Sharon.

"No, it doesn't sound that way," shrugged Crissy. At this point someone knocked on the door.

"I'll get it," said Crissy. She walked through to the door and pulled it open.

"Hello, Honey," said a voice. Crissy didn't respond. Clay and Sharon exchanged glances and walked over to stand next to their ward.

"Hello, Clay, Dr. Gray," said a tall woman. "May I come in?"

"Who are you?" asked Clay.

"My name is Grace DeRosa," said the woman.

Chapter 23

Clay embraced Crissy, who looked as pale as a sheet. She still couldn't talk. He led her over to a sofa and sat her down.

Sharon poured a glass of water at the desk in the room and gave it to Crissy. Grace sat down next to Crissy and embraced her.

"I'm so sorry, Honey," she said, stroking the teenager's hair. "It's okay. I'm alive, yes, and I've always been close. I just couldn't approach you."

Clay heard the love in the woman's voice. The devotion was unmistakable, the concern sincere.

Sharon hadn't spoken. Now, she managed a few words.

"Mrs. DeRosa," she said. "How dare you?"

Grace looked up. "I'm very sorry, Dr. Gray. I must apologize to you and to Crissy. Especially to you, Clay. I'm so sorry I involved you."

"That isn't quite what I meant," said Sharon. "I want to know how you could do this to that girl. To say she's been distraught wouldn't begin to. . ."

"Dr. Gray, please," said Grace. "She didn't know it, but I've always been close by. Always. I've never abandoned her. But I had to vanish. I almost killed that man, after all."

"The man in the house, I presume you mean," Sharon asked.

"Yes," said Grace. "I understand your indignation at what I've put you through. Please let me apologize."

Now Crissy spoke up. "Mom, it's really you, isn't it," she said. "I'm not dreaming, am I?"

"No, Honey," said Grace. "Please try to forgive me. I believe that I can explain."

"Well, it'll take a lot of explaining," said Clay, his tone as hostile as Sharon's.

"Could we go someplace private?" said Grace.

"What's wrong with this cabin?" said Clay.

"They know we're here," said Crissy.

"Who?" said Sharon.

"The Coven," said Grace. "Crissy's right. They've been waiting for the opportunity to attack in combination. They think they can overpower your efforts."

"Are they on the ship?" asked Clay.

"No, I don't think so," said Grace. "They managed to use their thought shield as a group to protect four or five of them on a flight over here. They're the ones who came after you, Crissy, when you went ashore."

"Why don't they just come on the ship?"

"They can't," said Grace. "They are terrified of water, as you deduced. They'll go home on a plane, protected by the Coven and drugged to near insensibility."

"So we're safe if we stay aboard?" said Sharon.

"They can't get at us in a physical sense, no," said Grace. "But they can try to shred us with their mental skill."

"Why didn't they do it on the way over here? While we were in port?" asked Crissy.

"Honey, they tried," said Grace. "I've been able to fend them off to some extent. But also water jams their ability. They didn't feel you while we were at sea because they can't overcome water. That's why you haven't felt me until now. To be sure you didn't know what I was doing, but I've had you covered for some days. It becomes too much at times, though, and I fall asleep."

"Then we're vulnerable?" asked Sharon.

"Somewhat," said Grace, "though Crissy's been blocking them to some extent without realizing it."

"Mom," said Crissy. "How could you do this to me? To us?"

Grace sat in silence, staring at the floor. When she looked up, she had tears on her cheeks. "Honey, I know you've read my letter," she said.

"We all did," said Clay.

"I know," said Grace. "Let me try to explain. When I wrote that, I was convinced that I had only moments to live. Then, I came up with the idea of the flare."

"What flare?" asked Clay.

"I knew that they couldn't stand light," said Grace. "When that man came in, I knew at once that he intended to kill me. I led him upstairs—talk about humiliating, the way he leered at me—knowing that he intended to have brief sex with me and then yank my soul out of me. When we got into the bedroom, I took off the negligee and posed."

"I don't want to hear this," groaned Crissy.

Grace paused, seeing the mortification on her daughter's face. "I'm sorry, Honey," she said. "I'm sure this is embarrassing for you. Please believe me, I've never been so insulted myself. Still I knew it was the only way."

Crissy nodded. "Okay, go on."

"He had intended to kill me, of course," said Grace. "Then I said, 'why don't you take off the sunglasses?' He did, and I dimmed the light. He started to take off his clothes. When he looked down, I ignited a flare and shoved it in his face."

"It paralyzed him, didn't it," said Clay.

"Yes," said Grace. "I had sunglasses on the table and shoved them on as the flare caught. He staggered and fell, and I hit him with a baseball bat. I knocked him unconscious."

"Oh, my God," said Sharon.

Grace nodded. "I can still hear that clunk as the wood hit his head."

"Regrets, too?" asked Sharon.

"I haven't had time to consider that, Dr. Gray," said Grace. "You must remember that the water takes away morality and I've been no exception. I have no qualms about defending myself now, and defending my daughter, and that's what I was doing."

Sharon nodded. "Then what happened?"

"I dressed and ran out of the house. I went back to the street in the next block. I was planning to grab Crissy and just get out of there," said Grace. "But then the bus didn't come on time and I had to make a decision. I hid behind the house. The Coven came in and took the man away."

"Then who did I see?" said Crissy.

"You saw no one," said Grace. "I used all my strength to convince you that you were seeing me dead on the floor."

"But Mom—" Crissy choked. Now she stood and ran to her adopted mother and embraced her, weeping and coughing, unable to speak.

Clay and Sharon stood by, silent. Clay slipped his arm

around Sharon and embraced her.

Crissy and Grace embraced for some moments, with Grace murmuring some comfort to her daughter. "I'm so sorry, Honey," she said. "So sorry."

Sharon poured Crissy another glass of ice water. The teenager drank it in silence, and then sat on the couch.

"What now?" asked Clay.

"They'll be waiting for me," said Grace. "And for Crissy. They'll kill me, I think. This time, they won't fail."

"Mom, why don't you escape?" said Crissy. "Go ashore, catch a plane—"

"No, Honey," said Grace. "I have to do the right thing here. We have to try to end this clan of death and evil even if they kill us. You and I have to go after them."

"Not alone, Grace," said Clay.

"No, that's correct," said Sharon. "We'll help."

"I don't think you can," said Grace. "That's very sweet and very courageous, too."

"We love Crissy," said Sharon. "We can't let her be destroyed."

"But you can't fight this group," said Grace. "You don't understand their power."

"We do understand that they're dim-witted," said Clay.

"Huh?" said Crissy.

"Their attempts to catch us, and catch Crissy, have been ham fisted and stupid," said Clay. "They don't have any fighting skills, and they have no honor. That's our advantage."

"But how can we fight them?" asked Crissy. "Think of the power of the group combined together. They can bulldoze us, can't they?"

"They didn't get us on the way to Norfolk," said Clay. "We stymied them with the static. Can we do it again?"

Grace shrugged. "I couldn't read any of you during that time."

"You were out of touch those two days, then?" asked Clay.

"Yes, and it was very scary," said Grace.

"Okay," said Sharon. "Okay. But we can't have a fistfight or a brawl getting off the ship, can we?"

"At this point, I'm about ready to say 'Bring it on,'" noted Clay, his mouth in a grim line.

"Thank you, Clay," said Grace. "But what do we do when we get off the ship?"

"I'm thinking we should go to Salem and blow up this well that pumps out the Kickapoo Joy Juice," said Clay. Sharon nodded.

"What good would that do?" asked Crissy. "Our enemies already have the power."

"But they can't get at our minds if we stifle them with white noise," he pointed out.

"But we can't do that all the time," said Grace. "And I can't put a protective shell around you by myself. Not even with Crissy's help."

"Do we have to kill them, then?" asked Sharon. "That seems barbaric, doesn't it?"

"What happens when you shine the light on them?" asked Clay.

Grace shrugged. "It stymies them for a time," she said. "They can't take the light. Well, I can't either, for all that. It doesn't take the power away for good."

"That guy who came to – er –" Clay began.

"You mean at my house," said Grace. "Some months ago."

"Yeah, him," said Clay. "Did he recover?"

"I'm sure he did, yes," Grace said. "I've sensed him. He wants revenge."

"Of course he would," said Sharon. "These people think in very basic human terms, don't they—revenge, personal gratification, no pain, no effort. . ."

"Yes, they do, Dr. Gray," said Grace. "Their lives are simple ones, consisting of a great deal of sensual indulgences."

"We have the rest of today and then tomorrow and Friday to come up with a plan," said Clay. "Can we do it?"

"I think we have to try," said Sharon. "Otherwise they revenge themselves on Grace and take Crissy anyhow, as they planned to some months ago."

"True," said Grace.

"Mom?" said Crissy. "They still want to kill you?"

"Yes, they still want that," said Grace. "They also still plan bring you into the cult to fornicate for profit. That hasn't changed."

"They won't do it," said Clay, and Sharon nodded.

Chapter 24

Sharon and Clay went up on the deck and watched the beautiful paradise of Bermuda recede into the Eastern Horizon. Crissy and Grace needed some time to talk and reconcile after the events of the last few months and weeks.

"Will we see them at dinner, do you think?" asked Clay.

Sharon shrugged. She wiped at a tear in one eye.

"What's the problem?" Clay murmured, embracing her.

"I liked having a daughter," said Sharon. "I'm back to being childless."

"Yeah," said Clay. "Yeah, I know what you mean."

"Tears at your heart," said Sharon.

"I agree with you, but I'm mad," said Clay. "I feel used. This woman conscripted us to protect her daughter."

"At this point, though, we aren't hurt, injured, we're not out anything that can't be replaced. . ."

"Except the last several days of our lives," grunted Clay.

"That's true," shrugged Sharon. "But we have gained a lot in these last several days. We have each other, we've helped out a girl who has come to love us and wants to know us, who we'll watch grow up and marry—"

"Assuming we don't get shot, stabbed, lynched, electrocuted or have our minds blown up," he noted.

"We won't," said Sharon, with a grin. "We can defeat those

big dopes."

"Maybe," said Clay.

The air was chilly, but the ship had arranged for a belly flop contest among the passengers. They made their way to the pool and watched the hilarious competition for some time. "Come on," said Sharon after about an hour. "We need to go back to the cabin."

Clay entered the cabin and they found Crissy sitting on the couch, staring at the Atlantic Ocean through the sliding glass door. Sharon went over and sat down next to her.

"Are you okay?" asked Clay, leaning against the wall. Sharon put an arm around the girl and stroked her hair.

"Yeah, I guess," said Crissy. "It's not easy to feel much after your insides have been torn out, then replaced, then torn out again."

"You've had to deal with a lot," agreed Sharon. "How did the conversation go with your mother?"

"Not well, I'm afraid," said Crissy. "I'm struggling with mixed feelings."

"I can understand that," said Clay. "You must have been thunderstruck at seeing her."

"Yeah," said Crissy. "Not that I wasn't glad to see her, I mean. And the way she constructed everything with the mind trick stunned me. I don't have anything like that ability."

"Didn't you say the ability increased with use?" asked Sharon.

"Well, yeah," said Crissy. "I try not to use it, though. I don't like invading someone else's mind."

"You did it with us," said Clay.

"I know, of course that's true," said Crissy. "But I only did that to protect myself from my dad. It turns out that Mom burned the notion of killing me into his mind to the extent that she couldn't turn it off when she survived, so she had to hang around me to protect me from him."

"That's interesting," said Sharon.

"I've apologized for what I did to you," said Crissy. "I promise it won't happen again, Clay and Sharon."

"Okay," said Clay.

"There's something I want to ask," the girl said.

"Sure," said Clay.

"Are you two getting married?"

"Yeah, you betcher butt we are," swaggered Clay. "Er—isn't that right, Sugar Dumpling?" he asked, his voice high pitched and whiny.

"Yes, dear," chuckled Sharon. She reached over and patted his head, and both laughed.

Crissy didn't giggle, as she usually did. "Have you decided when?"

"No," said Clay. "But we both want to make it happen as soon as we can."

"Well, then—" began Crissy, but her eyes teared and she swallowed.

"Yes?" said Sharon, gentle and loving, hugging the girl.

"Do you think..." she began. "I mean, this is hard to ask. Would you mind if—I mean, once this thing with the Coven is over—Could I please come to live with you?"

Clay and Sharon couldn't speak for a few moments.

"Look," said Clay. "I don't know if you should. It should be obvious that we love you, and we want to be part of your life from now on, but moving out from your parents is a pretty big deal."

"I know what you mean," agreed Crissy. "So is that a 'no'?"

"Honey," said Sharon. "You'd always be welcome with us, in our house, in our lives, whatever happens. But I don't think that's what you really want. Also, this is too big a decision to make now. You shouldn't even consider something like moving in with us until we get this thing concluded. Assuming we do get it concluded."

"Oh we will," said Crissy. "Those cult creeps are no match for you two and my mom. I know."

"Don't you think that would break your parents' hearts?" asked Clay.

Crissy snorted. "Break *their* hearts?" she said. "My mother scared me, betrayed me, hurt me—"

"She was trying to protect you," said Sharon.

"Ah. So that's why she gave me a shot of that water? To protect me?" sneered Crissy. "No, that's not what happened at all. She didn't want to help me out, make my life better, give me some advantage. She injected me because she wanted to see what would happen. She used me as a guinea pig in a science experiment."

"She was affected by the water," said Sharon. "She wasn't thinking as clearly as she would have under normal conditions."

"You know what Sharon means," said Clay. "We could see how much she loves you. It flows out of her. We saw that love surround you and envelop you just now."

"And then my father tried to kill me," said Crissy. "Not once, but several times. He wanted to drown me in a freezing lake. He hired mercenaries to help kill me. We had to have him arrested."

"We know all that, Crissy," said Clay. "And your mother enchanted your father into doing what he did."

"I know just what you're saying," said Crissy. "I mean that by contrast you two have risked everything to protect me: Everything you own, everything you've worked for, your jobs, your homes. You've risked your lives to save me. In that cabin, Sharon, I'll never forget how you put yourself between me and that thug with a gun. Not to mention Clay jumping into a lake, leading a guerilla attack at the warehouse and everything else. Then you took me on this trip that cost you a fortune."

"Crissy, we wanted to do all that," asserted Clay.

"Yes, we did," agreed Sharon.

"I know it," said Crissy. "So now you tell me. Who should I now consider my real parents?"

Clay and Sharon didn't say anything. After a few moments, Clay spoke up. "Okay. Where's your mother now?" asked Clay.

"I asked her to leave me," said Crissy. "She told me that now that her secret was out, she wanted me to move my stuff into her cabin. When I recovered, I told her to take a flying leap into the ocean."

The girl was emphatic and serious, but Clay and Sharon exchanged grins over her head. "That wasn't very nice," Sharon said, just managing not to laugh.

"Why not? The ocean's right here. She could just open the door and jump off the balcony." Now Crissy giggled a little. The three of them chuckled together and the tension was broken.

Chapter 25

Sharon insisted that Crissy, who had been operating for several days on very little sleep, lie down for a nap. When she was asleep, Clay took Sharon into the next room.

"I think I should have a talk with Grace," he said.

Sharon thought for a second. Then she shrugged. "You'd be better than me, that's for sure," she said. "I have to struggle to be civil with her. Also you seem to have a better sense than I do about when you're being charmed. I don't get the impression she would be above doing that to you."

Clay nodded, grabbed a room key and headed down the corridor. He stopped in front of Grace's door and knocked.

The door opened and Grace stood there, staring at him through bloodshot eyes and mascara streaked cheeks. "Hello, Clay," she murmured.

"Hey," he said. "Crissy told us what happened. I imagine you're pretty upset."

"Yes, I am," said Grace. "Our reunion couldn't have gone worse, to say the least."

Clay gave her a sympathetic nod. "I thought I'd come over and ask," he said. "Crissy fell asleep a bit ago. We thought that maybe you could use a little support. How about if I take you up to the lounge to get a drink and talk a little?"

"Come on in," she said. "That would be wonderful. Give me

a minute to try to repair the ravages." She went into the washroom for a few moments to fix her makeup.

Ten minutes later they sat at a small table in a deserted lounge on the pool deck floor. Clay ordered them each a special martini.

"I'm sorry about what happened with Crissy," he said, aware that this sounded a bit lame. "I'm sure it wasn't what you imagined your reunion would be like."

She nodded. "It was just the opposite of the way I hoped it would go," she said. "I guess I thought that she'd be glad to see me and understand that I'd been working on her behalf."

"Yeah," said Clay. "It must have been tough for you, seeing us floundering around like we did. It was scary enough for us."

"I'm sorry," Grace said, staring into her glass. She sipped for a moment and wiped at her eyes. "Clay, please understand. I surrounded Crissy that night, for example, when she went to hide in the hotel. Then I shielded her from the Coven thugs at the ship gangway. I've also been protecting you in every way I can."

"I guess that's true," said Clay. "It's been an unusual experience, to say the least."

Grace sighed and looked out the porthole at the gray ocean swirling by. Clay had a chance to inspect her in more close detail.

Crissy had been right in her description of her mother. Grace had turned into a stunning woman with a lovely figure, her hair and skin beautiful. But Clay could sense a deep seated feeling of despair under the beauty.

"Why did I do it?" she asked after a few moments. "I guess I should apologize. No, wait a minute. Let me rephrase what I said. I take that back. I do apologize. I've been awful. This stupid ability has just twisted me."

"You don't have to do it," Clay said. "You can decide not to. Then help your daughter not to. Move along and repair your marriage, build your home and your career again."

"You don't understand," she sighed. "This stuff infiltrates you, becomes part of your identity, gets to the point that you can't remember being normal."

"You never were normal, Grace," he said.

She looked up in surprise. "What do you mean?"

"Memories of you in high school have been coming up," he said. "I'm remembering that you were the smartest girl in the class, near perfect on the ACTs, top grades, all that. . ."

"You're right, I was," Grace acknowledged. "Teachers and administrators fawned over me. But I did that well in academics because that's all I had. I was way too shy to get involved with athletics, or dance, or student council. So I just settled into achieving what I could."

"Then you got the chance to be extraordinary," Clay said. Grace shrugged, and then nodded. "That's why you took the serum."

"You don't know what I felt like," said Grace. "I used to stare at you and your girlfriend and think 'what a perfect couple.'"

"You mean Gail," he said. "Yeah, well, that fell apart two years ago. She dumped me for some guy in our subdivision, took the girls. . ."

"I know that," said Grace. "I saw it in your mind when I drafted you to save Crissy."

"Uh, huh," said Clay.

"I picked you when I saw you one day in Hyde Park," said

Grace. "I was hiding near Crissy's room and I saw you jogging through the neighborhood with your dog."

"Her name's Hephzibah," he smiled.

"Yeah," she said. "She's a real cutie. I love dogs."

"So you followed me home, I suppose," he asked.

"Yes, and filed the knowledge away," she said. "When I saw Jim go into the coffee shop after Crissy, I read in his mind what he wanted to do. I sped to your house and was lucky enough to see that you were not only home—Thank God—but coming out for a run."

"So you used the mind trick to bewitch me?"

"Uh, huh," said Grace. "I guess I was lucky that it worked with you. You say it doesn't always work with you, and. . ."

"I see," nodded Clay.

"I apologize," said Grace, and he thought that she was indeed being sincere. "Clay, I know that if I'd just gone up and asked you, you would have gone. But I guess I couldn't take the chance of re-introducing myself, of going into detail about what was going on, then we'd involve police..."

"Okay," he said. "I suppose that makes some sense. But why didn't you take the suggestion away from his mind?"

"I tried," she said. "I couldn't remove the suggestion. I tried and tried, in fact. Somehow I burned the idea into his mind so that he couldn't let it go."

"Couldn't you have called the police?" he asked.

"I suppose so," she said. "But then they'd have questions, not to mention how much trouble Jim would be in..."

"He's in plenty of trouble now, Grace."

"I know," she said. "I know. I just couldn't...well..."

Something else occurred to him now. "Grace," he asked.

"Does your husband know you're alive?"

"No," she said. "I'm ashamed of that. But I was afraid that if he knew I was alive, he'd want to help, and then the Coven would go for him too—"

"So it was okay to risk me and Sharon? Two complete strangers?"

Her eyes teared up again. "No, it wasn't okay," she said. "Of course it wasn't. I apologize again."

He considered for a few moments. "How have you been living?" he asked. "You haven't had an income in all this time, have you?"

"I set up a personal account when Crissy came," said Grace. "I thought it would be a college fund for her. I'd invested a lot of money in it. I got a cheap room near Crissy's Grandmother and used the gift to keep track of her."

"Why did you whack the guy who came to the house?"

"I couldn't think of a way around this," she said. "Hitting the man who came was a stopgap. So were you and Dr. Gray. I keep trying to come up with ways to neutralize them. I haven't hit on anything yet."

"What about having them thrown in jail?"

"On what charge?" she asked. "Reading my mind?"

"I see your point," he said.

"That's the whole dilemma," she groaned. "I'm all alone in this thing. If I involve Crissy, they'll kill her. If I kill them, I'll be regarded as the greatest mass murderer in history."

"How many of them are there?"

"Maybe a hundred," she shrugged.

"So we're going to fight a hundred vicious, amoral mind-readers, just the four of us?"

"Do you see any other way?"

"What about if we escape?"

"Where to?" she asked. "They've learned how to shelter the minds of their operatives to protect them from fear of water. I can't shield us all the time."

"I'm sure you're under a vast strain."

"Does Crissy hate me?" she asked in a tiny voice, full of despair and defeat.

"I don't know," he admitted. "I do know she wants to stay with me and Sharon. She doesn't want anything to do with you or with your husband at this point."

"I could see that," she said, and again the tears.

"Okay," said Clay. "Let's get Sharon and Crissy and we'll have a good dinner together tonight. Then, in the morning the four of us will try to review what we can do and come up with a plan." She nodded.

"Buy you another drink?" he asked.

"Please," she said. "It helps dull the pain."

At that moment Sharon joined the group. Clay called the bartender over and ordered a fresh round of drinks.

"How is she?" asked Grace, her voice tiny and fearful.

"She's sleeping," said Sharon. "She burned the candle pretty far on this cruise."

"I know," said Grace. "I followed her and protected her when I could, but again I fell asleep a few times. I was as frantic as you were when you couldn't find her. She was hiding with the static trick."

"Did you lose us when we went to Iowa?" he asked.

"Yes," she said. "But I really wasn't worried because she was with you and Dr. Gray."

"Tell Sharon what's going on," Clay suggested. Grace filled Sharon in, adding a few details.

"Is there anything we can do to neutralize their abilities?" Sharon asked at last.

"I'm not thinking real well right now, Dr. Gray," said Grace.

"I think you should lie down too," suggested Sharon.

"That might be a good idea," said Grace. "I guess we'll need our strength."

"Should I walk you to your cabin?" asked Clay.

"That won't be necessary, but thank you, Clay," Grace said, and drained her glass. "You've been very understanding and kind."

"Meet us here at 7:00," Clay suggested. Grace agreed and wandered off.

"Oh boy," said Clay.

Sharon nodded. "I think we need to get off the ship before it docks," she said.

"Yeah," he said. "That ought to be interesting to accomplish."

"She is beautiful, isn't she?" said Sharon.

Clay shrugged. "I guess," he said. "She didn't look enticing now, of course."

"Well, no," she giggled. "It isn't easy to look glamorous when you're under the strain she's been dealing with for several months now."

Clay grinned back at her. "Good to hear you laugh," he said. "It's been a while."

They looked out at the ocean. In a moment, Sharon reached over and took his hand. He smiled at her, and everything felt okay for a little while.

Chapter 26

"How's your dinner?" Grace asked Crissy, in another lame attempt to start a conversation with her daughter. The four of them sat at a table on the pool deck, overlooking the ocean which swirled by in the darkness.

"My dinner is fine," Crissy nodded. "And for God's sake don't apologize again, Mom."

"Okay," said Grace. "I'm trying to make things right if I can, Crissy."

"I know, Mom," said Crissy. "Look, I need some time here, you know?"

"Yes, Honey, I do know," said Grace.

Clay fixed his eye on his salad, embarrassed. Sharon picked at her dinner as well, despite the beautiful presentation and remarkable wine that Clay had ordered.

"Did you sleep?" Sharon asked Grace.

"Yes," she said. "We are safe here, at least for the time. None of the Coven managed to get on board."

Sharon nodded. "Well, that's something, anyway, right?"

"Can we relax for a bit, anyway?" said Clay.

The three women nodded and agreed to try.

Sharon turned to Clay. "Have you given any thought as to how we might get off this ship without encountering these cult thugs?" she asked.

"Yeah," said Clay. "I have a plan. I need a volunteer." For the next several minutes he laid out what he'd come up with.

"It sounds dangerous," said Sharon.

"Does anybody have a better plan?" he asked.

"I'll do it," said Grace.

"That's helpful," said Clay.

***

A loud noise awakened the occupants of the cabins at the top of the ship early the next morning. A helicopter landed on the top deck of the ship and several crew members carried a stretcher to the helicopter. A teenage girl and two other adults also climbed aboard, the girl holding the hand of the person on the stretcher.

"The girl's mother," said one of the early risers. "I heard the crew say that that girl's mom had a heart attack. Strange. I saw her dancing yesterday and she sure looked healthy to me."

"Remarkable," said his wife, as they watched the helicopter take off, heading north toward Baltimore and a cardiac care unit there.

But the helicopter didn't land at Baltimore, as planned. Instead, the crew took it inland to a landing site, where a man in an SUV opened the door and stepped out.

The afflicted woman thanked the crew of the helicopter and told them they were outstanding paramedics. She considered herself fortunate to have received such outstanding care.

The crew smiled and the helicopter lifted off, heading back to Norfolk. In their minds, they believed that they had revived the stricken woman, and indeed that they had placed her in the hands of a competent cardiac care unit.

Craig Foster embraced his brother and greeted Sharon and Crissy. They had to be careful that they didn't step on a very excited Hephzibah, who greeted her master and his friends with the overwhelming enthusiasm of the dedicated and loyal Canine.

"Everything okay?" said Clay.

"Yeah," said Craig. "I sprung DeRosa from jail and told him we had a job to do. He thinks that we're going to be saving Crissy and doesn't know anything else."

"Any trouble getting the material?" asked Clay.

"No," said Craig. "DeRosa had quite a few connections and we're ready."

The group entered the SUV and headed north. They reached Boston in the late afternoon and found a small motel west of the city.

James DeRosa came out of a motel room and greeted the party as they dismounted. Then he spotted his wife and stood dumbfounded as she crossed to him and embraced him. He and Grace had an emotional reunion.

Crissy stood off to the side and watched the people she had regarded as her parents embrace, holding Clay's hand while Sharon embraced her from behind. She hadn't seen her father for several days and was having a difficult time looking at him.

"Crissy," asked Sharon. "Are you all right?"

"Yes," said Crissy. "But stay right there, okay?"

"Sure," said Clay.

At last DeRosa and Grace came over. "Crissy," said DeRosa. "I'm—I'm glad you're all right."

"You are, huh," said Crissy.

DeRosa stared at the ground. "Please try to understand," he

stammered. "I became convinced that you'd killed your mother with that mind thing you two do. I wasn't thinking straight."

"And now you're thinking straight, is that right?" said Crissy.

"I'm trying," said DeRosa. "I know it wasn't right, and I scared you and hurt you…"

"Uh, huh," said Crissy. "You didn't just scare me. You drugged me. You threatened and imprisoned me. You kidnapped me. You held Clay's family hostage. You kept trying to kill me until we had you thrown in jail. And now you're glad I'm all right."

"I'll make it up to you," said DeRosa. "Whatever you want. I'll do my best."

"I'm not sure you can," said Crissy. "I'm also not sure I want to give you a chance." DeRosa looked at his wife, who nodded at him.

"Crissy," said Sharon. "Don't burn any bridges, right?"

"I'll try," said the teenager. "Thanks for getting us the stuff we need, Dad."

The group went into a meeting room where a local restaurant delivered pizza and drinks. The group went to bed early. Crissy stayed in the room with Clay and Sharon.

At three A. M. two SUVs left the motel and headed northward. They arrived at Gallows Hill Park just before sunrise.

"What now?" asked Clay. Grace directed Clay and Craig down into a woods.

"There it is," she said at last, pointing to a ramshackle hut hidden in the woods. Two sleepy guards lounged in the cold outside. With a nod at Grace, he and Craig slipped forward to the two men.

Within moments they had surprised and disarmed the guards. Then they bound them hand and foot and pushed them into the cottage. Next the brothers began wiring explosives to the cabin.

They rejoined Grace within moments. "They'll be okay," he said. "And we're ready."

"They're coming," she said.

"Good," said Clay, and Craig smiled.

***

Five minutes later, the woods around them crackled with the sound of approaching people.

Five men came forward. They held pistols at the head of Crissy, Sharon and DeRosa.

"All right, Foster," said one. "You're surrounded."

"So I see," said Clay.

His calm demeanor surprised the men. "You don't get it," said the man. "We're going to kill all of you. You can decide if it's going to be fast or slow."

"No, I get that you would do that," said Clay. "If you could."

Again the people exchanged glances. "What do you mean?"

"One thing that happens when you've got everything," Clay said, "is that you forget how to do some things. The state police can be here within minutes. Have you ever seen a S.W.A.T. team work?"

The leader stood with his mouth open as his followers stirred in discomfort. "What are you saying?"

"This is a hostage situation," said Clay. "You are holding us, with weapons, against our will. They'll shoot you and destroy this place."

The men stammered. "We can stop them," the leader said. "They can't resist us and what we can do to their brains. We'll fry them before they can get close."

"Maybe you could," said Clay. "But as you did it, you'd see an impressive fireworks show."

"What does that mean?"

"Two of your men are tied up in the shed," Clay answered. "They are wired with a large amount of what's known as C-4. It's a plastic explosive."

Three men came forward and started toward the old, broken down shed out of which flowed a small spring of water.

"If they open the door, they trigger the C-4," said Clay. The men stopped.

"We can blast your mind to perdition, you know," said the spokesman, a grizzled looking man with a grim cast to his face.

"I know," said Clay. "But I urge you to consider this. I can sense when you try the stun. If I sense any kind of probe, I let this trigger go." He held up a device. "Now, the stuff won't go off with a fire, or with an accident. Even if I was to shoot the explosive with a rifle, that wouldn't trigger the reaction. No, you need a detonator, or a blasting cap."

"What is that?" asked a woman who stood just behind the leader, pointing to the device in Clay's hand.

"A triggering device," said Clay. "This is an electronic detonator. As long as I'm holding it, the C4 doesn't go off. If I let it go, it'll transmit an electronic pulse that will trigger the detonator. That explosion will trigger the C4. Want to see? If I let it go, it'll rival the Boston Harbor Fourth of July display. That'll be the signal to the State Police, and they'll move in with all the firepower they've got."

"But you'll be killed too," said another woman.

"Yeah," said Clay. "But I'm not afraid to die. Neither are any of the rest of us. We don't intend to spend the rest of our lives being harassed by this group of losers."

A silence fell on the group. "What do you want?" asked the leader.

"First, get out of Crissy's life. Get out of Grace's life. Never— never—come near us again."

"What if we don't?" said the leader.

"Then I destroy the Spring," said Clay.

"But we can make this agreement, then go in and destroy the explosive anyhow," said a man.

"Funny, I thought you'd say that," said Clay.

"What do you mean?"

"I mean I've set up sensors. If you open that door to the shed, or tear it down and go in the back, or otherwise try to enter the shed, I'll know. At that point, I use this cell phone—" he held one up—"type a number on speed dial, and ignite the explosive. From anywhere in the country, or anywhere in world, for that matter."

"Then how do we get the water?"

"You don't," said Clay. "Not while any of us are alive. And if anyone of us dies, or gets hurt in some strange way, this Coven ends with this group right here. You don't get to infect anyone else, ever again."

The group murmured among themselves. "One other thing," said Clay. "You'd better guard this place well. If some traveler, some scientist, some young woman, some wild animal comes near here, I'll know and I'll blow it to hell."

"You think you've beaten us, don't you, Foster," snarled the leader.

"Yes, sir, that's exactly what I think," said Clay. "I'm glad we understand each other."

The conversation went on for some time, but Clay held all the cards and the group knew it. One by one the Coven of the Spring melted back into the woods and were gone.

"Crissy, maybe you and Craig would cut loose those two creeps in the shed," said Clay.

"How do we get in?" asked Crissy.

"Just a second," said Clay. He flipped a switch on top of the handheld trigger. "Okay," he said. "It's safe."

Within moments Crissy and Craig had released the men, who also disappeared back into the woods.

Sharon took Clay's arm. "Is this going to work?" she asked.

"Maybe," he said. "I think it's our best chance. Unless I go in and start blasting away with an AK47."

"True," said Sharon. "Now can we go home?"

"Yeah, let's," he said. "And thanks."

She looked up. "For?" she smiled.

"For holding my hand," he said. "That way no one can see it trembling." They grinned together. Crissy came over and embraced them.

Chapter 27

Summer

Sharon came into the kitchen, pulled out a chair and sat down with an "Umpf." She set down her briefcase and looked at Clay, who sat opposite her at the kitchen table, pouring over some architect's drawings.

"Tired?" he smiled, as she exhaled with apparent relief.

"No, not tired," she said. "Busy. All day. It's good to relax."

He put a finger to his mouth, pointed to a stack of mail and winked. Then he spoke a bit louder. "Crissy passed the G. E. D.," he said. "She found out today."

"Well, *that's* a shocker," said Sharon, feigning surprise, matching his volume.

"I heard that," said a teenaged voice from the other room.

"Hi Honey, just kidding," chuckled Sharon.

"Harumph," said Crissy.

"I'm going to get the kids tonight, up in Lake Geneva, rather than wait until tomorrow," he said. "Gail called earlier and asked if I could. They're supposed to play in some celebrity Pro-Am tennis tournament this weekend. You want to come with me to get them? We can get a bite with the girls on the way home."

"Sure," said Sharon. "Crissy going to come?"

"I don't think so," he said. "She has a test tomorrow."

"Is she going to see her parents this weekend?"

"If she does, she'll stay for an hour or so," said Clay. "Her mom wants her to stay the night, but Crissy told her that she wasn't ready for that yet."

Sharon nodded, stroking her swollen tummy with an absent smile. "I wonder if she'll ever be ready again," she asked.

"Good question," said Clay. "The mother understands, I think, that actions have consequences."

"Yes, they do," said Sharon.

"Work okay?" Clay smiled at her.

"Yeah," said Sharon. "Lots to do, but that's fine. Makes the day go faster. You?"

"I'm about finished with that West Side place," he grinned. "Carpet goes in tomorrow."

Sharon sat, and sighed. "It's a nice house," she said. "Some family will be very happy there."

"Not as nice as this," Clay pointed out and Sharon nodded. "There's something else," he said.

"What?"

"Gail may want to buy it," he said.

Sharon's double take almost made him laugh. "What do you mean?"

"I mean, this tennis weekend is Steve's last chance," he smiled. "She's ready to leave him as things stand now."

"Leave him?" asked Sharon.

"Yeah," nodded Clay. "That episode in the warehouse didn't sit well with her."

"I remember how mad she got with him," Sharon nodded.

"Well, things haven't improved, from what she said on the phone today," shrugged Clay. "He's not admitting he did anything wrong. They've had several major fights over that evening."

"I have to say," she said. "This isn't a real surprise, I mean, that they're having difficulty. Sex can only carry you so far. The statistics about second marriages aren't real encouraging. They don't do very well in a lot of cases. Particularly when they begin with a lie."

"Well, this doesn't sound very promising," he nodded.

"I hate to ask," she said, and hesitated.

He waited. "Well?"

"What does this mean to you?" she asked at last.

"You mean, would I consider starting things up with her again?" he smiled.

"I'd just as soon you have nothing to do with her," she said.

"I miss the girls," he nodded. "So she and I have to stay in touch. And I know what you're saying. But please believe me. This sale will be all business. I haven't any intention of lousing up our marriage. I never will. That's a promise."

She sat staring at her hands for a few moments. "You mean it," she whispered.

"In my house we have honesty," he said. "I would never consider anything other than business with her."

Sharon gave a little smile.

"Besides," he said. "I'm married to you and I *really* love you." He took her hand, and they were silent for several moments. At last, she gave him that smile he treasured above everything in the world and nodded.

"Anything else in the mail?" he asked.

"Just a second, I didn't check yet," she smiled. She picked up the stack of stuff and began riffling through it. "Oof," she said, holding her swollen abdomen.

Clay looked up. "What happened?" he asked.

"Your daughter," she said. "She kicked me."

"*My* daughter?" he grinned.

"Yes, well, no child of mine would kick her mother like yours does me," she sniffed. "Down, Hep," she said to the excited dog who was making a fine effort to climb into her lap. "Yes, thank you, it's a lovely coming home gift," Sharon laughed, accepting the gym shoe Hephzibah had brought her and petted the dog, laughing as she always did at the strange gifts the dog presented her.

Then she stopped riffling through the mail and held up an envelope.

When she didn't speak, Clay looked up.

"What's that?" he asked.

Sharon didn't speak. "Sharon?" he asked.

"It's from that testing lab," she managed. "The one that tested my DNA and Crissy's."

"Well, open it," he said.

"What if it isn't a match?" she asked, her face pale.

"Easy," said Clay, raising his voice for dramatic effect. "I say we bundle all of Crissy's stuff into plastic bags and toss them into the street. Then we boot her out into the snow and wind and ice to make her own way in the world."

"Just like that?" grinned Sharon, looking at the living room.

"You bet," said Clay. "Hup! Out! Pow! A good kick and we're done." He jerked a thumb over his shoulder.

"I heard that too," yelled Crissy from the living room. "And it's 90 degrees outside anyway."

Clay laughed. "Come on in here," he yelled back.

The teenager strolled into the kitchen, a textbook open in front of her. "Is this going to take long?" she asked. "I have a test in bio in the morning."

"Sharon got the letter," said Clay.

"Oh," said Crissy, after a brief pause.

Sharon still hadn't opened the envelope. "What if it isn't a match?" she asked again, looking from Clay to Crissy.

"Sharon," said Clay. "Give it to me."

Sharon handed the letter over. Crissy pulled a chair over next to Sharon and hugged her.

"I told you many times," Crissy said. "It's just a formality. I know who my real mother is."

"Thanks," said Sharon, with a weak smile. "Oof. This kid's in a bad mood." She stroked her abdomen.

Clay opened the letter. He pulled out the single sheet of paper inside and scanned the contents.

"Well?" said Sharon, looking fearful.

Clay didn't speak.

He just gave his wife a huge grin and flipped the letter to her.

THE END

Enjoyed this title
tell Jeff
Visit our page on Facebook TotalRecall Publishing

For additional titles by Jeff visit
www.TotalRecallPress.com

Title: ACID

- Author: Jeff Lovell
- Publisher: TotalRecall Publications, Inc.
- HARD COVER ISBN: 978-1-59095-116-3 $27.95
- PAPERBACK, ISBN: 978-1-59095-117-0 $19.95
- EBOOK, Nook, Kindle, ISBN: 978-1-59095-118-7
- Number of pages: 352
- Publication Date: 2013

Rick Howell, living in the shadow of two women who have the power to change reality, must risk his life to stop the genocidal exploits of a desperate lunatic who wants to acquire their powers. The discovery of a mind controlling drug opens a pathway to frightening mental abilities for Rachel Farrell, who can move backward and forward in time at will, while Donna Riske, Rachel's best friend, can control the thoughts of others.

www.ingramcontent.com/pod-product-compliance
Lightning Source LLC
Chambersburg PA
CBHW020330120726
47904CB00002B/359